Somewhere near

William quietly grabbed his sword, ever-present at his side, and sat up in his cot, waiting for the source of the noise to show itself. The curtain at his tent door rippled slightly and his heart began to beat faster, filling him with fear and dread at what was waiting for him outside. He gripped the handle of his sword tightly and prepared to strike as the curtain began to open.

Just as he was raising his sword over his head to surprise the intruder, a small face peered at him through the opening in the tent. A child! A girl, her veil pushed back from her dark hair. Still, it could be a trick.

"Who are you?" he asked in Arabic. After months in this part of the world, he had managed to pick up a few phrases here and there, enough to make himself understood when it mattered.

The child's eyes widened at the sight of the gleaming sword raised high in the air, ready to swing. She began to tremble and whisper in Arabic to William. He couldn't understand it all but he did manage to catch, "Please" and "Alone!"

1

He yanked the curtain out of her hand and looked around outside of the tent. Other than a few men sitting by their campfires, there was no one else about. He looked down at the girl, who was trembling like a leaf and he thought of his own small daughter and son back in England. He tried to give her a comforting smile and took her gently by the arm in to his tent, out of the cold night air of the desert.

He gestured for her to sit on the rug that was covering the sandy ground and he sat on his cot expectantly, waiting for her to work up the courage to say what she needed to say. Finally, she spoke, surprisingly, in halting English.

"P-p-please, sir", she began, her liquid-brown eyes full of frightened tears. "Please don't hurt my village", she begged.

William was stunned. What courage this child had! She had braved the sentries to sneak into the commander's tent to plead for her village. He smiled at her kindly.

"Such bravery, small one. Tell me, how do you know how to speak my language?"

"We have had soldiers here before. Sometimes they stay a long time. We listen to them speak."

William was impressed. Such intelligence! But he still wasn't satisfied that this was not a trick.

"Who sent you?' he asked.

The child shook her head. "No one. Everyone left but us. My mother has a new baby and can't travel. My father is dead, killed when the last soldiers were here. We are all alone. Please, please don't hurt us! I can give you this."

From a fold in her robe she pulled out a small wooden box. Sir William shrank back for a moment, suspicious of the box, but when nothing happened, he reached out to take it from her. It was a very old box, the wood dark and polished from many years of handling. He opened it gently and peered inside.

Four purple stones lay within, winking up at him as if they had a secret to share. As stones, they weren't worth much, but maybe they could buy food or supplies along the way for his men.

"What are these?" he asked the girl.

She waited a moment before answering. "My grandmother called them travel stones."

"They look like amethysts."

She shook her head. "No, not amethysts. These stones are magic. Very valuable! We have kept them hidden for many years."

"Travel stones? Why are you giving them to me? Won't your mother be angry?"

Again, the girl shook her head. "My mother told me to bring them to you. She said to tell you their secrets. Hold one in your hand." Perplexed, William picked up one of the stones. He felt a warm vibration in his palm as he held it.

"What is it doing?" he asked her. She smiled at him.

"It is waiting to take you, if you want."

"Take me where?"

"Wherever you want to go, in time. You can choose, but don't ever let go or you can't come back. Say it out loud. Try it, you'll see."

"But how do I come back?"

"Just think of here again, this same time and the exact same place. Say it out loud again." She shrugged, as if it were the most obvious thing in the world. "You try it now? I'll wait for you."

"Now? This isn't a trick, is it?"

She shook her head violently, afraid again, and grabbed his arm. "No, no, sir! We want to live in peace, no more soldiers. Please take these stones and make your men go away. Try them and see!" William felt ridiculous, but the girl looked so earnest that he decided to play along.

"All right, my young friend, where should I go?"

"Somewhere easy, to start. Go to the day you left your country. Say it out loud, the whole date, and don't let go!"

Still feeling ridiculous, Sir William held the small purple stone in his large calloused hand and felt the warm vibration again. Keeping his eyes on the girl he dramatically said, "I want to go to London, England, July 1, 1190!"

Instantly, he disappeared from sight. The girl smiled to herself. It had worked and was happening just as her mother had told her it would. She hoped with all her heart that it would be enough to send the soldiers away. Then, just as suddenly as he had disappeared, William appeared again, thumping down from the ceiling of the tent onto the carpet and nearly knocking her over. He picked himself up slowly, staring at her with amazement. He was the one trembling, now.

"Extraordinary! What kind of witchcraft is this?" She shrugged again.

"I have never used them. Just take them and please leave us alone!" Sir William nodded his head.

"You have my word of honor. Tell your mother not to worry. We will leave at first light. Your village is safe." King Richard would not be pleased if he spared the village, but he would think of what to tell the king later. The stones were too precious for him to let this opportunity go.

The girl dipped her head to him in thanks and departed silently as quickly as she had come. William sat back weakly and opened the box to slip the stone back inside, then put the box securely in his shirt. He couldn't let anyone know about this.

He needed to tell his men of the new plan. After what he had witnessed tonight, he wasn't taking any chances and besides, he was a man of his word.

The village remained unharmed.

Chapter One

April, 2013

Twelve-year-old boys are supposed to live ordinary lives.
They are at that wonderful age when the world of adults is beginning
to make sense but they are still comfortable enough to be able to
play games like Tag or War, running over neighborhood lawns and
through backyards screeching like banshees and firing foam darts at
one another. They are supposed to be able to play video games for
hours until their eyeballs feel as if they were going to fall out and to
try and cajole their parents into letting them see movies that are still
too violent and grown-up for them to watch. They are supposed to
live lives that consist of homework, messy rooms, dirty socks under
the bed, and noticing girls for the first time.

Tommy Andrews was fully aware of what a twelve-year-old
boy's life was *supposed* to be like and for the most part, his was
exactly that, except for one missing piece.

He watched from his bedroom window as his friends' fathers played catch with them, or showed them how to properly wash the family car in the big front yards of their little neighborhood. He wished that he had a father to play with, even if it was a father that he only saw on weekends, like many of his friends who had parents that were divorced. Tommy Andrews' parents weren't divorced. They were still married after many years. The problem was, simply, that Tommy's father had disappeared, almost twelve years ago, when he was one year old.

In spite of not having his father around, Tommy's mother really did everything she could to make his life a normal one. She worked as a schoolteacher in the little town in western Michigan where they lived. Each day, they would walk home together to the small farmhouse, the oldest on their street, that was very creaky and somewhat shabby, but clean and cared for.

While Tommy went to his room to start on his homework each afternoon, (he was very familiar with that particular part of a twelve-year-old boy's life) he could hear her humming and banging around pots and pans in the kitchen before starting supper for the night. Soon, the lovely aroma of something, often Italian with basil and garlic, would float upstairs and creep under the door to his small bedroom, tickling his nose and making his stomach feel like a bottomless pit. His mother would beam when he came down for dinner at the stroke of five-thirty and inhale all of the hard work that she had put into feeding him. She could turn something as ordinary as spaghetti and meatballs into the most delicious meal.

After dinner, he would help her with the dishes as much as he could before she shooed him away to go out to play catch or soccer with the neighborhood kids while she corrected papers and made lesson plans. Sometimes he would go out, but not terribly often. The other kids were nice enough, but he didn't feel as if he really fit in with most of them. They were obsessed with the latest video games or their new phones and Tommy wasn't really into all of that. He surfed the internet, but usually for information, not games, although some of the informational sites had games for kids on them that he enjoyed.

If he didn't go out after dinner, Tommy would often read to himself. He liked books about history and had a weakness for comic books that he would buy with his allowance. He felt silly talking about the history books with most of the other kids so he kept his reading a secret from them.

There was one boy, however, that Tommy considered a real friend, someone who he felt had more than video games for brains. Nick Jones was just his age and had no brothers or sisters, either, but his parents were divorced. This meant that for at least five days out of the week, there was someone sort of like him, without a dad. On the weekends, Nick's dad would drive up in a red convertible; a mid-life crisis, Tommy's mother called it. Nick's mother called it something else, but Tommy wasn't allowed to repeat it.

Nick even listened to Tommy talk about his favorite history books, when they had a good adventure in them, anyway, and they shared a passion for comic books, spending summer afternoons and their allowance in the small comic shop downtown. Because Nick's parents were divorced, though, they didn't get much time to spend together at each other's houses. He went with his father every weekend and for two weeks during summer vacation.

Nick's father seemed to sweep him away in a red blur every Friday afternoon for a weekend of water parks and laser tag. It had always sounded so exciting to Tommy until Nick confessed that his

11

dad didn't go on the water slides with him but sat talking on his cell phone or texting the whole time while Nick tried to find someone to pal around with. It was really very lonely and Nick said that he was always glad to come back home on Sunday nights. Tommy sometimes thought that even a lousy father might be better than having no father at all, but he kept that to himself so that he wouldn't hurt his friend's feelings.

The whereabouts of Tommy's father were a mystery, at least to him. No one seemed to know where he had disappeared to, except perhaps his mother. Tommy was convinced that his mother kept any evidence about his father locked in a box in her room. The box was somewhat large, about the size of a coffee table book, and made of wood. It was old fashioned looking and carved with spiraling, metal, decorations on the top and sides. The wood was dark, almost black, and the hinges were a dull brass. His mother kept it on her dresser along with a framed picture of Tommy on his first birthday. She wore the key to the lock around her neck and had never let Tommy look inside, no matter how much he begged and pleaded with her. She always promised that she would open it for him when he was older, and then made it clear that the conversation was over.

When Tommy would ask why he went away if he had loved them so much, his mother would get a sad smile on her face and say, "Sometimes, people don't have a choice." That part always made Tommy feel angry. To him it was a simple choice: stay with your family or run away to who-knows-where to do who-knows-what. It was maddening that he couldn't get the truth out of her.

Tommy had only one picture of his father and it was of whole family together, the only one that was ever taken, as far as he knew. In it, his mother was curled up in their blue reclining rocking chair, the same one that they still had in the living room. Her dark curls were neatly combed and held back with a green headband. She was looking at the camera with tired, but happy, eyes. It must have been just a day or so after coming home from the hospital with Tommy because she was holding him, all bundled up in a soft-looking blanket. Tommy had a small knit cap on his head to keep him warm and his face was all scrunched up. There were little mittens on his hands ("To keep you from scratching yourself", his mother said) and his eyes looked impossibly big and blue.

His father was kneeling in front of the chair, but had angled his body toward his family on the chair, his hand resting gently on the bundle that was Tommy. His face looked right at the camera, almost as though he were aware that this was the last picture that he would take with his new son. He had worn his brown hair long, gathered back into a neat ponytail. His eyebrows were arched in a way that made him look surprised even when he wasn't. He had dimples in his cheeks, something that he had passed onto his son, and his eyes were a clear blue, like Tommy's.

It was a happy family picture, even if it was taken with a self-timing camera. They all looked very content, like they were supposed to be together. In it, there was no indication that very soon Tommy's father, Geoffrey Andrews, would disappear from their lives forever.

Tommy often fantasized about how his family life would be if his father had stayed in the picture, if he had been a real father to play catch with and to teach Tommy how to fish. He didn't know much about him, but what he was able to squeeze out of his mother was that his father was a great outdoorsman, but that he also liked to read anything he could get his hands on, as though he wouldn't ever be able to get enough books. He liked to hunt with a crossbow rather than a gun and during the two years that they had been married and together, he had brought home enough deer meat to last for a long time in the freezer. Tommy's mother had sold the crossbow long ago. She was worried that Tommy would get a hold of it and shoot himself by accident.

"But what was he *like*?" Tommy would beg his mother. "What kind of job did he have? Where did he come from? Does he have brothers and sisters? Do I have cousins, or maybe grandparents? Is there anybody in his family that I can meet?"

His mother would sigh and close her eyes as if those were the most difficult questions in the world instead of being dreadfully ordinary.

"Tommy, your father's past was a difficult one. His family died when he was young and he grew up as an orphan. He wasn't a bad person, not at all, but he was always watching over his shoulder to make sure that no one was following him. There are evil people in the world and he wanted to make sure that you and I were safe. He was the kindest, gentlest man I had ever met."

"He was born in England, but he was very content living here in America with us." She was truly sorry that she couldn't tell him any more information. Tommy could see it in her eyes, pleading

15

with him to not make this any more difficult for her than it already was. For her sake, he'd stop the barrage of questions, but only to stop her from being sad. If it were up to him, he would have gone on forever, but he couldn't resist just one more question.

"Did he say if he was ever coming back?" he would ask her over and over again, as if the answer would change.

His mother shook her head. "No," she said, "He had to go; he didn't have a choice about it. He really didn't. It wasn't something that he made up. He left us some money to help out. Most of the money was very old; antique coins and such. Some of them were more than four hundred years old! Some of it I sold to help us out and some I've saved for you for when you're older. Then you can do with it what you want to, but to answer your question, he just didn't know and neither do I. I'm sorry."

The story sounded stranger to Tommy the older he got. His father thought people were following him? He had left antique money for them? What kind of person was Geoffrey Andrews, anyway? The more he learned about his family history, the more of a mystery it became. Tommy was more than determined to figure things out, once and for all. He began to hatch a plan inside his head,

16

a plan that would certainly get him into trouble if his mother ever found out, but it might just help him find out what had happened to his father. Heck, it might even help him *find* his father, a possibility that Tommy hardly dared to think about.

He was weighing the consequences of his plan one night when he was supposed to be working on a research report about the American Revolution. He tried to keep his mind focused on Samuel Adams and the significance of the Boston Tea Party but instead his mind kept drifting to the significance of his father leaving behind old money and wondering who could possibly have been chasing after him. It occurred to Tommy that he would most likely need some help in the matter; help from someone who understood his father dilemma and who might be willing to help, even with the threat of being discovered by whoever his father was afraid of or worse: his mother. Someone who liked a good adventure. He decided to talk to Nick after school the next day.

***

The next day seemed to drag on forever, each class more boring than the last. Tommy was so focused on talking to Nick later and not sounding like a complete idiot that he couldn't wrap his mind around the new algebra formulas first thing that morning and was reprimanded by the math teacher, Mrs. Beydoun, for not paying attention. He got through gym class all right. They were only swimming laps mindlessly and he could think about what to say at the same time.

Home Economics, however, was a nightmare. He was supposed to be measuring and timing, but as a result of his daydreaming, the egg whites did not turn into a meringue; they looked more like the suds at the car wash. Mrs. Ferris, the cooking teacher shook her head as she prodded the sodden mess with Tommy's spatula.

"Mr. Andrews, where is your head today? I've never seen a meringue look so… flat." She wrote something in her grade book and moved on to the next person, Susan Wright, who always did a perfect job at everything. She had giggled at Tommy's meringue mess and now had her nose up in the air, smiling smugly as Mrs. Ferris praised her perfect meringue, stiff with white peaks, like a mountain range.

"Susan's meringue is perfect enough to go on top of a lemon pie right this minute!" Mrs. Ferris proclaimed. Susan smiled pointedly at Tommy. Tommy scowled and looked at the floor. What he really wanted to do was to take her perfect meringue and shove right in her face. He smiled as he imagined Susan's shocked face, dripping with egg white while the class laughed. Maybe the sugar would even attract a swarm of bugs that would all go after her. He smothered a laugh as he imagined Miss Perfect running down the hallway, dripping with meringue and pursued by a cloud of flies and gnats, maybe even a yellow jacket or two. It was difficult, but he did manage to get himself under control and began to clean up his mess before Mrs. Ferris noticed.

The last half of the day dragged even more slowly than the first half. Lunch was a blob of something that they had had for lunch a few days ago, meat loaf perhaps. The President's new rules on lunchroom nutrition had obviously not made it to Michigan yet. At least the chocolate milk was actually milk. After lunch it was English grammar in Language Arts, boring under the best circumstances, followed by Social Studies.

Social Studies class was the one place where Tommy was usually really interested. He was fascinated by the explorers who had traveled the world, the problems that they had faced along their journeys, and where they ended up. Then, they had studied about the Puritans and were now, at the end of the year, studying the Revolutionary War. There seemed to be an endless networking of spies and strategies, just like in some of the video games that he played at his friends' houses; but this had not been a game that the Americans were playing. He found it incredible that people were willing to die for what they believed in. He couldn't imagine being able to do that, or the neighborhood kids being able to do that.

Tommy's teacher, Mr. Barnhart, was very interested in the American Revolution. He was from England and would joke with the students about what would have happened if the Americans had lost the war. It wasn't unusual for him to supplement his lessons with real historical objects that he owned himself; *primary sources* he called them.

During their unit on European explorers, he had brought in artifacts from daily life in the 1500's and 1600's. For the American

Revolution one day, he brought in some first-hand accounts that soldiers had written home to their families.

One of the letters spoke of a drummer boy, just eleven years old, who had been killed in battle. The soldier wrote of the young boy's bravery under heavy fire and how the remaining soldiers wept when they buried his body. That passage hit Tommy hard. For the rest of that day he wondered what it would have been like to be that boy, who was a year younger than himself and playing his drum while bullets flew through the air around him. It was a difficult feeling to shake off.

But on this day, like in all of his other classes, Tommy found it unusually hard to concentrate in his favorite class, even while they were having a debate, something that he loved to do. Mr. Barnhart noticed it, too, and asked Tommy to stay after for a minute.

Tommy sat there nervously while the other kids shuffled out, curious why Tommy had to stay. Of course, Susan Wright was whispering with all of her annoying friends, about him, he was sure, but he wasn't worried. He didn't want to tell Mr. Barnhart what was going on, but he knew that his teacher wouldn't push him too hard about it.

When the classroom was empty, Mr. Barnhart shut the door and turned to look at Tommy for a moment.

"Is everything alright, Tommy?" he asked.

Tommy nodded and fixed his eyes on the history book in front of him.

"I'm just asking because usually, you participate in the class discussions. It's not like you to sit quietly out of it, especially when we're discussing alternate perspectives." Mr. Barnhart was right. Tommy usually loved looking at historical situations from all points of view, not just the popular ones. For this particular lesson, however, he just couldn't seem to focus. Talking to Nick had been at the forefront of his mind all day.

He realized that Mr. Barnhart was staring quizzically at him and was waiting for Tommy to respond somehow.

Flushing red, he stammered out, "I'm sorry, sir. My mind is just on other things today. It won't happen again."

Still concerned, Mr. Barnhart asked, "Is it anything that you'd like to tell me about? I'm a pretty good listener."

Tommy felt torn. He really would like to spill everything out to his favorite teacher. His father's mysterious disappearance, the

22

other clues that he wanted to follow up on, bringing Nick into the situation, it was all too much. In the back of his mind, though, there was a little voice whispering to him, *Not yet, not yet.* Grudgingly, Tommy shook his head.

"No, but thank you. I'll be back to normal tomorrow." *I hope*, he thought as he gave Mr. Barnhart his best grin under the circumstances and gathered his things to head for the last period of the day. He was well aware that Mr. Barnhart didn't believe him and felt his eyes watching his back all the way out the door. He often got the feeling that Mr. Barnhart knew more about him than he thought. He was aware that his mom knew Mr. Barnhart. They were both teachers in the same small town, after all. It just seemed that somehow Mr. Barnhart *knew* him. He shook the feeling off and went to his next class.

The last hour, Computer Technology, passed by surprisingly quickly. There was a substitute and the teacher had left instructions for a free day. In that time, Tommy used a few different search engines to look up whatever he could find on crossbows and old coins and while the information that he found was fairly interesting, it wasn't anything that he felt would help him. When the final bell of the day finally rang, he bolted out of the door to his locker in order to catch up with Nick. He usually waited for his mother to finish teaching at the elementary school, but he had told her in the morning that he and Nick might hang out for a while that afternoon.

Stuffing his homework into his backpack, he caught up with Nick down the hallway at his locker. Although Tommy's locker was messy, it was nothing compared to the nuclear explosion that seemed to have happened in Nick's locker. Old lunch bags, crumpled papers, and even banana peels were all part of the disgusting mess. It was impossible to see where Nick put his school books or backpack.

"Wow", Tommy said as Nick wrestled some papers from the mass inside, "Gross! How do you find anything in there?"

Nick just grinned as he smoothed out a math worksheet. "I have a system. What's up?"

"Get your stuff and walk home with me. I've got a proposition for you."

"A proposition, huh? This isn't anything that going to get me into trouble, is it? I have enough to worry about as it is. My mom's gonna kill me when she sees my math grade."

Tommy shook his head. "Nope. If anyone is going to get into trouble, it's me." He glanced around, not wanting anyone else to hear what he had to say, especially Susan Wright who was only a few lockers away. He leaned in closer to Nick and whispered, "I want you to help me find my dad."

Nick looked at him strangely. "Your dad? Is he still alive? Where is he?" Nick knew that Tommy's dad wasn't around, but he knew that it made Tommy uncomfortable, so he never asked him about it.

"I don't know. My mom doesn't know, either, or so she says. He left behind some stuff that I think will help us, almost like a map, but there are a lot of pieces missing. I need you there to help me figure it out, from a different perspective, you know? Maybe you'll see something that I don't." Nick was looking interested now.

"I have to warn you, though. I'm going to need to break into something of my mom's. I'll do it so you don't get into trouble, but I need your help. I think that there's something in this box that she has that will help us."

"Like a clue?"

Tommy nodded.

25

Nick stared at him. "You're going to break into a box of your mom's? Won't you get into trouble?"

Tommy's stomach churned. He didn't want to break into the box, but the pull of finding something useful in there was so strong that he just couldn't help it.   Looking at Nick he said, "I hope not. We'll have to make a plan for when we can do it and put the box back before she notices that it's missing. We aren't going to steal anything. I just want to see what's in there and copy down any information that we find. We'll put everything back exactly the way it was. Then we can figure out if it will lead us anywhere or not. What do you say?"

Nick looked at him skeptically. "You really think we're going to be able to find your dad with whatever is in your mom's locked box?"

Tommy nodded.

Nick let out a heavy sigh and thought for a moment. "What's in it for me?"

Tommy thought for a moment and then had an idea. "My mom has a lot of old coins that she's been saving for me, ones that my dad left behind to help us out. She said that some of them are

26

over five hundred years old. If you help me out, when she gives them to me, I'll let you pick out whichever one you want. For keeps."

"For keeps?"

"Yep."

"Swear it."

Tommy sighed and tried to think up a good pledge. "I do solemnly swear to give Nick Jones his choice of old coins once we are done solving the mystery of where my father went. There, will that work?"

Nick stuck out his hand and tried not to laugh. "Jeez, you're a cornball. Shake on it."

They shook on it and immediately Tommy felt better. Knowing that he had a partner in all of this was going to make things a lot easier, so he thought.

***

All the way home, Tommy and Nick talked about how they were going to get into the box. Nick wanted to dress all in black and sneak into her room in the dead of night while she was sleeping, like a spy would in a movie, but Tommy shot that idea down.

"She's up late at night, correcting papers and watching old movies on TV. Plus, she sleeps really lightly. She'd wake up in a minute and freak out when she found us. We have to do it when she's out of the house. It's the only way."

"Okay, so when is she going to be out? She can't sit and correct papers all the time. Does she ever go out on dates? When my mom goes out on dates she's gone for hours."

Tommy shook his head. "No good. She hasn't ever gone out on a date. That's another reason I think my dad is still alive out there. It would be weird if he came back and she was dating another guy, right?"

"Maybe you just don't know that she's going out on dates." Nick smiled mischievously.

Starting to get annoyed, Tommy said firmly, "No dates. No way. We're getting off the topic." He thought for a moment. "She goes grocery shopping on Saturday mornings. That's only two days away. We can do it then."

Nick thought. "I'm supposed to be at my dad's this weekend, but I'll tell him that I'm going to do homework with you in the morning, so he can come and get me Saturday night instead. How long is your mom gone for?"

"A couple of hours. I think that'll be plenty of time for us to get in there and do what we need to do. By the way, how are you at picking locks?"

"Well, I never have, but I think I could practice on the tool shed lock. My mom never goes in there anyway. I'll look online, too and see what I can find out."

"Great, me too. We need to make sure we do it without damaging the box. It looks really old and valuable."

They were nearing the point where they would split off and head to their separate houses. They stopped and went over the plan one more time.

"Okay, so Saturday when your mom leaves to go shopping, call me and I'll come right over. We'll pick the lock, see what's inside, and decide what to do after that." Nick was getting excited now. He was talking fast and little splotches of pink were showing up on his cheeks.

"Yeah, but don't forget that we can't break the lock, or the box." Tommy ventured nervously. Now that they had a plan in the works it actually was beginning to feel slightly devious and that made him uncomfortable. He had never really lied to his mom before; he really hadn't ever had a reason to and she trusted him. It made him feel bad that they were going to sneak into her room and snoop in her things, but he told himself that he wasn't actually telling her a *lie*, he simply wasn't telling her what he was going to be doing.

Even with all of the reassurances he was giving himself, he still felt like a weasel, but was determined to see what was inside the box. Somehow he knew that whatever was in there would give him the clues to help find out what had happened to his dad. He could feel it! But still... He looked at Nick for a moment

"Uh, I feel kind of like a jerk for doing this."

To his surprise, Nick looked slightly sheepish, too. "Yeah, I know how you feel. Your mom's a nice lady. She was my third grade teacher."

Tommy knew that. Nick hadn't been in his third grade class and his mom had taught almost half of the kids in the town. He felt better, knowing that Nick felt the same way.

"I still want to do it, okay?" Tommy asked him.

30

A mischievous glint appeared in Nick's eyes. "You're on!"

He clapped Tommy on the back and turned toward home. "See you

on Saturday," he called over his shoulder.

Chapter Two

On Saturday morning, Tommy awoke with butterflies in his

stomach. He hadn't slept well, knowing what he and Nick were

going to do. He felt horribly guilty about sneaking around behind his

mom's back. A lot of kids at the middle school he attended seemed

to be embarrassed by their mothers or were always complaining

about them, but Tommy really did like his mom. She didn't smother

him, like some mothers, and she was never too busy to hear about

his day or to help him with a problem.

He wondered to himself why he didn't tell his mother about what he was going to do. For one thing, she would certainly try to stop him. She didn't think that he was old enough to even look in the box, never mind using what was in there to begin his search. He knew that it could truly be something dangerous, otherwise why wouldn't she let him see? He also wanted to prove to her that he was growing up and felt like he could handle anything that came his way. As for the coins, maybe Mr. Barnhart could help him figure out where they fit in.

He got out of bed and took a quick shower before going downstairs to breakfast. He found his mom in their little dining room making out the grocery list for the week. She sat with the box of coupons next to her on the table, which she carefully clipped out from the ads in the Sunday paper every week. Saving money was a big deal to her, not because they were dreadfully poor, but because she wanted to save for Tommy's education. She wanted him to go to an important university like Harvard or Yale and she wanted to be able to pay for everything without asking for help.

He said good morning to her and got himself a bowl a cereal before sitting down with at the table. She gave him the grocery list to read over as he munched away, another of their little rituals. She wanted to give him some input into what she bought. This time, Tommy noticed that she had added his favorite cookies to the list. She didn't usually get them because of the price, but would buy them as a treat once in a while. They were huge chocolate and peanut butter chip cookies that remained soft as long as the package was kept closed up. Tommy practically drooled at the thought of them, but knowing that she was buying something special for him made him feel even guiltier. He nodded his head, his mouth full of raisin bran, and shoved the grocery list back across the table to her.

"Does everything look okay?" she asked. "Did you notice that I added your cookies on there? It's been a while since I bought them for you and you've been working so hard in school." It was true, Tommy's grades had been excellent. Well, except for his home economics class. Cooking just didn't seem to be his thing. He pointed that out to his mom and she laughed, reaching out affectionately to ruffle his hair.

"Your father couldn't cook either, although he did try." Tommy sat quietly, hoping that she would say more about his dad.

"He had a horrible time working the stove and could never remember to put things away in the refrigerator. One hot summer, before we had air conditioning, he left the butter out and by the time I got home from work, it was a puddle on the counter." She laughed to herself at the memory. "He would try to cook breakfast and almost burn the house down. After a while, he stuck to cereal and milk. He told me that where he grew up, his mother and sisters did all of the cooking and didn't teach him anything."

Tommy was really intrigued now. "What else did he do?"

His mother chuckled, "Oh, the first time he tried to light a fire in the fireplace by himself he almost set the house on fire. I told him it was no wonder that he couldn't cook. He and fire just didn't get along. He told me that he got the whipping of his life from his father and that it took him a full year to try it again."

Eager for more, Tommy asked, "What else?"

"His sisters once tried to dress him up like a girl when he was little. He was the youngest and they trapped him in the barn, made him wear one of their dresses and braided his hair. He said that he had long hair when he was a little boy."

"But he has long hair in the picture that we have!"

"I guess it was even longer then. That time, it was the sisters that got in trouble."

"Did they get whipped, too?"

"I don't know. He didn't say. And now", she broke off the storytelling, "I need to get to the grocery store. Did you see anything else that I could add to the list?"

Tommy shook his head. "No. Mom?" His stomach was churning.

"Yes, Sweetie?"

"Is it okay if Nick comes over this morning? We want to hang out for a bit."

"Sure. Don't eat all the food in the house. And no TV or internet until I'm back."

"Okay, Mom. Thanks!"

"And don't destroy the house".

He knew she was goofing around now. "Anything else, Mother?" he asked in mock exasperation.

She pretended to think for a moment and then shook her head. "Bye now!" She gave him a wink and headed out the door. As soon as her car was gone, he raced to the phone and dialed Nick's number. Nick's mom answered on the third ring. Tommy politely asked for Nick and he heard her yell for him through the house. When Nick got to the phone, he sounded like he had just woken up.

"'Lo?"

"Nick, it's Tommy. She just left. How soon can you get here?"

Nick cleared his throat. "I'm on my way. I have to get dressed and then I'll be there."

"Hurry up… she'll be back in about an hour and a half. I want to have everything put back by then."

"Okay, okay; I'll be right there." *Click*. Nick hung up the phone. Tommy slowly put the receiver back in the cradle. He had set things in motion. There was no turning back now. He forced his feet to move toward his mother's room, feeling the dread sinking down in his stomach like a lead balloon. He also felt a rush of excitement at the thought of finding something of his father's and clues to where he was.

His mother's room was filled with bright sunshine from the windows. He loved this room. It was where he had crept into bed with his mother when he had bad dreams as a little boy and where he used to watch her fix her hair in the mornings before work. Of course, he was way too old to do any of those things now, but he had warm memories of feeling safe and very secure here. The bed had a large frame and headboard made from black walnut that she kept brightly polished. The bedspread was soft and comfortable; a cream-colored one with patterns of green leaves spread over it. Across from the bed was a tall, black walnut dresser. On top of the dresser was the box.

It was definitely an old box. It had little metal decorations on each corner and a lock that matched. The keyhole was old fashioned and looked like one would find in the door of an old house, but miniature. Tommy slowly picked the box up, grateful that his mother dusted regularly so there wouldn't be any tell-tale slide marks, and tried to look through the keyhole, but it was blocked by something. He gently shook the box and could feel some things moving around. He wished that Nick would hurry up. He had a sense of urgency and was fervently hoping that his mother would not come back early from the store.

When Nick did knock on the door a few minutes later, the sound nearly made Tommy jump out of his skin, even though he was expecting it. He carefully set the box down on the coffee table in the living room and opened the front door. Nick's eyes were still puffy from sleep, but there was a spark of excitement in his eye. Tommy took a quick look down the road to see if his mom was coming, then shut the door behind him.

Nick wandered around the living room, looking at the stacks of teaching manuals, papers, and general books in the corner where Mrs. Andrews usually sat. It wasn't messy, there was just a lot of stuff there. He reached down and picked up a book.

"*Charlotte's Web*. I remember this book! It was the one with the talking spider, right?"

"Yeah", Tommy said watching him. "What are you doing?"

"Just looking. It always looks so normal in here, not like a teacher's house."

"It *is* normal. We *are* people, you know." Tommy rolled his eyes at him. It wasn't anything he hadn't heard before. When they

38

periodically ran into one of his mom's students at the store or at a restaurant, most of the time the student would act amazed that she actually had a life separate from teaching, as if teachers didn't go shopping or out to eat. Tommy thought it was stupid, but to be fair, he knew that it felt strange when he saw one of his own teachers outside of the classroom.

"Are you done looking around?"

Nick, who had been flipping through the pages of *Charlotte's Web,* looked up at Tommy.

"Oh, yeah. Sorry, I got carried away for a minute there. So, is that it?" Nick pointed to the box on the table. "Wow, it does look really old."

"Yep. Did you bring something to pick it with?" Nick reached into his jacket pocket and pulled out a few interesting looking instruments: a paperclip, two screwdrivers of different sizes, and a credit card.

"What's the credit card for?" Tommy asked.

"The internet said that sometimes you can get an old door lock to open with one of these. I really didn't know what kind of lock it was, so I came prepared. Ready to start?"

Tommy nodded. He just wanted to get it over with. Nick examined the lock for a minute and then chose the paperclip. "I figure that this will do the least amount of damage", he said as opened the paperclip up and stuck one of the ends into the lock. He gently wiggled it around, trying to feel for the mechanism inside. After a long moment, his face brightened. "I think I've got it!"

Sure enough, the top of the box popped up, not enough to see what was inside, but it was open. Nick generously handed the box to Tommy. "Here, you open it."

With shaking hands, Tommy took the box from Nick and set it on his lap. He lifted the lid and let the light fall on the contents inside.

The contents were completely covered with a dark green piece of cloth that looked like silk. Tommy slowly lifted the silk cover off and looked for the first time at what his mother had kept concealed from him for so long.

There were some coins on top, old ones, too, by the look of them. Tommy lifted each of them up slowly, one by one, and passed them to Nick to examine. Some were silver, some were gold, and they had pictures on them of what looked like a king. There was a crown on the image's head.

Next to be taken out of the box were some old, folded letters. Tommy carefully opened up the first one and saw that it was a poem dedicated to his mother. He supposed that his father had written it and saw that he had guessed rightly. At the bottom of the page was his father's signature, *Geoffrey, 2000*, the year before he was born. He didn't read the poem; he felt that was private between his mom and dad, plus it was probably mushy. He set it aside.

"Is that anything good?" Nick asked.

"Nope. Just a love note from my dad to my mom."

"Ew."

Tommy hurriedly lifted out the next piece of folded paper. This one seemed really old. It was yellowed with age and was folded only once in the middle. Tommy carefully unfolded it, hoping that it wouldn't rip. What he found made him gasp in surprise.

It was another love poem to his mother, but it was the part at the bottom where his father had signed it that had made him gasp. He had to blink and look twice to be sure of what he was seeing:

Geoffrey Andrews, London, August 1540. Nick came up beside him to look.

"What is it?"

Tommy shook his head. "This can't be right. 1540? That was almost five hundred years ago."

Nick said excitedly, "Look at the next one. Maybe that will help."

Tommy lifted out the next yellowed paper. Actually, he began to think that the papers weren't normal paper, but parchment. It felt thick. He carefully opened it up and began to read what was there. It was from his father, but it wasn't a poem this time. It was addressed to his mother; it was a letter. Before reading what the letter said, he glanced down at the bottom again to find his father's signature: *Geoffrey, 1540*. Nick's eyes widened.

"1540 again! It can't be a mistake! Tommy, do you know what this looks like?"

Tommy shook his head, confused. Nick shook his head, annoyed at Tommy being too slow to catch on.

"Your dad was from a different time! He's a time traveler! He has to be! Look at how old this paper is."

42

"Parchment. They didn't have real paper yet", Tommy corrected automatically, feeling his stomach going all quivery.

"Whatever. It's not fake; look how brittle the papers are, not like that first one. It has to be real!"

Tommy stammered, "But time travel is impossible! No one has ever done it!"

"It looks like your dad figured out a way. Read the letter."

"But it's to my mom! What if there's gross stuff in there?"

"So what? If he was back in time already, maybe it won't be so bad."

"Fine." Tommy looked down at the letter. "It's kind of faded but I'll try."

My Dearest Mistress Elizabeth,

Long it has been since I have seen your lovely face. I miss you and little Tommy so much. How is he growing? I yearn to be back with you both and to watch him grow into a man. Every day, I search for a new way. It is to my greatest sorrow that I had to leave you, but it could not be avoided. I shall continue to hope for a way of coming back. Until then, I shall keep writing to you and entrusting Edward to bring them to you. I hope that they have all survived the traveling. Please burn these letters when you've read them so they don't fall into Abraham's hands.

Well now, there was something. Abraham was a name he hadn't heard before. He could be the bad guy. And who was Edward? Obviously, she hadn't burned the letters, or at least not this one. He read on.

I am back in England, but I dare not tell you where. There is quite a bit of talk of the king and his new bride, Katherine Howard. She is quite young, being about sixteen years old, and is from the prominent Howard family. Many are wondering how many wives he will have, her being the fifth one, and I sometimes find it difficult to keep silent about what I have learned in your time. Who here would believe that there will one day be a cold box to put food into or that people will be able to fly through the air and across the oceans in great, silver bird? These are things that I will have to write about only to you and pray that these letters reach you somehow.

In the meantime, kiss our son for me and tell him things only when he's ready to hear them. I hope that I may return one day to see him again.

Your loving husband,

44

Geoffrey Andrews, London, August 1540

Tommy slowly put the letter down in shock. His father was from the past? It was impossible! There was no such thing as time travel, he was sure of it. How could his mother have known this for years and not have told him about it? With his head spinning in disbelief, he jumped a mile when Nick clapped his hand on his shoulder.

"Tommy, do you know what this *means*? Nick had gone pale and his freckles were standing out. Tommy shook his head.

"We have to go back in time to find him! We have to try! If he could do it, so can we. What else is in the box? There must be something to explain it and how it works."

Nick reached around Tommy and gently dug further into the box. Tommy was still standing in shock, holding the letter. His brain just couldn't process what was going on. It certainly appeared as if his father was from the past, but how had he gotten to the future? If it was true, it certainly made sense then that his father hadn't been able to cook on a modern stove or remember to put things away in a refrigerator. Heck, the very idea of airplanes, electricity, even cars, probably made his head spin when he was in modern times. What would it be like to come from a time of horses, weird clothes and castles to a place where people had cell phones? Nick must be right; there must be something else in the box that would help them make sense of it all.

He looked down to see Nick drawing out a long, delicate, silver chain from the box. It glittered in the sunlight as if it hadn't been buried in a box for many years. At the end of the chain was a silver amulet. It was a circle shape and was carved with tiny leaves. Set in the center was a large, smooth, purple stone that sparkled and shone as if it contained a million stars. Tommy grabbed the amulet and looked closely at it. It was looking into a deep sea; he couldn't see the end to it. When he held it, his fingers felt tingly as if it was full of electricity.

"Cool", Nick breathed, gently taking it from Tommy. "It looks like an amethyst. That's the name for it, right? Do you think this is it? Do you think this is what does it?"

"I don't know." Tommy couldn't take his eyes off of it. It almost seemed to be speaking to him. Shaking his head, he forcefully looked away and reached into the box again. There weren't any more letters from his father. He gently pawed through

46

the box to see if there were any more clues to what the amulet was. Maybe his father had just given it to his mother as a gift. Perhaps it wasn't magical at all and the tingly feeling was just his imagination. He pushed more coins out of the way and then he came to another parchment at the very bottom of the box. As he opened it, he noticed that it wasn't a letter but a set of what looked like directions. With great excitement, he pulled it out.

"Nick, look at this. I think it's important!" Nick blinked his eyes and set down the amulet to look over Tommy shoulder at the parchment. It definitely looked older than the other papers and was written in very strange lettering that was hard to read. Some of it had faded, but it was still readable. The edges were beginning to crumble.

Nick let out a low whistle. "Wow, that's in worse shape than the other papers, er, parchments", he corrected himself.

Tommy nodded. "I think it's directions on how to use the amulet. I think that the amulet is how the time travel works!"

"Well, come on, read it!" Nick was getting excited.

Suddenly, Tommy happened to glance at the clock. It had only felt like a few minutes, but it was close to the time that his mother was due to be back from the grocery store. He decided not to risk it.

"Listen, Nick, we'll have to figure this out later. My mom's going to be home any minute. We'll have to put this away until we can get it out again." He started putting the coins and the letters carefully back into the box.

"Tommy, if we use it, if we really use it, do you think it will send us back to your dad's time? Will we go back to 1540?"

"I don't know. I've never done it before. I hope it does. It would really stink to be sent somewhere randomly."

"Seriously." Nick looked worried. "I'd hate to go back to caveman times, or to go back during the Black Plague. And how do we get back *here* once we get *there*? This might all just be a bunch of hocus pocus, too. It might not do anything at all. It *probably* won't," he said, sounding like he was trying to convince himself to not get too excited, just in case.

"I don't know. I'll hide this paper in my room and read it tonight. Maybe it'll tell us more. Right now we have to get everything else back into the box exactly the way we found it and lock it back up. She might read these to herself sometimes. Do you think you could open it again?"

"Pu-leaze, the lock is so old it's a piece of cake. Should we try it again next Saturday when she goes again?"

"Yep, and this week let's find out everything that we can about the year 1540. If we're really going to go back and do this, we need to know how to act and all of that stuff. Maybe my dad's in a history book somewhere."

"I'll bet Mr. Barnhart could help. He knows a lot about history."

"That's what I was thinking. We'll have to be sneaky about it though. He's cool and all, but he'll think we're absolutely nuts if he finds out we're thinking about time travel."

"Sounds like a plan."

Quickly, Tommy covered the items in the box with the green silk again and locked it. Tommy didn't know if his mother ever looked inside of the box but he didn't want her getting suspicious. After all, the letter showed that she knew that time travel, or whatever, was possible. His father had made that perfectly clear, and he didn't want her trying to stop them if she found out what they were up to. Heck, she might even get rid of the amulet; lock it up in the bank or something.

The boys finished putting the box back, and just in time. As soon as Tommy had slid it back on top of the dresser, he heard his mother's car pull into the driveway. He and Nick quickly walked out of the room and went out to help her with the groceries. His mother was surprised.

"Wow, what have I done to deserve all of this help? Nick it's good to see you again. How is seventh grade treating you?"

"Fine, Mrs. Andrews", Nick mumbled. Tommy's heart skipped a beat, hoping that Nick wasn't going to blow it. If she thought they were up to something, she wouldn't let Nick come over on Saturday mornings any more when she wasn't home.

"So what did you boys do when I was at the store?"

"Uh, we talked about our history homework. We have a research report coming up soon."

"Oh, have you decided what you're going to do yet?"

"Maybe. We were thinking maybe something in the 1500s."

Tommy looked at his mother out of the corner of his eye. He thought he saw her jaw clench, just a bit; it was almost unnoticeable but it made his heart race faster. Maybe she did know something after all, or maybe he was just seeing things. She began unloading bags out of the car, handing them to Tommy and Nick.

"The good old sixteenth century, hmm? Why are you interested in that?" She kept her voice purposefully light, Tommy noticed, but he also heard the note of concern that was behind her question, like when he was eight and said that he wanted to be a race car driver. He would have to tread very carefully here.

"Well, there was a lot of cool stuff that happened back then, like that king with all the wives and stuff. We're thinking about doing our history report on him." That wasn't entirely a lie. Mr. Barnhart did tell them that they would have to do a joint report. Why not do it on that king that his dad had written about?

"Oh, Henry VIII." Tommy thought that he saw his mother relax a little bit. "Yes, he can be very interesting to study. A bit of a tyrant, really." All of the bags were unloaded and the three of them began walking up to the house. In one of Tommy's bags, he could see the package of his favorite cookies that his mom had promised him when she left and felt another stab of guilt.

"Do you know much about him, Mrs. Andrews?" Nick was trying to help it along.

"A bit."

"Do you think you could help us with some of the details? Tommy, maybe we should just focus on him and not on the sixteenth century in general."

"That's probably a good idea." After all, if they wanted to avoid suspicion with his mom, focusing on Henry VIII seemed pretty harmless. Besides, they would need that information for when they would try out the amulet.

"He's definitely an interesting person to study, not only for how many wives he had but how he changed the religion in England."

"What do you mean changed the religion?" Tommy was getting genuinely interested now.

Mrs. Andrews began taking the groceries out of the bags and putting them away in the cupboards and refrigerator. Tommy took the used plastic bags and gathered them up for recycling later.

"Well, he wanted a divorce from his first wife, Katherine of Aragon, and the Pope wouldn't give it to him so he decided to make himself the Head of the Church of England. It was a big scandal because pretty much everyone in Europe was Catholic and if you spoke out against the Pope or the Church, you could get into big trouble."

"Did the Pope try to execute Henry?" Nick's curiosity was piqued now.

"No, but he was excommunicated, along with the entire kingdom. That means that the pope said that he would be kicked out of the church and, essentially, couldn't go to Heaven when he died. Understandably, his subjects were not pleased. A lot of them were devoted to being Catholic and didn't want to change. Many of them died for their beliefs."

"They died because of a religion? Why couldn't they still be Catholic?"

"Things didn't work that way back then. You had to follow the official religion, or else."

"Jeez", Nick said, "and I thought just getting up for Mass was tough."

Mrs. Andrews chuckled and said, "Things were a lot different then." They finished putting the groceries away and then Nick said that he had to go home.

"I'll start doing some more research online, Tommy."

Tommy nodded, "Yeah, me too. I'll catch up on the reading, too."

"Okay. See ya."

"See ya."

Nick headed out the door and Tommy was alone in the kitchen with his mother. He didn't have Nick as a distraction now and the guilt about what they had done was beginning to weigh on him. His mother noticed that something seemed wrong.

"Everything okay, Honey?"

"Yeah, fine, Mom. I'm just thinking about the project." Another lie, sort of. "Was Henry VIII really that bad?"

"I really haven't studied him all that much, I just know the basics. Maybe you should ask Mr. Barnhart. He's probably a bit more qualified than I am to tell you about it."

"I'll ask him on Monday." Tommy shuffled out of the kitchen to his bedroom feeling slightly betrayed. He wanted to ask his mom the questions about his dad that he really confused about. Why could she not tell him what she knew?

He shut the door to his room and had to make himself not pull out the parchment that he had hidden under his bed until nighttime. If his mother walked in on him reading it, he didn't know what he'd say. *Sorry, Mom, but I broke into your box and found out that my dad is from 1540, so Nick and I are figuring out a way to go back in time and find him. What's for dinner?* Yeah, that sounded totally crazy. This whole thing was crazy. He sighed and flopped down on the bed. Maybe after he finally got to read the paper things would make more sense.

***

Later that night, after an uncomfortable, but delicious, dinner of shrimp fettuccini with his mom, he waited until he heard her turn out the lights in the living room, walk across the creaky floor to the bathroom, and then walk back across the creaky floor to her room and shut the door. He glanced at his alarm clock: 11:07 pm. He waited a few more minutes until he felt sure that she had settled in and then retrieved his flashlight from his nightstand drawer. He frequently read at night and his mom didn't mind as long as he was able to get up for school the next morning. Some kids that he knew had televisions and computers in their rooms and they would stay awake half the night chatting online or watching late night re-runs. His mom was vehemently opposed to having that stuff in his room and although at first he felt a little put out by it, secretly he was kind of glad to not have the distraction. He didn't want to look like a zombie or to fall asleep in class like some of them did. This time, however, was a different matter and the next day was Sunday. He could zone out in church during the sermon if he needed to and no one would be the wiser for it.

Carefully, he stretched his arm out under his bed until he felt the folded parchment. He pulled it out, switched on his flashlight, and began to try and make out the lettering.

At second glance, it was incredibly old looking, older than the other papers. The heading at the top read: *The Amulets of the Moors*. That part was written in different writing than the rest of it. Tommy didn't know who or what the Moors were, but he could look that up on the internet tomorrow. His mom wouldn't mind. He went on to read:

Beware to he who wears this amulet!

A journey like no other will he take

To lands beyond description

Sights terrifying and wonderful to the eyes

With no guarantee of ever coming home alive.

This amulet was taken from the Moors

During the Holy Quest of Jerusalem by the servant

of

His Highness,

King Richard of England

To begin the magik, the bearer must hold the amulet

in his hand and make known His desire where he wants to

go.

He must not lose hold.

If the amulet is lost, the bearer will never return.

Tommy stopped reading for a moment and thought: *That's why Dad couldn't come back; the amulet is here! He needs it to travel back and forth.* He continued reading the last part of the parchment.

𝕿o return, he must hold the amulet securely and make known his desire to return home.

𝕬 warning to all who read this.

𝕸uch can go wrong.

-𝕷ord 𝖂illiam 𝕭arnhart, 1309

Much could go wrong. That was obvious. His father somehow ended up in the 1990s, got married, had a son, and then disappeared back to his own time without the amulet to bring him back. It must have been a mistake to leave the amulet here because in one of the letters, he wrote that he was searching for a way to return. It was all so confusing!

Tommy's heart was pounding. He desperately wanted to try out the amulet right then and there, but of course it was impossible. The amulet was locked back up in the box on his mom's dresser and besides, he needed Nick to come with him. Tommy gave a long sigh and put the parchment back under his bed. He didn't want to wait, but it seemed as if he had no choice. To look on the bright side, he reminded himself that he still had a lot of information to find out about the sixteenth century before they went. He pulled out a book from the collection on his nightstand and tried to read himself to sleep.

Chapter Three

Monday morning couldn't come soon enough for Tommy.

He hadn't been able to call Nick on Sunday because he had gone to

be with his dad. He really wanted to talk to him about the parchment.

When he finally saw Nick in the morning at school, Nick looked at

him questioningly. Instead of spilling it all then, as he was dying to

do, Tommy simply said, "I'll tell you all about it on the way home.

There's too much to say now."

The school day dragged on and on. When the last bell rang,

Tommy leaped out of his seat and walked as fast as he dared past

Susan Wright and her clique to his locker to meet Nick. Nick must

have been just as anxious as Tommy because he scurried up not long

after, still stuffing papers into his overflowing backpack.

"So, did you read it? What did it say?"

"Hang on. Let's get out of the school first. Just play it cool for a few minutes." Tommy wanted to dodge the eyes of the annoying Susan Wright, who was looking at them suspiciously. His and Nick's reputations would be unsalvageable through the end of high school if she thought that they were dabbling in time travel. They'd be the laughingstock of the entire school! Of course, if it worked, she'd never know a thing. He grinned, knowing that he could possibly do something that she and her stuck-up friends had never even fathomed. Maybe someday, he'd have a chance to show her up.

When they were a safe distance from the school, Tommy leaned toward Nick, who was looking at him expectantly.

"Okay, I read it Saturday night. It said that the amulet was taken from the Moors during the Crusades."

"Who are the Moors?"

"I looked it up online and the Moors were the people who lived in the Middle East and Africa. A bunch of kings in the Middle Ages went on Crusades to try and capture the city of Jerusalem but it didn't work. The parchment says that the amulet was taken by the army of Richard, King of England. I looked that up, too, and it turns out that it was the army of Richard the Lionheart."

Nick looked confused. "Who's Richard the Lionheart?"

Tommy sighed and rolled his eyes. "Don't you remember the story of Robin Hood? With Prince John and Maid Marian?"

It was as if a light bulb went on in Nick's head. "Oh *yeah*! That was one of the best movies ever! Robin Hood was a fox and Little John was a bear…"

"Yeah, well", Tommy interrupted him, "Richard the Lionheart was a real guy and a King of England, too. Someone in his army brought the amulet back from when they went on his Crusades. It has some rules with it, too."

"Like what?"

"Like you have to hold on to it and tell it where you want to go, but you can't let go of it. If you do, you won't be able to get back to where you want to go."

"Maybe that's what happened to your dad. That's why he's still stuck there."

"That's what I was thinking. So maybe if we go back and find him, then we can take him back home with us."

"But how do we know where he is?"

"Well, his letters are from London. I'm thinking that London will be our best bet"

"How do we do that?"

"We can look at the letters again and find one that's close to that date we're at now. That way, we can end up close to where he is. Once we get there, we can ask around. Someone will know him."

"So we're really going to do this." Nick stopped walking and looked at Tommy. He looked a little nervous.

"Sure, if you're still in."

"Yeah, I'm still in. I just want to make sure that we're coming back. We could get into big trouble for this."

"Nick, when are you ever going to have this opportunity again? How many kids can say that they traveled through time? You're the one who was all excited about it on Saturday." Tommy couldn't believe it. It sounded like Nick was starting to chicken out.

"I still want to do it. I'm just thinking about things."

"Like what?"

"Like what my parents are going to think when I disappear. Can we come back to the same minute that we left or if we stay for five days will we come back five days later?"

Tommy paused. He hadn't really thought about that. It wasn't like there was a manual or anything for explaining all of the rules of time-travel.

Tommy answered, "I don't know when we'll come back. Just to be safe, why don't you tell your mom that you're going to spend the night at my house on Saturday? I'll ask my mom if it's okay but don't worry… it'll be fine. Then your mom won't get worried. I'll leave a note in my room for my mom to find, since she knows all about this time travel stuff anyway. She'll know what we've done then. She's going to find out anyway and at least then I won't be there to see her face when she finds out that we left."

Nick started walking again, slowly. "Don't get me wrong; I really want to do this. I'm just a little nervous."

"Me too", Tommy admitted.

"What are you worried about? It seems like you've got this all planned out."

"Honestly, I'm worried that one or both of us will let go of the amulet and we'll be stuck in 1540, just like my dad. I'm worried that it will hurt, somehow, and I'm worried about what my mom is going to say, even though I'm kind of mad at her for not telling me all of this in the first place."

They walked on in silence for a few minutes, neither one knowing quite what to say. Finally, Nick broke the silence.

"So, are we going to do it on Saturday when your mom leaves again?"

Tommy grinned. Nick would come through after all.

***

For the rest of the walk home, they began to plan their strategy. Tommy would be in charge of talking to Mr. Barnhart about the time period; finding out what people wore, what they did for fun, and most importantly, about the king, Henry VIII. If their trip was to land them in London, they needed to know everything they could about the king.

Nick would be in charge of getting things together in a bag for them to take that would contain things from the twenty-first century that would come in handy; things like aspirin, antibiotic ointment, and toothbrushes, none of which existed in the sixteenth century. Nick didn't care so much about the toothbrushes but Tommy was insistent. It might make his mom a little less angry when she found out if she knew he was brushing his teeth.

On Tuesday morning, Tommy left for school half an hour early to talk to Mr. Barnhart. He was a little nervous about it. He knew that Mr. Barnhart really cared about history and he was a pretty cool teacher besides, but he didn't want Mr. Barnhart to think that he was crazy or anything.

Just as he had planned, almost no students were there yet. His shoes squeaked down the nearly empty hallway as he approached Mr. Barnhart's door. He peeked around the corner, feeling stupid, and saw Mr. Barnhart sitting at his desk going over some papers. Tommy gulped and knocked hesitantly. His heart jumped a little when he saw his teacher turn and look at him.

"Uh, Mr. Barnhart, are you busy?"

"No, Tommy, come on in. I'm just correcting last week's pop quiz. You got a 92%, by the way."

"I did? Great!" Tommy was surprised. As preoccupied as he had been yesterday he wasn't even sure if he would pass, much less get a good grade. Mr. Barnhart patted the top of his desk.

"Come on in, have a seat. What's up?"

Tommy slid into the desk right in front of Mr. Barnhart's. "Well, I was hoping that you could answer some questions for me about Henry VIII. I'm thinking of doing my big report on him and I need some information." Tommy squirmed and tried not to look as if he were up to something.

Mr. Barnhart paused and eyed him for a moment before speaking. "Henry VIII, eh? There's a lot of information about him. What specifically do you want to know about him?"

"Well, I'm curious about all of the wives that he married. Were there really six of them?"

Mr. Barnhart nodded and smiled. "Everyone is curious about that. He was one of those monarchs who were as famous for what he did in his life when he was alive as he was after his death. Did you want to know about them? The king and his wives, I mean."

Tommy nodded, figuring that any information that he could get would be helpful.

67

"I'll make it short… there are many books written about him as well as each individual wife. The first one was Katherine of Aragon. She was a Spanish princess who had first been married to Henry's big brother, Prince Arthur. Arthur died after only a few months and six years later, Henry married her. In almost twenty years of marriage, she only had one daughter that lived; not a son as Henry had hoped for, so he divorced her."

"Was divorce legal back then?" Tommy wanted to know.

"Only if you got special permission from the Pope. The Pope is in charge of the Catholic Church. In Henry's case, the Pope wouldn't give him a divorce so he broke away from the Church, created the Church of England, and made himself the boss."

Tommy laughed, surprised. "I guess that's one way to get what you want!"

"You bet, and he wanted a lady named Anne Boleyn. He married her and, again, had only one daughter, Elizabeth. No other children were born alive after that so he had her beheaded."

"Just for not having a son?" Tommy was amazed.

"In a round-about way. It was pretty important to him to have

son to succeed him and he finally got one with his next wife, Jane

Seymour, but she died right after having Prince Edward."

Tommy guessed, "So... he got married again?"

Mr. Barnhart grinned. "You've got it. Having only one son

was a start, but Henry wanted to make sure that if something

happened to Edward that there would be another prince, just in case.

He arranged a marriage with a duke's daughter, Anne of Cleves,

from near Germany. She came all that way and when she got to

England, Henry decided that he didn't like her. Right after they were

married, he began the process of getting the marriage annulled."

"That's four wives so far. Jeez, it's just like Hollywood!"

Tommy figured.

"Right. Next was Katherine Howard. She was a lot younger

than Henry; fifteen or sixteen years old when they got married. She

was beheaded the next year because she was seeing another man

behind his back and he found out about it. For a queen, that was

committing treason." Tommy couldn't believe it. Katherine Howard

had been so young!

"Why did she marry the king if she didn't like him?"

"She didn't have a whole lot of choice. Most people didn't marry for love, they married to make alliances or to get the land that the other family had. In Katherine's case, her family was very Protestant, or against the Pope, and they were hoping that by marrying her, Henry would make the Church of England stronger. Plus, Henry thought she was really pretty"

"So who was his last wife and what happened to her?"

"Ah, Katherine Parr. She was the lucky one in many ways."

"He sure married a lot of Katherines."

"Yes, she was the third one. She actually outlived him, though. Do you know that there's a rhyme that schoolchildren in England learn to help them remember the order of his wives?"

Tommy shook his head.

"It goes: Divorced, beheaded, died; divorced, beheaded, survived. That was what I practiced for my first test on him in primary school."

"That's pretty gruesome." He made a face.

Mr. Barnhart laughed again. "It *is* gruesome. A lot of the things that they did back then were gruesome, especially to our modern ways. Did you know that after someone was beheaded in

London, the head would be put on a spike on London Bridge, or in the marketplace for everyone to see?"

Tommy shuddered. "Ugh, why? But wouldn't everyone see it? Would they hide it from the kids?" That was so gross, putting a severed head out for everyone to see!

Mr. Barnhart shook his head. "You would think so, but no. The heads were to serve as a warning that England meant business and the king would leave them up there until they rotted away to just a skull. Kids were treated like small adults back then, not kids. At your age, you would have been apprenticed already and learning a trade or helping your father on his farm, not going to school. You still wouldn't be considered as a full adult until you were eighteen, but you were expected to behave like one." Tommy allowed himself a moment to think that perhaps his father might be a farmer, and then shook the feeling away. Time travelers probably wouldn't make good farmers.

"But didn't people get married really young back then? Could they get married if they weren't officially adults?"

"Good question." Mr. Barnhart nodded and Tommy felt a surge of pride. It was cool to have this kind of adult discussion with Mr. Barnhart, but he had to be careful not to give anything away.

Mr. Barnhart went on. "People usually only got married really young if they were from the nobility: kings, queens, princesses, princes, dukes, duchesses, that kind of thing. Henry VIII's grandmother, Margaret Beaufort, got married at twelve, but even that was pretty young for nobility. Regular people, like us poor peasants, usually got married a bit later.

"So, if I were a prince", Tommy ventured, "I could possibly be married right now?"

"Or at least engaged. Royal children were often engaged to someone when they were very young, some even as babies. But that could change. It happened to Henry's oldest daughter, Mary. She was engaged several times when she was small but none of them worked out."

The bell rang for homeroom, effectively ending their conversation. The time had passed so quickly! Even though Tommy had set out only to get information for his own gain, he found that he really was beginning to be fascinated with the sixteenth century,

72

which would definitely be an uncool thing in the eyes of his fellow students, most of which thought that last year's Superbowl was ancient history.

Mr. Barnhart seemed disappointed, too, but he gave Tommy a smile. "I was just getting revved up", he told Tommy. "We'll have to do this again sometime."

"Can we?" asked Tommy, not wanting to sound too eager. "Could we do it this week?" Thinking fast, he added, "I want to do some more research over the weekend."

Mr. Barnhart flipped open his organizer on the desk and found the current week. He ran his finger down the page and stopped on Wednesday.

"How about Wednesday after school?" he asked. "I don't have to be anywhere and we can talk for a longer time. You'd better let your mom know, though. I'm sure she'll get worried if you don't come right home."

"Can you call her tonight? I want to make sure that she knows I'm really meeting you instead of hanging out with Nick."

"Sure, no problem. Your mom still works at the elementary school, right?"

"Yeah, she teaches third grade."

"That's right. Why don't I give the school a call and leave a message? That way it'll be legit."

"Thanks, Mr. Barnhart."

"You'd better get to class now. You don't want to make Mrs. Sosinski cranky." Tommy's homeroom teacher was notorious for not being a morning person. It seemed to take several gallons of coffee to get her into a good mood most mornings.

Tommy scuttled out the door. "Bye, Mr. Barnhart…and thanks again!"

Mr. Barnhart lifted a hand to Tommy to say goodbye and tried to focus his attention to the lesson plans on his desk, but his mind kept turning over Tommy's sudden interest in the sixteenth century. He knew that it was normal for kids to go through phases and Tommy was definitely one of his better students, always interested in history. That part made sense.

Still, in the back of his mind, his intuition told him there might be something else behind the sudden and ferocious interest. He was sure that Tommy couldn't possibly know anything about his father. His mother was going to wait until he was older; that had been the agreement, and he knew that she would keep her word. They all wanted to keep Tommy safe. His knowing the truth would lead to opening up the past again. Much of it would be unbelievable to a boy Tommy's age.

He shrugged off the uneasy feeling and told himself to relax and enjoy the fact that his best friend's son actually liked his class. All thoughts of Tommy's possible ulterior motives left his mind as his homeroom group of twenty-five seventh-graders came streaming through the door.

***

When Tommy got out of school that afternoon and went to meet his mother, he was anxious to see if Mr. Barnhart had called her about their meeting after school. He waited restlessly on one of the swings as the elementary children streamed out of the school and attached themselves to parents, grandparents, babysitters, and older siblings who looked like they would rather have been anywhere else. As he watched them, a thought popped into Tommy's head: What if he had siblings in the sixteenth century? What if his dad had had a wife and family before he came here? Or what if he had gotten married when he had returned, thinking that he would never get back

75

to Tommy and his mom? These were questions that began to really bother him. If he did have siblings, or if his dad did have another wife, would he even want Tommy there? That was an unsettling thought.

He waited impatiently, his mind still turning and twisting as Mrs. Andrews exited the building shortly after the children had left. She looked young and pretty with her dark curls bouncing in the sunshine. He wondered if his father missed her and if he would still be in love with her when Tommy brought him back.

When his mom came within shouting distance, he jumped off of the swing and jogged toward her. Running would have been too much, he thought.

"Hi, Mom!"

"Hi, Sweetie! How was your day?" His mom gave him her usual big hug and kiss on the cheek. He took her bag to carry, as he always did, and they turned toward home.

"Fine, hey, Mom, did Mr. Barnhart call you today?"

Mrs. Andrews smiled and began walking. "Yes, he did. He said that you were really interested in learning more about Henry

VIII and wanted to talk about it after school on Wednesday. I'm proud of you for wanting to get your information early on."

"And?"

"And what?"

Tommy sighed. "What did you say?"

Mrs. Andrews paused for a moment. "I asked him to come over for dinner tomorrow night. That way, you two could talk as long as you'd like without worrying about being locked in the school or losing track of time, as you have been known to do."

Mr. Barnhart was coming over to his house? Excellent! Tommy would have to make absolutely certain that he didn't blow this chance. He couldn't let even the smallest suspicion arise that he was interested in all of this because of his dad, especially now with his mother there.

"Tommy", his mother asked gently, "is that okay with you?"

He realized that he hadn't said anything yet. "Oh, yeah, sure, Mom. Won't it be weird to have him at our house, though?"

Tommy's mother smiled. "No, I've known Edward for a long time. He used to come by quite a lot, years ago, actually. It'll be nice to catch up."

Tommy was shocked, but only for a moment. He had no idea that they actually knew each other outside of school, but they were both teachers, so it wasn't that unusual.

"When did he come over before? I don't remember that."

"Back before you were born. We both worked at the same school then and the younger teachers used to hang out together, before they all had families and such."

"Why doesn't he come over now?"

"Well, your dad went away and life just happens sometimes. Everyone is busy."

Tommy was still shocked but didn't want to ask too much about it now. This could be a clue as well, but he didn't think that Mr. Barnhart would know anything about his dad's disappearance.

"Oh. What are we going to have for dinner when he comes?"

"I was thinking of a nice pork roast. What do you think?"

"Actually, I was hoping that you would make something Italian. Everything Italian that you make turns out really good."

"Are you sure? You don't want something more American? Or what about something English, to make Mr. Barnhart feel like he's at home? Yorkshire pudding, maybe?"

"No, that sounds gross. I'm not saying make calamari or anything, but maybe your lasagna with all of the cheese, or that sausage and chicken thing. And we have to have garlic bread. How about that sausage and potato soup that you make sometimes…" Tommy's head was full of ideas. His mom was a very good cook and he really wanted to impress Mr. Barnhart.

Mrs. Andrews laughed. "Okay, okay, I'll think of something. We don't want to scare the man away with a five course meal, do we? What should we have for dessert?"

Tommy thought. "How about something with apples? Apple pie, or apple crisp, something like that."

Mrs. Andrews nodded. "Not very Italian, but I think I can manage. He'll be over around five o'clock so you two can start your talk without me eavesdropping in. I'll have dinner ready around six-thirty and if you're not done talking, you can continue. I'll only be an interested bystander."

Tommy was feeling happy about the whole business. It would be a good thing for his mom to have someone else to cook for. They didn't have any family that lived close enough to visit and they pretty much kept to themselves in the evenings, with the exception of town events and school programs. She certainly seemed to be excited about it; she had a little bit of a sparkle about her as they walked home. It made Tommy happy at first but then, after he thought for a minute, he got kind of a sick feeling in his stomach. He really hoped that his mother didn't think that Mr. Barnhart was cute, like the girls at school did. That would really be awkward. He shrugged the feeling off and began to plan out some questions to ask Mr. Barnhart.

***

Tommy called Nick later that night, after he had done the dishes and his homework. He took the phone into his room for privacy and shut the door. When Nick answered, Tommy asked quickly, "Can you talk?"

"Yeah", Nick answered, "My mom's outside vacuuming the car. What's up?"

Tommy told him about the conversation that he had had with Mr. Barnhart that morning and then told him about the dinner. Nick was astonished.

"No way! Mr. Barnhart's coming to your house? Can I come, too?"

"No. It'll look too suspicious. I'll call you after he leaves and we'll figure it out then."

Nick wasn't convinced. "I'm supposed to be doing this project, too! What will it look like if you're the one getting all of the information and I'm doing nothing? Mr. Barnhart will think you're doing all the work. I need to be there. After all, we're going to time travel together, right? I need to know what's going on. Maybe I'll remember something that you'll miss, something that will save our lives!"

Tommy had to admit that Nick was right. It would look funny if he was asking all of the questions by himself for a joint project and it wasn't fair to Nick if he couldn't be there, too.

"Alright, fine. Let me ask my mom. Hang on."

He went into the living room where his mom was grading papers. She looked up as he walked in.

"Hey, Mom, can Nick come to dinner on Wednesday, too? He wants to hear what Mr. Barnhart has to say."

"Oh, that's right. You're working on that project together. I guess, if it's okay with his mom."

"Thanks, Mom! You're the best!" He began walking back to his room, telling Nick, "She said yes! He'll be here at five and dinner's at six-thirty. Come hungry!"

"What are you having?"

"Something Italian. It'll be good, trust me. Make sure you ask your mom, though. My mom will check."

"Fine, I will, but she really won't care. See you at school tomorrow?"

"Yep, see ya."

"See ya."

Chapter Four

The last bell rang finally rang on Wednesday and Tommy

practically burst out of the school, giving Nick a quick wave, and ran

all the way home. Once he got home Tommy flew around the house,

straightening pillows on the couch, dusting the tables in the living

room, and running the vacuum cleaner over the floors. When his

mother got home, she laughed at how frantically he was cleaning.

"If this is how you act when Mr. Barnhart comes to dinner,

I'll have to start having him over every week! Maybe then you'll get

your chores done without me asking." She smiled as she said it but

Tommy knew that she was only partly kidding. He was supposed to

pitch in and help his mom around the house without being asked but

he hated housework with a passion. It usually took his mother more

than one request before it actually got done, especially when it came

to emptying the dishwasher. This time, however, he was powered by

his own initiative. He wanted Mr. Barnhart to see that he lived in a

nice place and was determined to impress him.

Tommy even lit the scented candles that his mother kept in the living room, the ones she got from a candle party that one of the teachers had. His mom came downstairs sniffing the air and smiling, then told him to wait until after dinner for that.

"The smell of the food will clash with a vanilla candles. Wait until coffee and dessert time. Why don't you clean out the fireplace and get it ready for a fire, instead, since you have all of this nervous energy?" she told him. The April evening would be perfect for a fire; crisp and chilly. Nervously, Tommy did as she asked and kept straightening things that he had already fixed. When he was finally satisfied, he ran upstairs, rinsed off in the shower, and put on some jeans without holes and a nice shirt. Then, he went back downstairs and tried, unsuccessfully, to read until the time when the doorbell rang at 4:55.

"I got it!" he yelled, ran to the door, then stopped short and opened the door slowly, as if he hadn't been cleaning feverishly all afternoon. He took a deep breath to greet Mr. Barnhart, but it wasn't him! Nick stood there instead, all cleaned up. His hair was still wet from an after -school shower and he was wearing a plaid, button-down shirt with pressed khaki slacks and dress shoes, something that he would normally only wear to church or on picture day. Despite knowing that his friend had been due to come over, Tommy felt a short stab of disappointment.

"Oh, it's you. C'mon in."

"Don't sound so excited."

"I know; I'm sorry. I thought it was Mr. Barnhart, that's all." Tommy shut the door behind Nick as he came in. He caught a whiff of aftershave as Nick passed by him and coughed. "Did you put on cologne?"

"Just a little bit of aftershave that my dad got for me."

"But you don't shave!"

"I know, but it smells good and I only put a little bit on."

Tommy rolled his eyes. Nick held out a brown bag to Tommy. "My mom sent over a bottle of wine for your mom and Mr. Barnhart. When I told her that he was coming over, she got a goofy smile on her face. I know that she was thinking that he and your mom are going to start dating or something."

"Ugh. Well, why don't you go give it to my mom in the kitchen? She'll love it."

"Okay." Nick went through the kitchen door and found Mrs. Andrews working on dinner. As Tommy listened to her asking Nick about his mom and telling him that she would call and thank her later, the doorbell rang again, making Tommy jump. He smoothed down his crazy hair and tried to look mature as he went to open the door.

He took a deep breath and then swung open the door to see Mr. Barnhart standing on his front porch and, like Nick, holding a bottle of wine. He formally stuck out his hand to Mr. Barnhart.

"Hello, Sir, how are you?"

With a surprised look, Mr. Barnhart took his hand and shook it. "I'm fine, Tommy, but really, you don't have to be so formal. It's after school… we can be friends now, right?"

Tommy relaxed a little, feeling a bit foolish. "Um, right. Okay, come on in."

Mr. Barnhart grinned and came in, shutting the door behind him. Tommy's mother came out of the kitchen, wiping her hands on a dishtowel. Tommy thought that she looked beautiful. Her hair swept up in the back and she had a few curls straggling down. She wasn't wearing anything fancy, but a soft grey-blue dress that looked nice with the silver locket that Tommy had gotten her for Christmas last year. The tiny chain with the key to the box was also around her neck, but was tucked into the dress, Tommy could see. Instead of holding out her hand to Mr. Barnhart, she gave him a small hug. As he hugged her back, Tommy's stomach flip-flopped with nervousness.

"It's so good to see you again, Edward. Thank you for coming over to help the boys." Mrs. Andrews stepped back and smiled her lovely smile at him.

Mr. Barnhart said, "It's good to see you again, too, Liz. Thanks for having me over. Dinner smells wonderful." He held out the bottle of wine to her and she took it, graciously.

"Thank you for this! We're certainly well stocked now. Dinner won't be for a while yet so you can all sit out here while I'm finishing things. I'll bring you a glass, Edward. Tommy, can you get a drink for yourself and Nick?"

"I'm guessing that we can't have wine, too", Tommy joked with his mother.

She playfully flicked the dishcloth at him, "Not for another nine years, young man! We have soda for the two of you. It's fizzy… you can pretend that it's champagne."

"Thanks a lot", Tommy joked and followed his mom into the kitchen, leaving Mr. Barnhart and Nick to get comfortable in the living room. He poured sodas for Nick and himself and watched as his mom used the corkscrew to open the wine and pour it into two glasses. She followed Tommy out to give Mr. Barnhart his glass and then lit the fire that Tommy had set up before she went back into the kitchen to finish making dinner, which was becoming more delicious-smelling every minute. Tommy wondered how they were going to have a serious conversation with the smell of lasagna filling the room but he needn't have worried.

"So how does this whole thing start?" Nick asked, starting things off.

"Well, you guys wanted to know about Henry VIII, right? Let's back up a bit and start with Edmund Tudor, Henry's grandfather, who lived back in the fourteen-hundreds. Edmund married Margaret Beaufort. She was from a royal family, too, but not a princess or anything. She was only twelve when Edmund married her." Nick gave a low whistle at that.

Mr. Barnhart went on. "They had their only child, Henry Tudor, the next year. To make a long story short, when Henry grew up, the king thought that he was a threat to the throne and had him banished from England. He raised an army and came back to defeat the king, Richard III. Henry became king in 1485 and married Elizabeth of York, ending the War of the Roses, which is a tale for another time."

"Where does Henry VIII come in?" Tommy asked. He was getting confused about where this was going. There were too many people in this story already.

Mr. Barnhart smiled. "He was the second son of Henry VII and Elizabeth of York. His older brother, Arthur, was supposed to be the king and Henry was going to be given to church to become a priest or a bishop. The plans changed when Arthur died a few months after marrying Katherine of Aragon."

"After Arthur died, Katherine was forced to remain in England and basically wait for Henry to grow up so that she could marry him and keep things good between England and Spain. They

89

weren't able to get married until Henry VII died, seven years later and Henry VIII became king.

"Wow, it sounds like a soap opera that my mom likes to watch!" Nick exclaimed.

"It's pretty close", Mr. Barnhart admitted.

"So then what happened?"

"Well, Henry and Katherine tried to have a son, a prince, to be Henry's heir, but they only had one living son. He died when he was less than two months old. Their only surviving child was Mary Tudor, who would grow up to be Queen Mary I. Henry got tired of Katherine eventually and began to pay a lot of attention to Anne Boleyn, who was one of Katherine's ladies at court. He desperately wanted to marry her and tried to get Katherine to agree to a divorce, but she wouldn't. To solve the problem, Henry decided to change the religion and declared himself to be the Head of the Church instead of the Pope. That way, he could get the divorce and marry Anne to have sons, but things didn't work out that way."

"He married Anne Boleyn and they had Elizabeth, who would later grow up to be Queen Elizabeth I, but they weren't able to have sons. Henry got tired of Anne even more quickly then he got tired of Katherine so he had her beheaded three years after they had gotten married."

"Wow!" Nick breathed. "Was all of that legal?"

"Unfortunately, yes. Back then, the king had tremendous power and most people believed that the king's power came from God. Many people knew that Anne Boleyn was executed on false charges, but to stand up for her would have been like committing suicide."

Nick, who hadn't been in the classroom to hear Tommy's conversation with Mr. Barnhart asked, "He had six wives, right? Who was next?"

Mr. Barnhart then told him about Queen Jane, who died after giving birth to Edward VI and was therefore Henry's favorite wife. "She's the wife that he wanted to be buried next to because she was the only one to give him a boy."

He told about Queen Anne of Cleves, who was perhaps the luckiest of all the wives because she had agreed to a divorce, and of poor, foolish, Katherine Howard, who lost her head for really cheating on the king. When he said the name "Katherine Howard", Tommy suddenly remembered that that had been the name in his father's letter. It had said that the king had just married her. *That wasn't going to end very well*, Tommy thought to himself.

When he finished telling them about Katherine Parr, Henry's last wife, the boys felt as if they had been listening to a story in a book. Some of the characters were just too outrageous to be believed, especially Henry. Being married *six* times was almost unbelievable! Mrs. Andrews peeked around the corner into the room.

"I'm sorry to interrupt this harrowing tale", she said, "but dinner is ready. You can all come to the table." Tommy couldn't believe it. It was six-thirty already.

"That's fine, Liz. We're at a good stopping point." The boys and Mr. Barnhart made their way to the table, which was set with Mrs. Andrews' best china and linen napkins. A huge, steaming pan of gooey, cheesy, lasagna sat in the center of the table and Mrs. Andrews was bringing out a large soup tureen.

"The lasagna is really hot so while it sits for a few minutes, we can have some potato and sausage soup." The soup was Tommy's favorite and he was glad to see that Mr. Barnhart enjoyed it, too. They all conversed easily through the dinner, only falling silent a few times as they enjoyed the hot, salty soup and the rich lasagna, oozing with tomato sauce and Mrs. Andrews' own personal mixture of cheeses.

Tommy noticed that his mother drank two glasses of wine rather than one, her usual. Her eyes were bright and while she wasn't flirting with Mr. Barnhart, she certainly seemed happy to be talking to him, almost like she had missed him. Mr. Barnhart also seemed happy to be there; he complimented Mrs. Andrews' cooking and asked her several questions about what she had been doing lately. Mrs. Andrews, in turn, asked about teaching in middle school and asked if he had been back to England lately. As they went on, Nick gave Tommy a kick under the table and rolled his eyes during one point when the two of them were laughing at some teacher joke. Tommy glared at Nick and turned his attention to the last remaining bits of lasagna on his plate.

His stomach was suddenly doing flip-flops and the feeling of happiness that he had when Mr. Barnhart first came was being replaced by fear that his mother may fall in love with his teacher. It wasn't that he didn't like Mr. Barnhart; he was the greatest teacher in the world as far as Tommy was concerned, but he didn't want his mother falling in love with anyone, especially now that he was going back in time to try and bring his father home. In his mind, the perfect scenario was to find Geoffrey Andrews, find a way to bring him back home, and the three of them would be a family again to live happily ever after.

He tried to shake the feeling off as he looked at the pair of them. It wasn't Mr. Barnhart's fault that his mother was pretty or that they liked each other. He knew that his mother had been lonely for a long time and had probably given up any hope of Geoffrey ever coming back. Before now, he really hadn't thought much about it, but it occurred to him that it had to be very difficult for his mother. His fear was turning to a mixed feeling. He still didn't want her to fall in love with Mr. Barnhart but he also wanted her to be happy. He just hoped that everything would work out the way it should.

The doubts about this whole plan came flooding into his brain. Maybe his dad wouldn't want to come back. Maybe they wouldn't even find him. Maybe the people who were following him captured him. Maybe he was even dead. The possibilities were endless, and maddening. Not one of the endings to the story that he thought of would make every single person happy.

Tommy was jolted from his thoughts by his mother saying, "Tommy, do you all want to go back into the living room to talk for a while? I'll get the table cleared up and start getting dessert ready."

"Dessert?" Nick groaned, "I don't think that I could eat another thing. I'll be full until next week."

Mrs. Andrews laughed. "I'm glad to hear that, Nick. I'll wash up some of the pots and pans first. Perhaps by the time I'm done cleaning up your appetite for apple crisp may have increased a little."

Nick's eyebrows shot up, "Apple crisp? Why didn't you say so? I'll definitely want some of that!"

Mrs. Andrew's ruffled Nick's hair, just like she did to Tommy's. "That's what I like to hear", she said and shooed them all out of the kitchen and into the living room, moving a great deal more slowly now that their stomachs were full of lasagna, garlic bread, and sausage soup.

Mr. Barnhart settled on one end of the couch with his hand on his stomach and a contented sigh, Tommy at the other side. Nick curled up in the overstuffed arm chair next to the fireplace and leaned his head on the arm of the chair, looking full and comfortable.

Mr. Barnhart spread his hands open, "Well? Where did we leave off?"

"You were telling us about Katherine Parr, and how she outlived Henry", Nick mumbled from his chair where he was curled up with his eyes only half open.

"Oh, yes, lucky Katherine Parr. She was smart enough to escape the plot to kill her and took care of Henry until the end of his days, something that couldn't have been an easy job to do. He was a bit of a mess by the time he died, very overweight and extremely cranky. He also had a sore on his leg that hadn't healed for years and had to be taken care of constantly."

"When did he die?" Tommy wanted to know.

"January 28, 1547. After he died, his son, Edward became king, but only for a few years."

"What happened to him?"

"He died when he was a teenager, probably from tuberculosis, a lung disease. Then Lady Jane Grey was proclaimed queen, but only for nine days. Then Edward's oldest sister, Mary, invaded London with her army and took the crown from Jane. She became known as Bloody Mary."

"Bloody Mary?" Tommy asked.

Mr. Barnhart nodded. "She ruled for only a few years as well and then died from some kind of tumor, then Elizabeth took over and was queen until 1601."

"Why was Mary called "Bloody Mary"?" Nick interrupted.

Mr. Barnhart sighed and shook his head as he smiled "Everybody wants to know that! She was very Catholic and believed that the only way to make people come back to the Church was to threaten to have them burned at the stake. Many people were turning Protestant at that time and wanted nothing to do with the Catholic religion any more. Hundreds of people died for their beliefs while she was on the throne."

"Just for not believing the same religion? That's really sick!" Nick was astonished.

"Religion was a tricky thing back then, much more so than today. We live in a country and a time where we have the freedom of religion and separation of church and state, so we're not used to the idea of an official religion that everyone has to follow."

"Are there any countries like that today, where following a religion is the law?" Tommy wanted to know.

"Unfortunately, yes. Some countries in the Middle East and Africa have official religions and many religions are banned in China. We're very lucky to live in a country where our personal choices are respected."

"What did the normal people do?" he asked Mr. Barnhart impatiently. "What kinds of jobs did they have?" He really wanted to find out as much as he could about the place and time that they would be traveling to. It wouldn't be a good idea to just show up and have no idea about how people lived. The idea was to blend in as much as possible.

"Well, most people were farmers of some sort, living out in the country. People in the city did all kinds of jobs: carpenters, wheelwrights, weavers, millers, and bakers; all of the jobs that were needed to support the cities. There was also the clergy, with every position from simple priest to archbishop. Then there were the gentry. They were the families that owned the land and had a lot of wealth and prestige in England: earls, dukes, duchesses."

"So what kind of people would we be?" Nick asked.

"Most likely you'd have been just plain, common peasant people out working on a farm somewhere. You boys, though, may have been apprenticed to someone, especially if you were sons of merchants."

"Apprenticed?"

"When some boys were around nine or ten years old, especially boys that weren't going to inherit the family farm or business, they were sent away to live with a master of some sort, to learn a trade, such as wheel-making or blacksmithing. If you were sent to be an apprentice to a blacksmith, you would spend the next seven years learning the trade and he would give you a place to live, clothes to wear, and food to eat. In return, you would work for the master blacksmith; cleaning the shop, delivering orders, and fetching the things that he needs."

"Would an apprentice get paid?" Tommy asked.

"Nope. You were paid in training and having a roof over your head. Sometimes the master would be a kind one or you could end up with a cruel master, but it was better than ending up hungry in the street. At the end of an apprenticeship, you would have a trade, a job, rather, and you could support yourself."

"What about school?"

"School usually wasn't an option. You might have learned your alphabet, but most people didn't. As an apprentice, you would probably be able to write your signature and know how to do basic math to run your business, but chances are that you would never even own a book. They were too expensive, for one thing, and you probably wouldn't be able to read it anyway."

Nick let out another low whistle from his chair. "No school? I could live with that!"

Tommy turned to him, "Yeah, but you'd have to work every day! It's not like you would get to watch cartoons or play video games."

Mr. Barnhart nodded. "That's right. You'd be up before dawn lighting fires and getting water from the well. Chances are that you would be pretty busy all day long. Apprentices got the worst jobs around a place, especially the newer ones." Tommy laughed at the thought of Nick having to be up before the sun every day. He stumbled through much of the morning every day and was lucky to wake up before lunch!

Nick was coming out of his food coma, looking a little worried. "Didn't they do anything for fun?"

Mr. Barnhart smiled. "Sure. There were dances and parties, especially on saints' days and holidays. Sundays were days of rest and as an apprentice, you might get to go and visit your family for the day."

"I don't know if I'd want to live back then. It sounds like a lot of hard work", Nick countered, shooting a concerned look at Tommy.

"Things would certainly be different", Mr. Barnhart acknowledged. Just then, Mrs. Andrews came back into the living room and their talk was sidelined for a moment.

"Would you gentlemen like your dessert served out here or back in the dining room?"

Tommy asked, "Could we have it out here, Mom? I don't think Nick can get up."

Mrs. Andrews and Mr. Barnhart chuckled at the sight of Nick, somewhat more awake but still curled up in a ball in the overstuffed chair. "Sure. Edward, would you like some coffee?"

"Sounds great, Liz. After that, I should get going. It's a school night, you know."

Tommy groaned. He had completely forgotten about school the next day. *Just get through it*, he told himself, *only a few more days and we'll actually be there!* He hoped that Nick wasn't too frightened and that he would keep his promise to come with him. The more he learned about the sixteenth century the more he knew that he was going to need a friend to come along. Between the two of them, Tommy hoped that they could remember everything that Mr. Barnhart had told them.

They finished their apple crisp and vanilla ice cream with a few more questions and tidbits of information. They found out that people used to use the bathroom in chamber pots and dump them out close to the streets, something that grossed them all out. They also learned that although the knights and ladies in the movies were always glamorous and clean-looking, in real life, they probably didn't smell very good. "Some people washed themselves regularly", Mr. Barnhart told them, "but many people only washed the parts of their bodies that showed every day: hands, face, and feet. Everything else was only washed once in a while." Mrs. Andrews shuddered at this, making them all laugh.

As the dessert plates were cleared away and Mr. Barnhart got up to leave, Tommy thought that the evening had been a success. He watched Nick stagger back down the street to his house, half asleep from all of the good food and conversation. He didn't even mind that much when Mr. Barnhart gave his mom a friendly hug goodbye at the door, even if the hug did last a little too long for Tommy's taste.

When the guests were gone and all of the dishes loaded into the dishwasher, Tommy thanked his mother for having everyone over.

"Dinner was great, Mom, and we really found out a lot about Henry VIII."

"Yes, well, I was glad to do it. We should have Edward over more often. He doesn't have any family around here, you know." She had a little smile on her face that worried Tommy.

"Mom", Tommy began. He wasn't sure how to say what he was feeling.

"Yes, Tommy?"

"Do you like Mr. Barnhart?"

"Why, of course I do. It was nice to catch up with him. He knew your father, too, way back when. They were great friends and had a lot in common."

That was news to Tommy, but he didn't want the conversation with his mother to go that way just now. "That's not what I mean. Do you *like him* like him?" There. It was out in the open now.

"Oh, I see." Mrs. Andrews put the towel down that she had been drying the countertop with and looked at Tommy with a small smile. "You want to know if I'm interested in Edward, romantically, right?"

"Well, I saw the way he was looking at you and you looked pretty happy. You don't go out on any dates and I don't even know if you and Dad are still married! Are you going to date Mr. Barnhart?" Tommy was flushed and upset all of a sudden.

Mrs. Andrews held her arms open and he rushed into them, feeling like a little boy again. He felt her sigh and then talk to him as his head was buried in her shoulder.

"Tommy, it's a very difficult situation. Yes, I've been lonely. Your father has been gone for so many years now, but the situation is so complicated."

If only you knew, Tommy thought.

Mrs. Andrews went on. "When he left, your father and I agreed that if he was gone for more than ten years it meant he probably wasn't coming back, not that he wasn't going to try. At that point, he thought it would be simply impossible or something may have happened to him. He wanted me to move on after that and although it's been more than ten years, I haven't wanted to move on."

"I guess I hadn't thought about it much until Edward came over tonight. I haven't talked to him in a long time because it was too painful. He reminded me of all the good times we had together, before your dad left. I don't expect you to understand any of this. I want you to know, though, that I don't plan on jumping into anything. I will take things very slowly"

"But what if Dad came back tomorrow? Or next week? What would you do?"

His mother let out another huge sigh and stroked Tommy's cheek. "We'll cross that bridge when we come to it. He may have another life, another family somewhere. It's been a long time and I can't wait forever to have him back. He may not ever come back. Can you understand that? I know I'm asking a lot and I know that the idea of your father is important to you, but believe me when I tell you that I'm almost one hundred percent certain that he isn't going to come back."

Tommy felt deflated, his happiness about the evening all but gone. "Maybe he just didn't want to come back to us."

His mother pushed him back gently and took his chin in her hand so that he was looking straight into her warm, loving face. "Thomas Geoffrey, if you have believed anything that I've ever told you in your whole life, believe this: your father loved us with all of his heart. He had to leave us; he didn't have a choice. We tried to think of every way we could to stay together but it was too dangerous."

"What happened?" Tommy burst out. "Why won't you tell me why he left?"

His mother sighed again, released his chin, and looked up at the ceiling, as if she were looking for the right answer up there somewhere. Finally, she said, "I won't tell you why he left yet because sometimes even I have trouble believing it, even though I know it to be true."

Tommy was more anxious than ever. She was *so* close to spilling the truth about his father to him, time travel and all. It was killing him to not let on that he already knew the unbelievable part. He watched his mom's eyes fill with tears and she took a deep breath before she spoke.

"Tommy, I promise you that I will tell you the entire truth on your birthday, the whole thing." Tommy's birthday was three weeks away.

"Why do I have to wait until my birthday?"

"For one thing, I think that turning thirteen is a pretty big deal. You're not a little kid any more and I think that you're finally ready to handle the truth. Waiting until your birthday will make it even more special and it will give me three weeks to decide how exactly I want to do it. You'll understand after you know the story, but there's a lot that may be very hard to you to accept and understand. Please, can you wait just this little while longer? It's more for me than for you. I've always hoped that I'd never have to do this, that he would be back by now but I don't think that it's going to happen. I'm asking you to wait, for my sake." He could see that she was having a hard time telling him even this little bit and even though he was disappointed, he nodded his head.

"Can you at least tell me one thing? Something to last me until then. Please?" Tommy begged.

His mother thought for a moment and then said, "He would have been able to help you so much with your Henry VIII project. He would have known much more about it, just as much as Mr. Barnhart knows, just as if he had been there."

A tear trickled down her cheek and Tommy felt so sad for her that he almost told her right then and there about all he had discovered, but he kept silent. He knew that she would stop them. He wrapped his arms around her waist like he used to do when he was a little boy and let her squeeze him tight while he wondered to himself what was going to come out of this adventure.

The next few days passed very quickly for Tommy. Now that the reality of what he and Nick were about to do was sinking in, there didn't seem to be enough time to prepare for it all. They searched the internet, learned about how people wore, what they did, and what they ate.

Tommy was excited, but a little nervous. The most important thing of all was to make sure that he didn't let go of the amulet during the trip so that he and Nick could return home. He knew that if anything happened to him his mother would be devastated, not to mention what Nick's family would think.

Meanwhile, Nick was *extremely* nervous. He'd never even been to sleep away camp, never mind another century. He was afraid that they wouldn't be able to come back, that they'd lose the amulet, that he'd never see his parents again, even if they did fight like cats and dogs over every little thing. Still, he was excited, although if he had picked the time period, he would have gone back to the ancient Roman times to see the gladiators. Maybe if this trip went well, they could use the amulet to go there next.

The arrangements had all been made. Tommy's mom had given him permission to let Nick sleep over on Friday night and

Nick's mother had approved. The boys planned to pack a small knapsack with things like toothbrushes, toothpaste, and soap to bring along.

Nick had been smart and suggested packing some snacks to take along. They figured that modern snacks, like peanut butter crackers, wouldn't blend in very well but beef jerky and cookies might work, without the wrappers, of course. Nick had also suggested bringing water, but Tommy vetoed the idea. He reminded Nick of what Mr. Barnhart had told them: that people didn't drink water very much because the quality wasn't very good and could make them sick. They would have to find milk or ale to drink while they were there if they wanted to fit in.

"What's ale?" Nick asked.

"Mr. Barnhart said that it was kind of like beer, but everyone drank it, even the kids."

Nick's eyes widened. "We're going to drink beer?" he asked incredulously.

"Mr. Barnhart said that it wasn't that strong, that most of the drinks were pretty watered down and the alcohol killed a lot of the bad germs."

110

"Oh." Nick sounded partly relieved and partly disappointed.

Chapter Five

Friday night came quickly. After school, Nick went home with Tommy. As they walked, he told Tommy, "Man, it sure is going to be hard trying to play it cool in front of your mom tonight."

"I know. I told her that we had a lot of work to do on the project so we'd be in my room the whole time after supper."

"Tell me how tomorrow morning is going to go again."

"We'll wake up, my mom wants to make us pancakes and sausage for breakfast, and then we wait for her to go out shopping. As soon as the car leaves, we'll go and get the amulet, grab the knapsack, and go. Are you ready?"

"As ready as I'll ever be," Nick mumbled. A pause, and then, "Tommy, are you scared?"

Tommy didn't want to admit it but he knew that Nick was scared, too. "Yeah, but I'm excited, too. It's like going on a roller coaster for the first time. Terrifying, but I know that after it rolls down the first hill, it'll be better."

"I don't know if we should do this. What if something happens?"

"Nick, don't back out on me now! I'll make you a deal. If we don't find anything out in three days, we'll come back, okay? I really don't think that I can do this without you, at least the first time. Maybe, if it all goes well, I can go back by myself if you really don't like it, but I don't want to try this alone. At least we'll have each other to help, right? Please?"

"Help with what?"

"Remembering everything that we need to know."

"So I'm just there to help you remember stuff?" Nick was starting to sound a little angry.

Tommy stopped walking and looked at him. "No, Nick. You're my friend, my best friend, really. I need you there to just be with me, you know? Please, don't change your mind."

Grudgingly, Nick nodded his head. "Okay. I'll still go. And just for the record, you're my best friend, too. Hanging with you, I feel like we're actually doing something important. It's actually interesting. Maybe I'll even become a history teacher someday.

"Well, if you become a history teacher, you'll be able to tell your students all about the past. Maybe we can visit more than one place, even the future. That's how my dad got here!"

"I didn't think about visiting the future!" Nick said excitedly. "Do you think it works that way? We could go forward in time and find us! We can see what happens, if we get married, or if we have kids. That would be so cool!" He thought for a moment. "And so weird."

"Well, for now, let's get through this first trip and see what happens. At least when we go backward, we can read about what we're getting into. If we go to the future, we won't know anything abut it. Earth could be taken over by aliens, for all we know, or maybe it gets hit by an asteroid."

They were walking up the front walk to Tommy's house by now and although Tommy knew that his mother wasn't home yet, he told Nick, "Okay, let's change the subject. We need to start doing something else or my mom will get suspicious."

They went in and put their backpacks in Tommy's room before going back out to watch television in the living room. When Mrs. Andrews came home a little while later, they were innocently chomping down pretzels and drinking juice while watching a show about Florida's dangerous animals. Tommy felt nervous as he struggled to keep his focus on the show, but shoved it down deep inside and tried not to look fidget.

After dinner, pork chops with melted cheese, they disappeared into Tommy's room and went over everything they would need for the morning. Snacks, toothbrushes, toothpaste, and coins all went into Tommy's small knapsack. It fit on his back like a backpack and he thought it would stand the best chance of staying with them. They got out their history books and notebooks with everything they had learned. If Mrs. Andrews came in, it would look as if they were studying hard, which in fact, they were.

They went over their stories again in case someone questioned them: they were just travelers who had gotten lost and needed to find Geoffrey Andrews. They thought that he was probably in London. Tommy figured that even in a big city like London, somebody somewhere must know who his dad was. If they were pressed with more questions, they would just play dumb and say that they didn't know. It was the best they could come up with for the short time they had to plan. It had to work. It simply had to.

Just before going to sleep, when he had turned the light out, Tommy thought about what they were going to do in the morning. All of the doubts began marching through his head. Maybe he should call the whole thing off. Maybe his dad had another family by now and wouldn't want to see him. They might catch some horrible disease, like the Black Death or get killed somehow. Then he shook his head. No! They had come this far. All of the planning they had done, all of the studying, it couldn't go to waste. He had given Nick his word. Three days. He could do it for three days. Giving a little shiver, he rolled over and tried to get some sleep.

Morning came slowly. Neither one of them had slept very well, especially after Tommy had said, just before lights out, that it may be their last night sleeping in comfortable beds for a while. Tommy tossed and turned drifting in and out of sleep and he could hear Nick tossing and turning as well. When Mrs. Andrews knocked softly on the door to tell them that breakfast was almost ready and would they mind waking up now, Tommy was shocked to see that the clock next to his bed said that it was 9:30! They had overslept; now they would have to eat quickly in order to make everything happened according to plan. They really wanted to stuff themselves with food before going in case they weren't able to eat for a while.

Tommy and Nick quickly got up and headed to the two separate bathrooms, one upstairs and one downstairs, to brush their teeth and get quick showers. Nick took twice as long to brush his teeth, thinking that just in case their toothpaste got lost, at least his teeth would have had one last good cleaning. He even flossed and used some of the mouthwash that he found in the bathroom cabinet and swirled it around in his mouth until his eyes watered.

In the shower, he turned it on as hot as it would go and scrubbed his body with soap until his skin was red from rubbing. He shampooed his hair twice and when he finally stepped out of the shower he felt like a boiled chicken.

Nick saw Tommy coming down the hall from the other direction who had, from the looks of it, had given himself the same treatment. If nothing else, they would be the cleanest people in England in an hour or so.

They came to the table for breakfast, lured by the tantalizing aroma of breakfast sausage and Mrs. Andrews' melt-in-your-mouth pancakes. The pancakes were enormous, as big as their faces, and were as light and fluffy as a cloud. They topped off their stacks with real butter and pure maple syrup that Mrs. Andrews had gotten as a present from a student's family.

Nick thought he was in Heaven. His mother never cooked breakfast; she was always watching her calories and would never have fixed a breakfast like this. His dad usually went out in the mornings and brought home fast-food pancakes or breakfast sandwiches, both of which tasted like cardboard smothered in grease. This, Nick knew, was real home cooking, meant to be enjoyed.

While they were eating, Mrs. Andrews ate a bowl of cereal and worked on her grocery list.

"Mom, why aren't you having pancakes?" Tommy wanted to know.

Mrs. Andrews blushed a little. "Just trying to eat a bit healthier. I don't have the metabolism that you boys do. I'd like to lose a couple of pounds."

Tommy rolled his eyes as Nick smiled to himself behind his plate. Nick's mom was always counting calories and exercising. He thought, as he knew Tommy did, that their mothers didn't need to worry so much about their weight. They were perfect just the way they were.

"Can you think of anything to add to our list, Tommy?" Mrs. Andrews asked.

Tommy looked over the list, trying to behave the way he always did on Saturday mornings but finding the big, guilty lump in his chest difficult to deal with. "Nope, it looks like you have everything, Mom. Don't forget to get some mozzarella cheese, though. You said that you were going to make pizza this week."

"Oh, that's right," Mrs. Andrews said and wrote it down. Tommy blinked back tears. He knew that in a few moments his mother would walk out the door and he'd be causing her a lot of pain. He hoped that she would forgive him when he came back, and that she would understand why he did what he did.

All too soon, the list was finished. Mrs. Andrews got her coat and purse, and then turned to look at the boys for a moment.

"Are you two all right?" she asked. You don't seem quite your usual selves this morning. You're awfully quiet."

Nick looked down at his plate while Tommy stammered out, "We're fine, Mom. We stayed up too late last night and I didn't get a lot of sleep."

She eyed them for a moment more, raised an eyebrow, and then shook her head.

"All right, be good. Can you possibly clean up the kitchen when you're done? It would be nice to come home and not have to do it."

"Um, sure, Mom. We'll take care of it."

"Okay then. I'll see you when I get back." She dropped a kiss on top of Tommy's head and then to Nick's surprise, gave him one, too. Nick blushed to the roots of his red hair. He looked pleased and embarrassed as she mussed up his hair and made her way out the door.

"Mom, wait!" Tommy exclaimed. He jumped up out of his chair and gave her one final hug, right in front of Nick. In case they never came back, he wanted to remember everything about her: her vanilla and lavender scent from the lotion she used, her chin resting on his head, her tight squeeze. His mother looked down at him in surprise.

"What was that for?" she asked as he sat back down.

Tommy shrugged, not able to look at her. "Just… because. Thanks for the pancakes and everything."

"Oh, um, okay. Don't burn the house down. I'll be back soon." She smiled, but looked at them strangely as she walked out the door. They watched her get into the car and drive away.

"C'mon," Tommy said, "Let's get this place cleaned up quick and get this over with."

They cleaned the kitchen in record time: rinsing the plates and loading them into the dishwasher, hand washing the pans, and wiping down the table to get the little syrup blobs and crumbs off of it. Tommy swept the floor and Nick followed behind with the wet sweeper. In no time the kitchen was clean and Tommy turned to look at Nick.

"Are you ready?" Nick nodded.

"You get the box, I'll get the knapsack."

Tommy raced into his mother's room to fetch the box from under her bed while Nick ran back to Tommy's room to get the knapsack that they had carefully packed the night before. They met in the living room where Tommy was trying to pick open the lock on the box. Impatiently, Nick took over.

"Here, give it to me. You'll ruin it! I'll teach you the right way another time." In half of a second, Nick popped open the lock and there were all of the things that they had left the last time: the letters, the coins, and, most importantly, the amulet. Tommy slowly drew it out of the box by its long silver chain. It almost seemed to be a living thing, with its deep purple stone that you could look into forever. Even as he was just taking it out of the box it seemed to quiver in anticipation. Tommy figured that it sensed what they were about to do. After all, it hadn't been used in almost twelve years.

"Do you have the directions?" Nick whispered, even though they were the only ones in the house.

"Right here." Tommy took them out. "Let's put the coins into the knapsack, too. We may need some money while we're there/"

"All of them?"

"No, just some. Remember, I owe you one when we get back."

"Unless I just get one there."

"Yeah, well, anyway, don't put all of them in."

Once everything was in the knapsack, the boys looked at each other.

"We both have to hold it," Tommy said.

"The chain or the amulet?" Nick wanted to know.

"Let's both hold the amulet. It might not work if we're just holding the chain. Hey, it's a long chain. Let's see if we can put it around both of our necks." To his surprise, the chain was long enough. "We should both still hold onto it, though, just in case. We need to focus on London, England, August, 1540. We need to say it out loud together. Got it?"

"Wait, why August?" Nick wanted to know.

"Because that's when the letters were dated, remember? He had to be in London in August of 1540. If we go at that same time, we have a better chance of finding him."

"Got it," Nick replied. "Okay, let's do this!"

They both took a hold of the amulet, feeling the electricity inside of it vibrate to warm their fingers. They linked arms, the better to make sure they stayed together, and Tommy counted, "One, two three" They both said at the same time, "I want to go to London,

122

England, August, 1540." A cloud of smoke instantly filled the room and swirled around them with the scent of heavy perfume. Tommy was blinded by the smoke and began coughing. He couldn't see Nick, but he could hear him coughing, too, and Tommy managed to yell out," Don't let go of it!"

The room began to spin, faster and faster and Tommy felt sick to his stomach as the ground beneath him disappeared but he didn't let go of the amulet. He could still feel Nick's fingers on it, too, as they swirled through the perfumed fog. The pressure on his body was tremendous, like he was being pulled in two different directions and all of the air was squeezed out of his lungs. Just when he thought he was going to pass out and couldn't hold on any more, he felt them start to free-fall. He had no idea how long they had been twirling through the air but it seemed that their journey was ending just in time. His head was so dizzy that it ached horribly, like when he went on the upside-down roller coaster, only a hundred times worse.

The fog began to thin out as they fell and Tommy could see the outline of Nick's body again, both of them still hanging on for dear life to the amulet. Tommy stretched out his other hand and Nick did, too. They grabbed on to each other's shirts so that they wouldn't get separated in what remained of the cloud. Tommy looked down to see the ground spinning up toward him, coming too fast. It was like sky diving without a parachute! Panic crept up from his stomach.

"Hang on!" he called to Nick, who looked down and then back at Tommy in horror. They were going to hit the ground. Hard.

Tommy moaned, his head pounding, as if someone were hitting it with a hammer over and over. As he tried to sit up, the earth moved beneath him, his stomach retched, and he desperately tried to not throw up from the dizziness but it didn't work. He did manage to lean over far enough so that he didn't get any vomit on his clothes. Gross. He lay back down on the hard ground and waited for it to pass.

After what seemed like an eternity, the earth slowed and he groaned as his stomach gurgled in rage at the ordeal he had put it through. So much for stuffing himself full of pancakes and sausage. He felt all over his head with his hands, checking to make sure everything was where it should be. Although he was sore, nothing seemed to be broken. Maybe you fell just hard enough to not be seriously hurt. Whatever. He was all in one piece. Blinding sunlight made him squint for a few more minutes before he could actually get a good look around him and a new world came into focus.

He was in a field of some kind, with long grasses, waving in the sun. The sky was a crystal clear blue with tiny puffs of clouds scattered about it. The landscape looked strange for a moment before he realized that something was strange. There were no telephone wires anywhere and no airplanes flying overhead. It was perfectly still and quiet, except for the sounds of birds. He looked around to find Nick and saw him lying about ten feet away. He hadn't woken up yet.

All of a sudden, Tommy thought of the amulet and began frantically searching the ground around him. Without it, they would be stuck here forever! He ran his fingers over the ground, looking for a sparkle of some mind when he heard Nick begin to moan. Forgetting the amulet for a moment, Tommy quickly crawled over to Nick's side and began talking to him.

"Nick, hey, it's me, Tommy. We landed in a field. We're okay, but you're probably going to throw up in a minute."

Nick cracked open one eye slowly at Tommy and tried to prop himself up. "Throw up? Why would I…" Just then, Nick turned green, groaned, and Tommy pushed his head over to the side just in time. When Nick was finished, he weakly sat up and rubbed his eyes.

"Man, it's bright out here. I feel like my dad looks the morning after he's been to a big party."

"Don't worry, it'll pass," Tommy assured him, "Right now, we have to find the amulet. I know that we were both holding onto it when we fell."

"Yeah, we'd better find that, pronto," Nick agreed. "Just where are we, anyway? Did we make it to England? Where's the knapsack?"

"I think so," Tommy said. "Look around. There aren't any wires. I think that city over there must be London." He pointed to a large clump of buildings that looked to be a few miles away. "We can walk to that pretty quickly. I think the knapsack is gone, though." There was no sign of it. They could do without the toothpaste, no one else used it here, but the money was another matter. How would they be able to get around without it? Before

126

Tommy let himself think about that, he wanted to find the amulet. Without it, they had no hope of going home.

"Maybe we should have told the amulet that we wanted to land right in the middle of London so we wouldn't have to walk so far," Nick grumbled. His head was still foggy and while the pounding was lessening, it was still there. Maybe they should have thought to bring some aspirin with them.

"No, I think it's better this way," Tommy countered. "If we had dropped right in the middle of London, it would have caused a big stir. This way, nobody knows how we got here. Falling out of the sky would probably not be a good thing here."

Nick nodded. "So, we just start walking to London?"

"First, we need to find that amulet. We need it to go home. Let's look all over the ground where we landed." The boys began combing over the grassy ground inch by inch, looking for that wink of purple hidden in the weeds. They were beginning to get desperate after about half an hour when Nick finally spotted something that looked like a silver chain a few yards away. He gave a shout to Tommy and went to grab it. He reached it and pulled it up, the mysterious purple stone shining in the bright sunlight. Nick thought he had never seen anything more beautiful in all his life. Now they had their ticket home and wouldn't have to live out the rest of their lives in 1540. Tommy ran over to his side breathing heavily and grinned at him.

"Awesome job, finding it."

A minute later, Tommy noticed something else. The knapsack! The straps were torn and broken, but it was there. Tommy tied the ends together and looped it over his shoulder. He slipped the chain of the amulet over his neck and tucked it inside of his shirt. Amazingly, the chain that had been large enough for him and Nick to loop it around both of them was more of a normal size now. Maybe it had even more powers that they didn't know about.

They were ready to move on and began walking toward the city in the distance. A little while later, they found a road that made the walking a bit easier than walking through the tall grass. The sickness and pounding from their fall had gone away and in the clear, bright air, they were beginning to feel like they were actually on an adventure. They congratulated themselves on making it this far and figured that the worst was over. They had traveled through time; really, truly traveled through time! It was amazing!

"One thing we forgot", Tommy said as they trudged on their way. "Clothes. We don't really look like we belong here."

"We'll find some when we get to London", Nick countered. He was feeling pretty good right then.

They were feeling on top of the world when in an instant, their world came crashing down. About a hundred yards away, a group of four men on horses was rushing right for them on the road at a full gallop. There was no doubt in their minds that they had been seen.

Chapter Six

"Run!" Tommy yelled. He and Nick turned and began to race as fast as they could through the long, wavy, grass but it was useless. A horse can run much faster than a person, especially the big warhorses that the men were riding. Every few seconds, Tommy would glance back to see if they had managed to lose the riders but they were getting closer every second.

At the last moment, Tommy turned to see the sweat flying off the horses' bodies and noticed the bright green and white of the uniforms. Uniforms! They weren't just any riders; they were soldiers! Tommy's heart felt like it was going to pound right out of his chest and he quickly veered to the side to avoid being trampled by the biggest hooves he had ever seen. As quick as a wink, the soldier vaulted off the back of the horse and grabbed Tommy up by the scruff of his shirt. Glancing to the right, he saw that Nick was receiving the same treatment from one of the other soldiers. The soldier who was holding Tommy spun him around and eyed them both up and down.

"Well now, what have we here?" The soldier's breath, the worst Tommy had ever smelled, blew right into his face. It was all he could do not to gag. Instead, he breathed through his mouth and tried to think of something intelligent to say.

"My… my name is Tommy," Tommy managed to stammer out.

"Well then, Thomas, how is it that you came to be in the middle of this field near the road to London with your friend, here?" His almost-toothless smile showed that he was enjoying making Tommy squirm.

Tommy didn't answer, working frantically to come up with some sort of believable lie that didn't include a magic amulet and falling out of the sky. His brain was blank. In all of their careful planning, they hadn't been prepared to be captured by soldiers! Finally, he mumbled out, "I don't know."

"You don't know?" growled the soldier. "How about your friend here? Does he know?"

"N...n...no, sir," Nick managed to eke out. "We woke up here, in the grass. We both threw up, over there." Nick pointed in the direction where they both had, in fact, thrown up earlier, in case the soldiers wanted to check.

The soldier looked at them more carefully. "You're wearing the oddest clothes I've ever seen. Where did you get them?"

The boys shook their heads, now firmly committed to the lie. "We don't know, sir," Tommy volunteered, "We woke up with them on. We don't remember much of anything but our own names." It just popped out.

The soldier holding Nick shook him roughly. "And what might your name be, my fine lad?" he asked.

"Nicholas, sir," Nick squeaked. Tommy could see that Nick was getting more and more frightened all the time. He hoped that the soldiers would be letting them go before Nick completely broke down in tears. He tried to give Nick a look to reassure him, but the other soldier had Nick facing away. All of a sudden, Tommy had an idea to help save them. Without thinking of the consequences, he opened his mouth and said, "We can tell you what will happen in the future."

As soon as he said those words, he regretted them. He knew it was the wrong thing to say from the looks on the soldiers' faces. He wished that he could take the words back, but it was too late. He had their interest now.

"I think, sir," said the soldier who was holding Nick to the soldier who was holding Tommy, "we should take them to the king." At those words, Tommy's knees went as weak as jelly. The king?

Henry VIII in person! It was a terrifying thought. Things were definitely not going according to plan.

Tommy's soldier looked thoughtful for a moment and then nodded. "Yes, the king will want to know of this, especially with all of the Catholic plots flying about his head. These boys may be in on one of them; methinks they're lying about telling the future. If they are involved in a plot, we will be richly rewarded for bringing them in. Robin! Ride ahead and tell the king that we have a special case for him." One of the other soldiers, presumably Robin, nodded, wheeled his horse around, and took off at a gallop down the road to London. Tommy tried to protest, to tell them that he and Nick weren't a part of any plot, but the soldiers paid no attention to their pleas.

"Shut up now! No more of your filthy lies! You're going before his Highness and you'd better have a good reason for being out here alone and looking the way that you do. It would be a shame if two young ones such as yourselves would have to die for a traitorous cause, but that's how your people work, don't they?" He smiled wickedly as Tommy opened his mouth again to protest. "That's right, I forgot. You aren't part of the Catholic faction. Of course you're not", he said mockingly. "But do you carry the stink of sorcery about you? We'll just let his Highness decide that, shan't we? Do you know what the penalty for sorcery is, lad?" He leaned in closer to Tommy's face, grinning wickedly into his eyes and breathing out the same foul air. Tommy shook his head and held his breath, praying that this wasn't happening to him.

"It's not pleasant", the soldier growled.

Thoroughly frightened now, Tommy decided to keep his mouth shut and work on a story in his head to tell the king. He hoped that Nick would be doing the same.

The soldiers hoisted the boys up onto the horses, climbed up behind them, and began a fast gallop toward the city. The horses were so huge and the gallop so smooth that it felt like flying to Tommy. If it wasn't for the fact that they were being taken to a bloodthirsty king and could possibly have their heads chopped off, it might have been an enjoyable experience. As it was, the journey into London took a much shorter time than Tommy had hoped it would. In no time at all, the horses slowed to a walk and they were inside the City of London, proper, gazing at the spectacles that surrounded them.

As the horses slowed down even more to avoid the throngs of people and they were better able to take in the sights and smells around them, the boys remembered what Mr. Barnhart had told them about hygiene; it was very lax compared to the twenty-first century. The sheer smell of the place was overwhelming. Piles of household garbage stood next to doorways; mounds of horse poop cluttered the streets. Flies were buzzing everywhere, pigs roamed around loose, and Tommy had to close his eyes just to realign his senses to this new place. The smells alone were enough to make him gag and the sight of people everywhere overwhelmed him.

Nick was looking everywhere at once. The buildings were so close together! The stalls where vendors were selling their wares in the narrow streets were particularly interesting. It seemed as if everything was for sale: meat, vegetables, spices, herbs, furs, animal skins, even used clothing. If only he and Tommy had found their way here before getting captured by the soldiers, they could have bought some new clothes and blended in a little more. But that thought was replaced by what was coming in the next few minutes. Shortly, they would be standing before *the* Henry VIII, the most infamous king in the history of England. Nick began to panic as he thought of what the king could do to them. He hadn't bargained on getting into a mess like this. He might never see his mother again if things didn't go well. *At least we still have the amulet* he thought to himself. Although he desperately wanted to reach into the front of his shirt to see if it was still there, he didn't dare while riding with the soldier. It was his only way home and he didn't want it taken away from him.

The city, however, was enough to take his mind off of his predicament, if only for a moment. The reality hit him that he was in *London, the* London, and not just London, but London in 1540! It was at the same time both impossible and amazing that they had done it, that they had arrived here in one piece.

The smells were very strong and unpleasant but just the sheer fact that they were there took Nick's breath away. He looked over at Tommy on the back of the other soldier's horse to see if he was feeling the same thing. He saw Tommy was looking around in wonderment, alright, but his face was pale and pasty, as if he had the flu. He hoped fervently that Tommy wouldn't throw up again, not all over the soldier. That would really get them into hot water. He caught Tommy's eye and tried giving him a little grin, a look of encouragement, and Tommy gave a weak smile back. For the rest of the ride, Nick decided to focus only on the fantastic sights around him and tried to put off the thought of what they'd be meeting at the end of their ride.

***

After navigating for what seemed like forever through the streets of London, they arrived at a large river, muddy brown and extending as far as they could see in either direction. The soldiers stopped for a few moments at the bank to allow the horses a drink. As they bent their thick, sweaty necks down, Tommy ventured to timidly ask the soldier he was riding with, "Where are we going?"

For a moment, he didn't think the soldier heard him and he didn't dare ask him again. There was a long pause before the soldier finally answered. "Hampton Court, where his Majesty is currently residing with the new Queen." Tommy wracked his brain. In their conversations with Mr. Barnhart, he had never mentioned a Hampton Court. Tommy desperately wanted to know how far away it was. He didn't want to be stuck on this horse forever with the smelly soldier!

When the horses had drunk their fill, the soldiers turned them down a path that followed the river and picked up speed again. After what seemed like hours, a huge, reddish-brick building appeared on the bank of the river. As they rode closer and closer, Tommy's heart began its pounding in his chest again.

They entered the palace through armed gates and doorways, dismounted from the horses, entered an open doorway guarded by more soldiers, and then began walking through a dizzying array of passages. Tommy's legs were stiff from sitting for so long, but he didn't dare ask to slow down.

At the entrance to the palace, Tommy's soldier asked the guard, "Did the messenger come? Where is His Majesty today?"

"He arrived a little while ago. The king is in the Great Hall, holding court. He's expecting you", the guard replied. Tommy's soldier nodded and they entered the palace, twisting and turning through a maze of passages.

At last, they came to the entrance of a long hallway. It had a stone floor and walls and, despite the August heat outside, it was damp and chilly. Tommy presumed that the king would be at the other end and from the way the soldiers collected themselves, he knew that he was right. The soldier kept his sword uncomfortably pressed against Tommy's back, between his shoulder blades the entire way. As the soldier hustled him along, Tommy could once again smell his rancid breath coming from over his shoulder.

Tommy's stomach was churning with fear. He fervently hoped that Nick, also with a sword pressed to his back, would keep his mouth shut in front of the king. All of the stories that he had heard about Henry VIII made him out to be someone who would not be trifled with and Nick wasn't exactly a smooth talker. People around the king seemed to lose their heads for no reason at all, simply because they had disagreed with him, and here he and Nick were, appearing out of nowhere and wearing strange clothes.

He remembered again what he had said about being able to know the future and that it was punishable by death. He tried to gulp down the large lump in his throat and forced himself not to cry over the thought of losing his head in the Tower of London. He wondered if the king would believe that he had made it up because he was scared. He hoped so. Maybe he would be so angry that he'd just send them to get their heads chopped off today.

It seemed like ages until they reached the end of the hallway. The soldier reached around him to pull open one of the heavy, oaken, double doors to the Great Hall. The handles of the doors looked just as they should in a palace of Henry VIII; large, menacing iron rings with all sorts of other ironwork added for decoration.

As Tommy held his breath, the door slowly swung open to reveal a huge, sunlit room with a giant throne at the opposite end from where they were. Upon it sat a rather large, bearded man dressed in what looked to be very expensive clothing. He wore a purple velvet hat on his head topped off with an enormous white feather that bobbed as he talked. His purple coat had enormous puffed shoulders and his pants ended tightly just below the knee. He had on white stockings that were probably made of silk and large, black leather shoes with bright gold buckles on them. Seated around him were several other men and a few ladies, including one young lady who was more richly dressed than the others and sat directly at the king's side. Tommy assumed that she was Queen Katherine Howard, Henry's fifth wife, but he didn't have time to properly take it all in.

The soldier pressed the sword against his back, forcing him to begin walking toward the king, every step harder and harder to take. The closer they got to the king and the queen, the younger the queen looked and the older Henry looked.

Tommy's knees trembled and shook, threatening to give out. He noticed a peculiar smell in the room and tried to glance around to see what it was without anyone noticing. The odor seemed to be coming from the king himself and Tommy saw that he had a bandage wrapped around one of his massive legs. It looked as if something yellow was leaking through. Gross! Tommy tried not wrinkle his nose and breathed through his mouth so that the smell wouldn't make him nauseous. He remembered then what Mr. Barnhart had said about the king having a sore on his leg.

When he had walked almost all the way to the throne, the soldier forced him down on his knees to the ground.

"Bow before your king," he sneered, pushing Tommy's head down until his forehead touched the rug. Tommy glanced quickly over to see that Nick had been placed in the same position. The rug smelled funny, like horses and unwashed wool. He hated to think of what was stuck onto the shoes and boots of people who'd walked over this rug that he was now touching with his face.

The soldier yanked him upright onto his knees and before him sat *the* King Henry VIII; fat with a smelly leg, grandly dressed, and with an interested look on his face as he stared first at Tommy and then at Nick.

The room was silent. Everyone was looking at Tommy and Nick and waiting for the king to speak first. When he did, his voice did not match the huge body. It was rather high-pitched and would have been better placed on a thinner, smaller, man.

"Why have these oddly-dressed prisoners been brought before me?" he thundered. Even if his voice was high, it didn't make him any less intimidating. Tommy's knees began to shake again.

The soldier holding Tommy made a slight bow before answering. "Sire, we found them wandering about the fields in the outskirts of London wearing strange clothing that we've never seen before, then when we questioned them, this one," he pointed his finger at Tommy, "started blabbering about how they can tell the future."

"The future?" King Henry muttered, "Do you expect me to believe that you would willingly bring about a charge of witchcraft upon yourselves? Are you indeed sorcerers? *Are you?*" he thundered again, looking at them with laser-like eyes. There was nothing high-pitched about his voice now.

Tommy didn't know how to answer, or if he was even supposed to answer. He simply shook his head and cowered, silently begging for this to be over. His knees began to tremble uncontrollably and he tried not to let the tears come to his eyes. He knew that if he tried to speak at that moment, he would start bawling like a baby, something that was not looked kindly upon in Tudor times. At twelve, almost thirteen, years old, he was expected to behave like a man. He took a few deep breaths and quickly glanced at Nick. He had gone so pale that all of his freckles were standing out and tears filled his eyes. If anyone was going to speak to the king, it would have to be Tommy before Nick lost it.

In a shaky voice, Tommy managed, "Um, Sire, my name is Thomas Andrews and this is my friend, Nicholas Jones."

The king frowned. "And where do you come from, Thomas Andrews?" Tommy wracked his brain. In Tudor times, the New

World hadn't been settled by England yet. Heck, no one would even make it to Roanoke until 1585 when Elizabeth I, Henry's second daughter, would be queen. He knew that he couldn't just spill out that they were from a non-existing America. He decided to stick to the story that he had told the soldier.

"I... I... I don't remember, Sire. I think that Nick and I were both hit on the head pretty hard and some things are difficult for us to remember."

The king stared at Tommy full in the face for a long moment and then he looked at Nick.

"Is this true, Nicholas?"

Nick bobbed his head up and down, nodding ferociously, not trusting himself to actually use words. The king, however, wasn't impressed by Nick's inability to speak.

"Don't you know how to speak to your sovereign?" the king said, in a voice that was a bit softer.

Nick dared take a peek up at the king, but the sight of him, coupled with the nauseating smell coming from his leg, made him bow his head again, this time shaking it back and forth. Of course Nick had never had to speak to a king before. The closest he had come was when he had won first place in the city art competition and got to have lunch with the mayor. The mayor was far less scary than this giant sitting on a throne. He forced out a whisper, "No, Your Majesty". At least he remembered to say that.

The king gave a grunt, dissatisfied with Nicholas and turned his attention back to Tommy.

"You speak strangely, not like an Englishman. Perhaps you come from the continent? A country from the Far East, mayhap? You do speak the language tolerably well, however. Were you well educated?"

Tommy shook his head again. "I don't know, Sire. Small memories come back to me day by day." He was getting more creative with this lie. "Perhaps tomorrow I shall be able to tell you more about where I came from." A slowly returning memory might buy them some time, enabling him to string the king along for a while and keep their heads on their shoulders.

The king spoke again, "What of what my captain told me? Are you involved in witchcraft? Do you practice sorcery?"

Again, Tommy shook his head. "No, Sire. I don't know why I said that. I'm afraid that when your soldiers grabbed us, my head wasn't quite right and I was still a bit shaken up."

"Then how do you explain the strange clothing that you're wearing?" Tommy looked down at his jeans and tennis shoes. He and Nick didn't know exactly what to expect when they said the words over the amulet. Maybe they should have found some clothes before they left, the kind that people wore at the Renaissance festival that his mom liked to go to every year. Their clothes must certainly have looked odd to people who had never seen a zipper or rubber-soled shoes.

Tommy thought fast. "I don't remember how we got these clothes, these rags, Your Majesty."

Tommy hoped that he was speaking respectfully enough. He hated to think of spending the night in a dungeon because he said the wrong thing. He snuck a look at the young queen who was seated on the smaller throne next to the king. She seemed bored with the whole business, although she did not utter a word. She simply stroked the tiny dog that was lying on a pillow on her lap and stared off into space, once in a while focusing on them. As he had first thought

146

when he entered the chamber, she was very young, maybe fifteen or sixteen years old, not much older than them. She could have been Tommy's babysitter a couple of years ago!

She was pretty, in a different kind of way. Her nose was a bit large, but it fit nicely in her face. Her eyes were a light blue and the front part of her hair was a pretty shade of auburn. The rest of it was covered by some kind of hood, sparkling with jewels and gold trim. She wasn't exactly skinny, but short and slightly plump, although her waist was pulled in tightly by a corset. He tried to imagine what she might look like in the twenty-first century and decided that she would probably look very nice. He blushed slightly thinking about it. Tommy wondered how long it would be until Henry found out what she was up to behind his back and then her fate would be sealed. He looked away quickly, in case Henry saw him looking at her. He didn't need any more trouble!

The king scrutinized them with a menacing stare. "I don't know if I believe what you say. My mind tells me to have you tried as spies and executed immediately." Tommy's heart lurched and he heard Nick give a small sob, "But you are young and I have no evidence of any crime." He paused before he went on. "Maybe I shall wait a few days to see if your memories return. I shall warn you that spies are not treated kindly here, so if you are on a mission from another sovereign, he will be sorely disappointed. My men are quite, er, *adept* at detecting lies." Tommy shivered.

"Sire, we are not spies! Surely, you will find that out in the next few days as our memories return." He wondered how long he could get away with the memory-loss scam. Hopefully long enough to make an escape plan!

"Hmmm, we shall see." He turned to the soldiers that were holding Tommy and Nick.

"Put these two in the Tower tonight. Not the dungeon, mind you, we want them alive, but in a room alone. Lock it tight and guard the door, but make sure that they are fed adequately and for the love of God, get them some decent clothing. Send ahead to Kingston, immediately!"

The soldiers stood up straight and gave short bows from the waist. "Yes, Sire." One left right away, presumably to let Kingston know, whoever that was.

The king continued. "I want then brought back here tomorrow after dinner. We shall see how much of their memories have been regained and perhaps," a small grin played at the corners of his mouth, "if they speak the truth, we might find out something about the elusive future as well." With a wave of his ringed hand, they were dismissed.

Before the soldiers began to march them out, they saw the king haul himself up off of the throne with the aid of a cane and struggle to his feet, stubbornly refusing the hand of the servant next to him. He then offered his other hand to the queen, who took it daintily and nimbly stood beside him. She looked even smaller standing next to him than she did sitting down. Tommy wondered how on earth she could stand being married to a brute like that. He didn't have much time to dwell on that thought as the soldiers that had brought them into the chamber hustled them out of there in record time.

They traveled back down the same hallway and out into the cobblestone courtyard of the palace again. Tommy screwed up the courage to ask the soldier, "Where are we going?"

"To the Tower", the soldier grumbled.

"What tower?"

"What do you mean what tower? The Tower of London, of course. That's where all of the *important* prisoners are kept." He said the word "important" with a mocking sneer. "You should feel privileged. There aren't many commoners that end up there. If it were up to me, you'd be rotting at the bottom of a dungeon." Tommy had no doubt that he meant every word that he said, and that people really did rot at the bottoms of dungeons.

"So we're not going to a dungeon?" Nick piped up bravely.

"No, but you will be in a cell. They'll even put fresh straw down for you and your friend. It's almost better than my own house, but I'm free to come and go as I please and I don't have to face King Harry tomorrow." Tommy couldn't see the soldier's face, but he could hear the sneering grin that must have been spreading out his thin lips.

Tommy desperately tried to put on a show of bravery and not cry. He wondered if Nick was trying to do the same because he hadn't heard him whimper at all after they left the Great Hall. He hoped that Nick would pull it together and help him think of a way to get out of this mess. They hadn't even been in London for twenty-four hours and they had already been arrested, taken before the King and would now be put in jail.

He wondered if his father was out there, somewhere in the throngs of people that flooded London. Was it possible that maybe, just maybe, his father could sense that he was there? Just in case, Tommy tried to send him a message with his mind, but it only made him feel more hopeless.

They came to the banks of the muddy river again, this time to cross at a long bridge. Tommy's curiosity got the better of him.

"What river is this?"

"You're definitely not from London, are you, boy? This is the Thames River and we're about to cross it on Tower Bridge. Do you see those heads up there? You could be joining them soon."

Tommy and Nick both saw them; two heads stuck on the tops of spikes. They almost looked like Halloween decorations, except that Tommy knew they were real. He shivered, gulped, and forced himself to look away and think of a way to change the subject.

"Why not London Bridge?" he asked, remembering the old nursery rhyme.

The soldier looked at him strangely for a moment. "Because Tower Bridge goes right to the Tower."

"Oh."

All too soon, they crossed the bridge and suddenly, the Tower came into view. In Tommy's mind, he had seen the Tower as just one building, but as they came up on it, he saw that it was a collection of several buildings with towers surrounded by high, thick walls. It wasn't incredibly tall by Tommy's modern standards but he noticed that it was the tallest building he'd seen all day.

They crossed over the moat and the soldiers at the gate seemed to recognize the group of soldiers they were with. With a nod, the portcullis was raised and they crossed through the thick walls into the Tower of London. They dismounted from the horses as some boys about their age took led the horses away, no doubt to give them water and food.

Tommy's soldier spoke to another guard, "Where will they be held?"

"In the Bell Tower. Kingston has ordered it to be ready."

With the soldier still holding him tightly, they marched over to one of the Towers and began to climb the twisting steps inside.

Tommy and Nick hadn't realized that the steps that were inside of a tower curved up around and around until they got to each level. He felt very dizzy climbing them, having thrown up his breakfast and after all that had happened to them that day. For no reason at all, he thought about how the young queen, who he had only just seen, and wondered if she would soon be a ghost in that lonely Tower. It all seemed so long ago now, that night when Mr. Barnhart had come over for dinner. He had been warm, safe, happy, and *clean*; a far cry from what he was now.

They finally stopped in front of a barred door. Another soldier, better dressed, older than the first two, stepped forward with a ring of keys and unlocked the door. Tommy's soldier shoved him in and he fell on the floor. Before he could get up the other soldier shoved Nick in as well, who landed on top of him. The new soldier who had opened the door, and who the boys would find out was the Constable of the Tower, not a soldier, scolded the soldiers.

"Don't be shovin' these boys around! I've been given strict instructions that they be unharmed and I won't have ya breakin' their bones the first minute they get in here! Now, get on with you and I'll be speaking to your captain later." The constable commanded attention. This must be Kingston. He was tall and solid with the look of muscle that is slowly turning to fat from age and lack of exercise. He appeared to be in his late forties or early fifties. He would almost have been a grandfatherly presence if he were not holding a large ring of iron keys that were going to lock Tommy and Nick in the infamous Tower of London.

The lower ranking soldiers didn't look pleased, but stood up straight and said, "Yes, sir", before sneering at them and heading back down the hallway. Nick scrambled to get up off of Tommy and both of them cautiously sat up and looked around their new surroundings. The constable gave them a sympathetic look.

"You are young ones, aren't you? Well, at least they put you in here instead of in the dungeon. That's where most of 'em go."

"M-m-most prisoners?" Nick stammered out.

He nodded. "Most common prisoners, anyway. I beg your pardon, but the two of you sure don't look as if you have a penny to your name. And you're wearin' the oddest things! King Henry must have taken a liking to ye to put you in the Tower."

"A liking to us?" Tommy blurted out. "We were brought here with swords poking us in the back and they took us to the king himself! How can he like us?"

The constable leaned in and spoke in a conspiratorial whisper, "Aye, lad, he does think highly of you, or at least he wants to know more about you. In the dungeon, things are different. You'd be down in a dark hole with a whole mess of beggars, thieves, and cutthroats, the like of which you've never seen before. There's no clean straw or pot to relieve yourself, so men just piss all over the floor, and worse. Your food is tossed to you through the bars, if you get any at all and what lands on the floor has to be wrestled away from the rats. At night it's even worse. The rats are hungry, too, and they look for the weakest prey they can find." The constable's voice dropped to a whisper. "There's been many a prisoner who died in the dungeon and a few days later there's nary a trace of 'im left. The living men sometimes wake in the night to find the rats gnawing on fingers, toes, or ears and there's nothing to be done about it." He stopped for a moment and looked at their pale faces frozen in horror at his description of the dungeon. Pleased that he had gotten the reaction that he wanted, he leaned in even closer to them, pointing a finger at their chests in turn.

"And that, my good lads, is why I think that the King regards you highly. You're behind bars, but you won't die behind them. Now, the block is another matter, but we'll just have to wait and see about that, now won't we?"

Tommy screwed up his courage to ask, "What's the "block"?"

The constable gave a sad smile. "Why, the chopping block, of course, where those found guilty of crimes against the King are beheaded. All kings have done it for as long as there have been kings and if I had to be executed, I'd choose that way above all of the other ways. It's over in a minutes and you don't feel any pain. One swipe of the axe, or of the sword if the king likes you, and all of your troubles are over." He gave a small tight smile and locked the door to their cell, ignoring their fear at being left in such a place.

"Now, you're to be here until tomorrow afternoon at least so here's what I can tell you", he said to them through the small window in the door. "You may call me Mr. Kingston. I've been the constable here at the Tower for many years and I have served my

156

king well. My wife and I live here and I may be able to persuade her to share some of our supper with you lads tonight, otherwise you might not eat at all." He began to whisper again. "I can't do that for every prisoner, but seeing as that you two are without friends and family and so young, we can help you out for a day or so. Mind, though, if you're here longer, you'll have to do some chores in order to pay for your suppers", he said sternly, shaking a thick finger at them. Tommy couldn't tell if he was pulling their leg or if he was serious.

"Y-y-yes, sir," Nick stammered. Tommy was a little relieved that Nick seemed to be okay. He thought that Nick would have completely lost his mind by this point after all they had been through. After all, this was all Tommy's fault. They had traveled back in time to find *his* father, not Nick's. Nick had come along to keep him company and to help him. He knew that Nick was scared out of his mind and he couldn't blame him.

Tommy was scared, too, but actually traveling back through time had strengthened his resolve to find his father. He had to be somewhere in London, the letters said so, or somebody here would have to know where he was. There was only the matter now of getting released from their prison and escaping the King's wrath.

Mr. Kingston gave them one final look before leaving them to wait. They could hear his keys jingling as he descended down the winding stairs and then they were left in the lonely room.

Chapter Seven

Lying on the straw pile that night wasn't as uncomfortable as Tommy had first thought that it might be. He and Nick pulled the scratchy woolen blanket over them and in no time at all, Nick was snoring away. Tommy didn't think that he would be able to fall asleep with all that was coming up the next day but to his surprise, he found it incredibly hard to stay awake. His stomach was full of some sort of stew that Mr. Kingston had brought to them later that evening. It was made with a greasy kind of meat that Tommy didn't recognize and tasted fairly bland, but Tommy didn't care. He and Nick were so hungry that they practically inhaled the contents of the bowls that they were given. Mr. Kingston had chuckled to see them eating so quickly.

"Easy, lads, you don't want to make yourselves sick. Mrs. Kingston will be glad to know that her cooking was appreciated. She'll send breakfast over for you in the morning. I don't know what time the king will want you, but be prepared for a messenger to come at any time." He turned to leave, taking their empty bowls with him down the long corridor. When he was out of sight, Nick whispered to Tommy, "Should we go back now? Should we use the amulet while everyone is asleep?"

"No, not yet," Tommy whispered back. "Let's see what happens in the morning. If the king doesn't like us, he won't have us executed right away. We can get away then. We're safe for now," he tried to reassure Nick. "Kingston is looking after us. Don't worry, we won't die. Just keep that amulet with you at all times."

Nick didn't like what he had to say. He had half of a mind to take the amulet himself and leave Tommy behind to face the king on his own but after a minute of thinking about it, he felt guilty. He knew that he wouldn't be able to leave Tommy behind on his own.

They drifted off to sleep easily; first Nick and then Tommy. As they slept, they had no idea that Mr. Kingston had come back to quietly check on them several times during the night. Mr. Kingston had been Constable of the Tower for a long time and had attended many of its most notorious prisoners, including Queen Anne Boleyn. He knew that a lot of the prisoners executed by the king could very well be innocent and he tried to treat them with as much respect as he could in their final days. Queen Anne had been most appreciative at the end, thanking him for his service to her.

He didn't know where these boys were from or where they had gotten such ugly clothes, but he thought there was something about them that deserved special attention. He chose not to think about it any more and to go to bed to rest his old bones. That was the only way to get through what the job offered some days. If he thought about the prisoners too much, he might go mad. Too many of them never left the Tower alive.

In the morning, Tommy awoke to Kingston's voice coming down the hallway. "Up you go, lads, time to rise and shine! Mrs. Kingston has sent over some lovely porridge for you to break your fast with."

Nick looked confused. "Break my fast? What the..." he mumbled sleepily. "Oh!" His face lit up as he realized what that meant. "Breakfast!" Tommy rolled his eyes and smiled at him. He assumed that they would be learning a lot of new words in the next few days. As Tommy rose to his feet he ran his tongue over his teeth. They felt fuzzy and his mouth tasted gross, the result of not brushing his teeth last night or this morning. He hoped that the feeling would

161

go away after he ate something. The soldiers had taken away their knapsack with the money, toothbrushes and toothpaste. He didn't want to know what they thought of that stuff!

They took the steaming bowls of porridge from the constable and began to eat. It really didn't taste like much. It was a lot like the oatmeal that Tommy's mother had for breakfast sometimes on winter mornings, but not flavored with maple or brown sugar. There was a bit of salt in it for flavor and although it wasn't what he was used to, Tommy was glad that it didn't have any mystery meat in it.

When it was gone, Mr. Kingston took their bowls. "You lads sure have a healthy appetite. I hope we got clothes for you that are big enough."

"Clothes, Mr. Kingston?" Nick asked.

"Yes, they should be here soon. Mrs. Kingston is just finishing patching up a few rips and tears. Beggars can't be choosers, you know. Anyway, you can't go in front of the king wearing what you are now."

"Yes, sir; thank you," Tommy told him. He knew that Kingston was going out of his way to be nice to them and he wanted to show the old man as much respect as he possibly could. He might be able to put in a good word for them to the king. Mr. Kingston nodded in response and shuffled off down the stairs again.

A short while later, he came back with a pile of what looked like rags, but were actually the clothes that Mrs. Kingston had gotten from a second hand stall and patched up.

"These were the cleanest that she could find. Today isn't wash day, so you'll have to make due with the way they are. At least you won't be looking like some strange foreigners any more."

The boys thanked him and he left again to give them their privacy. It was bad enough that they had to use the chamber pot, really a bucket, in front of each other, even if they didn't look. Tommy decided that in addition to toothpaste and deodorant, toilet paper and flushing toilets were more great inventions of the modern age.

They quickly got out of their T-shirts and jeans. Nick was a little dismayed when he saw how long the stockings were ("They look like girls' socks!" he complained) but after the initial shock, they buttoned themselves into the pants and pulled the shirts over their heads. Tommy tucked the amulet down in the front of his shirt. Smoothing his hair down, Nick asked, "How do I look?"

Tommy gave him an appraising glance. Nick really did look like he had stepped out of the pages of a history book; not as a prince, but more like a peasant. At least they now looked as if they could fit in the time they had fallen into. The trick now was to convince the king that they were simply peasant boys who had been bonked on the head and had bad cases of amnesia. *No problem* Tommy thought grimly to himself. They clearly had to come up with a plan, though, of how they were going to talk to the king later that day. If they made one wrong move, they could end up missing their heads.

Tommy's stomach rolled with the heavy porridge inside as he thought of his mother. He and Nick had been missing overnight and she must have told Nick's mom by now. She must be horribly worried about him! Tears came to his eyes as he thought of her, but he calmed himself down by thinking that it would all be worth it when he found his father. He forced himself to pull it together so that he and Nick could strategize. Nick was thinking exactly the same thing.

"Tommy, what are we going to tell the king?" Nick whispered. Clearly, he was afraid of being overheard. Although

Kingston had been really decent to them so far, there was no telling if he, or someone else, was somehow listening in on their conversations. It was better to talk softly about the important things. They both remembered what Mr. Barnhart had said about King Henry being paranoid.

"We need to tell him where we're from. We need to come up with a place and a story about our families, something that will be hard for Henry to check out." Nick was right.

"I think we should just keep playing dumb. It's not like anyone is going to recognize us or anything. If we never come out and say, 'Oh, by the way, King Henry, we are from the year 2013. We found this magical amulet and decided to pop into your century to find my missing father, who also knows how to travel through time', then no one can prove we're from anywhere else. We just have to make sure that we stick to it and not mess up." Nick looked skeptical.

"I don't know, Tommy. I think we should just go home now, before we get tortured or something", he pleaded.

Tommy saw how scared Nick was and he felt bad. It would be so easy right now to just take the amulet and go home. But what then? Would he ever find his father? What had this whole thing have been about? He had to convince Nick to stay here with him.

"Nick, come on. I know this seems bad, but think of everything we did to get ready for this, all of that studying. We can do this! We just have to stick to the story, okay? Just a couple more days and then we'll go home. Please, Nick. This means a lot to me. I have to find him!"

"Keep your voice down!" Nick looked around worriedly, no doubt checking for Mr. Kingston but also at Tommy's sudden burst of emotion.

Tommy dropped his voice to a whisper. "C'mon, Nick, think about it. Do you really want to be home right now, listening to your dad yapping on his cell phone, fighting with your mom and them calling each other horrible names while you're bored at some arcade? This is a chance to do something that no kid has ever done before! Maybe we could even write a book about it later and make loads of money. Scientists will want to study the amulet and they'd have to pay us a fortune to get a look at it. Think about it! All we have to do is keep it together for a little while more. Just keep telling everyone 'I don't remember'. If we keep it up, we'll be fine! What do you say?"

Nick's face was brightening a little as he thought about it. If they could pull this off so that no one got hurt, especially them, then maybe, just maybe, they could get out of this room and back home. If Tommy wasn't there beside him, he would have used the amulet to get home a long ago. As it was, he had promised to help Tommy and if things went south, they could always escape with the amulet. It was a good plan, as long as, like Tommy had said, they kept to their story. He looked at Tommy, nodded his head, and smiled. "Let's do it," he said.

A short time later, they heard the familiar jingling of the keys that Kingston carried at all times coming down the hallway. Tommy figured that their cell in the Tower must face the west because even though it was morning, hardly any daylight at all penetrated the corridor where they were being held. Out of the small barred window that they had, Tommy could barely make out the buildings and streets of the city. Torches along the walls provided light enough to see in the hallway through the small barred window in the door, but there weren't any torches in their cell.

Mr. Kingston unlocked the door and came in cheerfully.

"Hullo, boys! Well now, you boys look a bit more proper, I'd say. King Henry ought to like that when he sees you later."

"Mr. Kingston, do you know when the king will ask to see us?" Nick asked anxiously. He wanted to get the whole thing over with.

"Nay, lad, I don't. The king has a lot of important business to attend to every day: meetings with his advisors, meetings with Parliament, taking requests from his subjects, hunting…"

"Hunting?" Tommy asked, "Doesn't the king have someone hunt for him?"

Kingston chuckled and shook his head. "The king has always enjoyed hunting, ever since he was a young boy. He's very proud that he can bring down deer to feed the palaces. He doesn't hunt as much these days, but he still likes to go out on occasion."

"Is it because he's so, well, *big*?" Nick couldn't stop himself from asking in a whisper, just in case anyone else was listening. He couldn't imagine the king hauling his huge body up on some poor horse. The king had to weigh more than three hundred pounds! Too late, he thought he might have said the wrong thing, but when he looked at Kingston, the constable was trying to hide a smile.

"He is a big man, that's for certain, but he rides a war horse, a strong one from France, although he keeps several of them for when he tires them out. Nay, he doesn't hunt as much, though, because of the sore on his leg. Did you not see it yesterday in the chamber? It gives him great pain, especially when he rides."

"What happened to his leg?" Tommy asked.

"He had a jousting accident, years ago, and the leg never fully healed. Now it just drips pus all day, every day and never stops hurting him. It can put him in a dreadful temper. Most times, only the presence of the queen can calm him down." Nick shuddered at the word "pus".

"Is it Queen Katherine Howard?" Tommy already knew who she was, of course, but he couldn't let Kingston know that.

"Aye, he married the young queen last month, all of sixteen years old or so, she is. He calls her his rose without a thorn. He's convinced that she will give the kingdom another son, but", he shrugged, "nothing so far. I don't want to be getting into that gossip with the likes of you lads, though. It's dangerous to talk about the

169

king's marriage", he said, in a tone that made it clear the subject was closed.

Kingston went on, "I've got some other prisoners to attend to. I'll check back with you boys later. Mrs. Kingston is preparing dinner as we speak. I believe you'll enjoy it today. She's really taken to feeling sorry for the pair of you and wants to give you a proper dinner, not just prison food."

"What is she making?" Nick's mouth was already watering, not because the food was spectacular, but because he was hungry. It was amazing to think that he couldn't just go and grab a snack any time he wanted to, like at home. It seemed as if they had eaten their porridge a lifetime ago.

"I'll keep that to myself for now. I think that a surprise will be good for you." Kingston gave them a smile and headed back, jingling, down the hallway.

Nick waited until he was out of sight and whispered to Tommy, "He's really nice to us. Do we have to lie to him?"

"I know, I feel bad, too, but how else are we going to get out of here?

"Maybe he'd understand", Nick argued, "Maybe he knows about time travel, too!"

"Fat chance!" Tommy retorted, a little irritated with Nick for even thinking of it. "He'd run and tell the king and they'd have us executed as sorcerers."

Nick was silent for a moment while he thought. He kicked a loose stone on the ground and thought about what Tommy had said. He was really scared but Tommy was his friend. He very much wanted to be there for Tommy, even if it meant being afraid for a while. He decided to trust that Tommy meant what he said and that at the slightest hint of danger they would whisk out the amulet and propel themselves back to 2013. He stopped kicking around the loose stone and slowly looked up at Tommy, who was anxiously waiting for Nick to decide. Tommy's face was hopeful and fearful at the same time as Nick made his decision.

"Okay", Nick said, finally. "I'll go along with it."

Tommy breathed a sigh of relief. If it all went well, if they could make the king believe their story then maybe, just maybe, they would find his father. Geoffrey Andrews could be in London this very minute and Tommy wouldn't know where to find him. It was frustrating to be so close, but no idea how close. His dad didn't even know that he was here.

As he sat in his pile of straw that was also his bed, another plan began to form in his mind. If he told the king his father's name, maybe the king would know who he was, or could find out. But then the king might try and reunite Tommy with his father and his father wouldn't know who Tommy was. Or maybe when he saw Tommy he would understand. From the one picture that he had, Tommy could see that he resembled his father a lot. They both had the same dimples, the same blue eyes, and the same nose. Tommy wondered what his father would do if he was suddenly brought to court to meet a son he thought that he'd left back in 2001. He might wonder if Tommy's mother had told him the secret of the amulet and that Tommy had come to find him. Tommy thought of how to broach the subject with Nick. He had put Nick through so much already. Would Nick go along with yet another part of the scheme? Tommy decided to find out.

"Um, Nick", he ventured. Nick was looking around the walls where prisoners had scratched their names into the plaster. From the looks of it, they hadn't been the only bored people locked up in here. There really wasn't much to do in the cell besides talk and sit.

"Yeah?"

"I have another idea."

Nick groaned out loud. "Tommy, seriously, I don't think that I can take another one of your ideas! If we add to it, we'll just screw it up and get ourselves into trouble. Then we'll have to leave and you won't find your dad! What else can we possibly say to make this story weirder?" Nick was clearly annoyed. Tommy tried to make it sound as good as possible.

"It's nothing big. I was just thinking that if I told the king that I knew my father's name, maybe he would know who he is, or he would find somebody who did. He might even bring my dad to court to see us."

Nick countered, "That would be brilliant, *except* for the fact that your dad has no clue that we're here! And even if he did come, where would that leave me?"

"Calm down! I think that if my dad sees me, he'll know who I am. I look a lot like him and my mom was supposed to eventually tell me the story, so hopefully he'll figure it out. As for you, we'll just say that you can't remember your parents yet, but we feel like brothers so we have to stay together. What do you think?"

Nick was still worried. He didn't want to let Tommy off the hook so easily. He nervously took the amulet out of his shirt and held it tightly. He could still feel the warm vibration that it gave off and it was a tempting thought to just use it and go home.

"Let's just say that this works. Your dad shows up, takes one look at you and knows that you're his long lost son. What if Henry won't let me go with the two of you? What if he keeps me around?"

"He won't!" Tommy said forcefully. I won't let that happen. No matter what, we stay together. We can't be separated, okay? Okay? We'll leave before that happens, even if my dad is here. I promise!" he said, gripping Nick's shoulders and looking into his eyes.

Nick looked back at Tommy, wanting to believe him. So much was at stake! Did he really have a choice? "Fine", he said grudgingly, "but you're going to do my homework for a year. Or two."

Tommy smiled at him. "As long as it's not home economics. You would fail." Nick managed a smile at this.

174

"We can do this, Nick! Just stick to the plan and let me do most of the talking. Agree with whatever I say. We can do this!"

Just then, the familiar jingle of Kingston's keys came up the stairs, getting louder with every step the old man took. Nick hurriedly tucked the amulet under his shirt before he came into view. The boys could smell the food before they could see it, warm and savory Nick's mouth was watering before he reached their cell.

"That smells great, Mr. Kingston! What is it?"

"It's a special treat for you today, lads! Mrs. Kingston has made some roasted venison for you, made from one of the king's own deer! Mrs. Kingston makes the best roast venison in the whole city of London, if I do say so myself!"

Mr. Kingston unlocked the door and gave them their meals, served in a wooden bowl called a trencher. They were famished after the long morning spent making up a believable story and being bored. Just as it smelled, the venison was delicious. Tommy didn't know anything about the spices used to make it, but he didn't care what they were. The meat was tender and slid off of the bones. The bread was tough, but when he used it to sop up all the gravy, it softened easily.

"Does the king have a lot of deer?" Nick managed to get the question out in between mouthfuls of savory venison stew. Mr. Kingston nodded.

"All of the deer are the king's deer, throughout the kingdom."

Suitably impressed, Nick's and Tommy's eyebrows rose up.

"All of the deer are his? In all of England?"

"Yes, one must have special permission to hunt them. The penalty for poaching one of the king's deer is death."

The boys stopped eating for a moment. "Um, Mr. Kingston", Tommy ventured, "these deer weren't poached, were they?"

Mr. Kingston laughed. These boys amused him to no end. It was as if they had never been in England before. "Of course not! Mrs. Kingston and I are allotted some for ourselves. We cook them for our more distinguished Tower guests." Apparently satisfied with his explanation and happy to be called "distinguished", Tommy and Nick dug back in to their stew with gusto.

Mr. Kingston watched them eat with satisfaction. His wife would be pleased. Her heart had been touched by their situation, especially after he had told her how polite the boys were and how scared they seemed. It made her think of her own children and how she would feel if they were imprisoned in the Tower. It was in her power to help them through their, hopefully, short stay until they could get home to their parents. She had set Mr. Kingston to the task of finding out more about them and how they got there. Perhaps he could help their case with the king.

Finally finished, and with a full stomach, Tommy looked up at Mr. Kingston with a grateful sigh.

"Please tell Mrs. Kingston that we say thank you for the wonderful food. We know that she went through a lot of trouble to make it for us."

"It will give her great pleasure to know that. She also wanted to know if you boys had remembered anything new."

Tommy glanced over at Nick. This was it. It was a trial run of what they would tell the king later that day.

"I've remembered a little bit more. I think it's my father's name."

Kingston's eyebrows shot up. "Do you, lad? What name is it? Maybe I can help."

Tommy took a deep breath before saying it out loud. "Geoffrey Andrews."

Mr. Kingston thought for a moment. "Andrews, you say? Geoffrey Andrews?" He shook his head sadly. "I'm sorry, my boy, I don't know anyone by that name. Do you remember what he did? Was he a tradesman or a merchant?"

Tommy decided that he'd better not say anymore before he wove the story too much. Kingston might get suspicious. He felt terrible about lying to him that way, but he thought that it was the only way to save both of their skins.

"I don't know what he did. That's all I can remember right now."

Kingston was silent for a moment, taking it all in. Then he said, "The king will want to hear about these new developments. Perhaps he will know who your father is. How old are you, lad?"

"I...I... I think I'm twelve years old." Tommy stammered, thinking quickly. If he had lost his memory, would he know how old he was? He hoped it sounded convincing to Mr. Kingston.

After a long moment, Mr. Kingston reached over and tousled his hair. "Well, wherever you're from, you were both kept clean, I'll give them that. No lice on you."

Clean! Tommy had now gone without brushing his teeth for more than 24 hours and it had been more than a day since his last, scalding, shower, but Mr. Kingston thought he was clean. It was difficult to keep a straight face.

"I'll send a message informing the king of what you have told me. I have a feeling that he'll be wanting to speak with you today. I'll be back later." Mr. Kingston gave them a final smile before locking them in again and jingled off down the hallway.

Nick waited until the sound of the keys couldn't be heard anymore and turned to Tommy.

"Jeez, Tommy, you should be an actor or something! He totally believed you!" he whispered.

Tommy sank down to his straw pile. He felt himself start to shake, lying didn't come naturally to him. He was a pretty honest person, normally. What would his mother say if she knew what he was up to? He took some deep breaths to steady himself and looked at Nick.

179

"We both have to be great actors, okay? We have to get through this with our heads still attached."

The absurdity of this struck them both at the same time and they began to giggle.

Nick looked back at Tommy, much less nervous than before. "No matter what."

Chapter Eight

The king must have liked what he heard from Mr. Kingston because it was only a short time later that the familiar sound of the keys came back up the stairs toward them. The boys looked at each other and each braced himself for what was about to happen. The thought of using the amulet right that very second was extremely tempting to Nick, but he only gave it a squeeze through his shirt before Mr. Kingston came into view.

As Mr. Kingston walked up to the cell door, he hurriedly began unhooking the keys from his belt. "The king wants to see you now, lads", he told them. "He has all of his councilors in the room and with what you've told me, they want to meet you. Smooth your hair down, boys; you're going in front of his Majesty."

"Are we going to be chained up?" Tommy wanted to know.

"Nay, he wants to sit and converse with you."

"Converse?" Nick was confused.

Tommy nudged him. "It means he wants to talk with us."

"Oh."

It felt strange to be out of the jail cell where they had been held for almost twenty-four hours. The sunlight was beginning to come through the windows on their side of the building now and it looked beautiful to Tommy. The air was fresh and sweet compared to the air in their room with the chamber pot. He thought that he would never take freedom for granted ever again.

Mr. Kingston marched them down the circular staircase and out into the Tower complex where he took a firm hold of each of their arms.

"We're not going to run away!" Nick protested.

"I can't take any chances", Mr. Kingston told him. "I have to have some hold on you out here. If you were to escape, it would be the end of me."

He walked them through the gates, past lots of soldiers, and over the moat to where there was a carriage waiting. Tommy breathed a sigh of relief. At least they wouldn't be riding on a horse in front of a soldier again all that long way to the palace! Mr. Kingston rode with them inside the carriage and they stayed silent while they were driven back, swaying and bumping over the uneven ground to Hampton Court.

When they got there, before he opened the carriage door to let them out, Mr. Kingston leaned forward to them and whispered,

"When answering the king, it is best to address him as 'Sire' or 'Your Majesty'". He then gave them a wink and stepped out onto the gravel driveway, took them by the arms again and, followed by the king's guards, walked them back into the palace.

They walked down the long hallway that the soldiers had dragged them down the day before until they were standing in front of that same, heavy oaken door with the enormous iron hinges. Mr. Kingston knocked on it and it slowly opened to admit them back into the king's chamber.

It was full of more people than it was the day before. Besides the king, there were several other important looking men dressed in long robes and collars. The queen was also there, but seated in the background with several of her ladies. This time, her gown was a deep blue that made her hair seem more red than blonde. She, along with the entire room, looked intently on Tommy and Nick as Mr. Kingston brought them forward. Tommy only looked at her for a moment before he remembered that he was supposed to bow. He gave Nick a little nudge so that he would remember, too. The last thing he wanted was to be shoved face-down into that smelly carpet again. He noticed that Mr. Kingston bowed with them and quickly

183

stood, with some difficulty, to introduce them to the king and his court.

"Your Highness, may I present to you Thomas Andrews and Nicholas Jones." He bowed slightly and stepped back so that there was nothing in between the boys and the enormous king.

Today, even though it was August, there was a chill in the air and King Henry had chosen to wear a purple velvet doublet, or jacket, lined with some kind of fur around the neck and wrists. His leg wound looked as if it had a fresh wrapping on it at the moment and the smell wasn't nearly as strong as it had been the day before. His beard looked freshly trimmed and he appeared to be in a good mood. Gone was the darkening between his eyebrows that seemed to foretell the coming of a rage, much like a storm cloud comes before the actual storm.

Tommy felt his heart lift a little, seeing that the king looked to be in such a receptive mood. He waited silently for the king to speak. The room was as still as death as the entire court waited to hear what the king had to say. He could feel the penetrating gaze of the king's small blue eyes on him, almost as if he was trying to see directly into Tommy's soul. Through small glances up, he saw the

184

eyes slide over and take Nick in the same way and finally, after an incredibly long moment, the giant king spoke.

"I hear that your memories are being restored to you in a small way", he said in that same high-pitched voice. Tommy waited to see if he was going to say something else but it seemed safe to reply.

He took a deep breath and, remembering what Mr. Kingston had told him, said, "A bit, Sire."

The king shifted his gaze to Nicholas. "Is this true?"

Nick nodded his head. "Yes, Sire. Tommy, I mean *Thomas*, has been filling me in on the missing pieces. I'm sure that it will all come back to me in time." Beads of sweat stood out on his forehead, but Tommy noticed with pride that Nick was able to answer the king without shaking in his shoes this time.

The king looked back at Tommy. "Tell me what you have recalled."

This was it. There was no turning back now.

"Sire, I can remember my father's name."

"Oh?" The king raised an eyebrow. "It's not one of my courtiers, is it? Is that what you've come here for?" A few titters went around the room. Apparently, that had been a joke.

"No, no, Sire. At least, I don't think that he's here. His name is Geoffrey Andrews."

"Hmmm…" the giant king pondered this for a moment, drawing his heavy eyebrows together and making creases appear all over his puffy face. He shook his head.

"I don't know of any Geoffrey Andrews. Is he a lord? A peer?"

Tommy shook his head. "I don't know, sir. I don't think so." That was the truth, at least. He had no idea what his father did for a living. For all he knew, he could be down in the streets on London at this very minute.

Amazingly, the king looked interested. "I am most pleased with this news. I like very much especially how you have both changed since yesterday, from showing cowardice to showing bravery. I don't know if I fully believe your story yet, but I am willing to give you some more time to regain more of your thoughts. I will be sending you back to the Tower, but not to a cell. You will have a larger room to yourself and Mr. Kingston will continue to attend to you. In the meantime, I will send a tutor to teach you your lessons. If your father is a learned man, he will no doubt expect you to read and write as well."

Of course, Tommy and Nick could both read and write, but they both knew that this was not the time to admit that particular fact. The king went on.

"I am going to send out some of my scouts to find this Geoffrey Andrews. Somebody somewhere must know of this man and if he is, in fact, still alive. It has been a long time and there have been many bouts of the plague and the sweating sickness. We will also see if any other families have lost a son, one about your age, Nicholas. Do you know how old you are?"

Nick answered, "I think that I am twelve as well, but I'm not sure." He thought that it was best to go along with what Tommy said.

"We'll say that you're between the ages of ten and thirteen years. That should be sufficient. You look to be close to Thomas' age. With any luck, we shall find both of your families and restore you to them. If not, we shall have to think of another plan. Perhaps

187

we can make you wards of the court or find you a place of employment on the palace grounds. I don't think that you are the sons of gentlemen, even though your hands look soft. No matter, no matter; there is plenty of time. Go back to the Tower now and let me think on this matter further. I shall call you to court again if I learn anything."

"Mr. Kingston", he called. Kingston stepped forward and gave a slight bow. "Mr. Kingston, install them in their new quarters and give them privileges in the Tower Gardens."

Mr. Kingston bowed low and said, "Sire, if I may ask a request?"

"You may."

"Might I show the young lads the menagerie in the Tower? I'll wager that there will be animals there the likes of which they've never seen and it will give them something to do until a tutor is secured."

"Excellent idea, Mr. Kingston. You may take them on the morrow after they've broken their fast. It will be a good place to begin their education. Leave me now. There are other pressing matters I must attend to at present."

That was their signal. Mr. Kingston marched them out of the chamber and down the long hallway as the next petitioner took their place before the king. He was silent until they reached the outside where he took hold of their arms again.

"It's simply what is done", he told Nick when Nick gave him a puzzled look. At least they didn't have to go back and sleep on a pile of straw. Mr. Kingston was explaining their new rooms to them as they were driven back to the Tower.

"You will have a bed chamber and a small sitting room where you can receive guests."

"We won't have any guests", said Nick.

"You will when the king finds a tutor for you", Mr. Kingston replied. "You can't very well expect to complete your lessons in your bed chamber, now can you?"

Tommy ventured to ask, "Is there a real bed in the bed chamber?"

Mr. Kingston raised his eyebrows. "Of course, you've probably never slept on a real bed, have you now? Yes, you'll have a real bed to share and a fireplace. The summer can still be chilly and you'll need a bit more heat at night, I shouldn't wonder. There'll also

189

be a washbasin so that you can clean up a bit and there'll be clean rushes on the floor."

"Will Mrs. Kingston still be cooking for us?" Nick asked hopefully.

Mr. Kingston chuckled. "Aye, I imagine she will. She rather enjoys cooking for the young ones, like you. When I told her how quickly you devoured that roast venison stew she was delighted! She was planning on making you a fine supper tonight after your long day with the king."

The boys looked at each other and smiled. A room like that, with Mrs. Kingston's cooking, would be heavenly after the first cell they were in. They had walked to a different section of the Tower. The building looked more like a house and wasn't made of the same kind of stone as the tower where they had been imprisoned. Tommy was a little bit disappointed to see that the door to their rooms was to be locked, but he knew that they were still considered prisoners.

The room itself was a bit larger than the one that they had come from but was definitely much cleaner and more home-like. There was already a fire roaring merrily in the fireplace and it cast a warm glow on the clean rushes that were covering the floor. A large bed stood in the corner with warm quilts stretched over it. It looked so inviting after their long day that the boys wanted to jump right in and go to sleep. A wash basin and pitcher with washing cloths was opposite the bed and at the back of the room was door that presumably led to the sitting room. The windows were still barred but they were bigger and the bars were further apart, allowing them a better view out onto the whole Tower complex. There were shutters on the windows that could be opened or closed from the inside to keep out the cold. If they didn't know that they were prisoners, the boys would have felt like they were in a sixteenth century hotel. It was a far cry from the dungeon that Mr. Kingston had told them about yesterday where the rats roamed freely. It gave Tommy a chill to think that they could be down there right now instead of in this cozy room.

"Well", said Mr. Kingston, "here it is. I have to lock you up, you understand, but during the day tomorrow you'll be free to walk abut the menagerie and the Tower gardens. I must say, they are quite beautiful here in the late summer. The leaves are at their best and there are plenty of flowers. I'll be back with your supper in a bit. Make yourselves comfortable until I return."

The boys thanked him and waited until the key turned in the lock. They looked at each other and smiled, still not quite believing their good fortune. They weren't sure what to do at first. It wasn't as if there was a Nintendo Wii or Gameboys in there for them to play with. There weren't even any books to read.

"So", Nick spread his hands open wide, "what so we do?"

Tommy shrugged. "I don't know. Maybe we should wash up. It's been a while and you stink."

"Yeah, well you don't smell so great yourself." Nick shot back at him, grinning, and gave him a little shove. It felt good to tease each other again, now that they were out of immediate danger. It turned out that someone else must have thought that they needed a wash, too, because the basin was full of steaming water and there was a lump of homemade soap in a ceramic dish. It was brown and looked nothing like the bars of soap that they had back home, but at least it was something. They stripped to the waist and spent the next half of an hour washing up.

When they were finished, they dried of with some extra towels and went to stand by the fire to get warm. While they enjoyed the heat from the red coals, they heard the key turn in the door and Mr. Kingston walked in with a bundle under his arm.

"Ah, you decided to take advantage of the warm water. I am very pleased to see it. You must feel better now."

"It did, Mr. Kingston. We really needed to wash up."

"Yes, well, tomorrow morning I'll see about getting you a full tub in here. Then you can each take a real bath and wash your hair if you'd like. There's no need for you to be as dirty as peasants anymore"

"I came to tell you that supper is on its way. Mrs. Kingston is just putting your tray together. I also brought you some clean clothing and will take the old ones back to Mrs. Kingston to wash tomorrow. It's not her usual wash day but she's decided that you must have clean clothes to wear while you're in the Tower, especially if you're going to be having audiences with the king. I'll turn my back if you wish while you change out of those and into these."

He placed the bundle on the bed and turned around so that the boys could wriggle out of the rags they had been wearing into some finer clothes. Nothing like the king would wear, of course, but nice enough so that they didn't look like beggars on the street. It only took a moment to change and then they gathered up their old clothes and gave them to the old guard. He nodded and bowed, then locked the door before going on his way.

"What do you say we take a little nap before the food gets here?" Nick suggested. Tommy thought that was a good idea. Ever since washing up and putting on clean dry clothes, his eyelids felt heavier than they ever had in his life. He nodded and they headed over to the bed.

"Do you want the quilt?" Nick asked him.

"No, we're only going to lie down for a minute. Kingston will be back soon."

But it seemed that as soon as Tommy had closed his eyes, Mr. Kingston was gently shaking them and the smell of something good was filling the room. He rubbed his eyes and sat up, yawning sleepily, and gave Nick a shove to wake him up.

"Come now, lads, your supper is here. Look what I've brought you: some boar stew with parsnips and bread that Mrs. Kingston made this afternoon."

The food did look good. Tommy had no idea what a parsnip was but he didn't care. His stomach was calling out for food. They eagerly took the trenchers that Mr. Kingston held out and tried to not eat as quickly as they had earlier that afternoon in an attempt at good manners. Mr. Kingston laughed.

"Now then, will I have to tell Mrs. Kingston that the food is bad because you didn't swallow it without chewing again?" They could tell that he was teasing but Nick felt obligated to say, "Oh, no, we love it! We're just trying to be polite. Please tell Mrs. Kingston that it's delicious!"

It was good and hot and it filled the empty corners of his stomach. As he finished, he felt the sleepiness come over him again and he wanted to do nothing but curl up underneath the quilt and go back to sleep. He handed Mr. Kingston the empty trencher, said his thanks, and struggled to stay awake while Nick finished up.

Mr. Kingston bid them goodnight and locked the door behind them. The room was almost completely dark now, with long shadows stretching across the floor. Tommy crawled across the bed and slid himself under the covers. Nick did the same. They didn't even say a word to each other and in less than a minute, they were

both fast asleep under the heavy quilts.

Chapter Nine

Tommy squinted in the bright light that came through his window, groaned and reached down to pull his sheet back up over his eyes. He couldn't remember if it was Saturday or not. Keeping his eyes closed against the too-bright sunshine, he sniffed the air to see if his mom had started making pancakes yet. He didn't smell anything cooking so he turned over in his bed and tried to go back to sleep, but the strange dream that he had been having made his mind race.

Nick. England. Henry VIII. Amulet. Kingston. Dad.

Tommy stretched his arms out luxuriously over his mattress and paused. His mattress felt different, scratchy even. He stretched out a little further and bumped something alive. It moved. With his heart jumping up into his throat, his eyes flew open to see what he had touched, only to see Nick sleeping peacefully at the other end of the bed. His heart thumping wildly, he gazed slowly around the room and realized that his dream hadn't been a dream at all but was in fact very real, down to the noises of the animals in the streets around the Tower where they were housed.

He sat up and took it all in: the washbasin where they had washed up the night before, the rope bed, the chamber pot on the

197

floor, bars on the windows. It was real, all of it. He and Nick were really stuck in England, in 1540, with Henry VIII and all of the danger that went with it.

Until now, Tommy didn't think that he had fully appreciated how much trouble he could be in if they were caught in their lies. He thought back to their dinner with Mr. Barnhart. It seemed so long ago.

Not for the first time he thought about what his mother was doing right at that moment. Was she afraid for him? Had she called the police or had she figured out what they had done? What about Nick's parents? What would happen when they went home, *if* they went home?

A wave of guilt washed over him as he contemplated those questions. What had he been thinking? He was all that she had, the only thing she had to remember his father, save the letters and one photograph, and he had run off without thinking things all the way through. He would have to spend the rest of his life making it up to her. Maybe if he managed to bring his father back, she would forgive everything.

Tommy pondered this for a while and then shook himself out of it. It was all well and good to feel guilty about everything that he'd done but quite another to keep his wits about him so that he could do what he came to do; find his father and get back home to his mother. Oh, and deliver Nick home in one piece as well. That was a tall order, but Tommy didn't see any other way around it

He reached over to wake Nick. Obviously, Nick wasn't having the same dream as he had been. He smiled in his sleep, mumbling to unintelligible things himself that Tommy would have dearly loved to have understood in order to tease him later. At the same time, he hoped that Nick wouldn't talk *too* much in his sleep. If Henry VIII as paranoid as Mr. Barnhart had said he was, he could very well have spies posted to listen to them sleep, just to see if they said anything incriminating while they were dreaming. Just the thought of the king finding out how they really came to London made Tommy feel queasy.

Tommy shoved Nick's shoulder a few times before he started to come around, rubbing his eyes sleepily and looking around questioningly at their surroundings. It was a shock to go from expecting to see your own room, with electric lights, posters, and schoolbooks to an almost bare room with rushes on the floor and a washbasin in the corner. Looking more closely at the washbasin, Tommy could see steam rising from it. Mr. Kingston had already been there to bring them wash water. He managed to get in and out without waking them up. It was only a matter of time before he came back with breakfast and Tommy didn't want to be caught in the middle of washing up. He noticed that there were also two fresh sets of clothes at the end of the bed.

"C'mon, Nick, wake up. Kingston will be here any minute."

"What? Oh, yeah. Kingston. We'd better get dressed then, eh?"

"He was already here to bring the wash water and some clothes. Let's get done before he gets back."

It was still humiliating to use the chamber pots with another person standing there, but they were getting more used to it. After all, when you have to go, you have to go. It was normal here. They washed themselves down the best they could with the slimy soap and rough washcloths. When he was done, Nick started using the washcloth to brush his teeth, explaining to Tommy. "I can't stand the feeling that they have fuzz all over them and I don't want my breath to stink."

Tommy laughed. "Could you see our mothers if we told them that we were going to meet a king and we didn't even have our toothbrushes? They would go ballistic!"

Nick shushed him as he heard footsteps coming down the hallway, accompanied by the jingle of keys hanging on Kingston's belt. He leaned closer to Tommy and whispered, "We're not supposed to have mothers, remember?"

Tommy nodded, impressed. Nick was more in the spirit of things this morning. Maybe it would turn out all right after all. He had just finished fastening the belt around his tunic when Mr. Kingston's kindly face peered into the room.

"Good Morrow, boys!" his big voice boomed in the morning quiet. "Up and about, I see? I wasn't sure if you would be or not. When Mrs. Kingston brought your water and clothes, she said that you were both still sleeping soundly."

Mrs. Kingston had brought their water and clothes?

Mr. Kingston laughed at their expressions. "Now, then, don't look so shocked. She wanted to get a look at the pair of you and see where all of that food was going. She rarely ever comes into this part of the Tower but made an exception this time. I daresay that she wanted to take you both home and fatten you up properly! It took quite a bit of convincing to put the thought out of her head."

"If you're up and dressed then, I'll go and bring your breakfast to you. I need to check on a couple of our other guests so it may be a few minutes. Try not to fade away with hunger before I return." He walked away chuckling at his own joke, leaving Tommy and Nick to wonder just who exactly the other guests were.

As his footsteps echoed down the hallway, Tommy leaned over into Nick's ear and whispered, "Remind me to sleep with my pants from now on."

Nick grinned and nodded.

A short time later, they heard Kingston returning. He was trailed by a small, round, grandmotherly-looking woman who was carrying a tray laden with steaming dishes. She bustled in busily behind Mr. Kingston and set down the tray upon the small table in the center of the room. Stepping back, she turned to face the boys, put her hands on her ample hips, and gave a loud sigh.

"Well then," she began in a gentle voice with a broad accent, "There you are, finally." She made her way over to the boys, who were sitting on the edge of Tommy's bed and looked them up and down.

"I dare say that you two have been through a lot the last few days, haven't you? Well, after more of my cooking and you'll be set to rights soon enough. My cooking and some fresh air will help with that. Mr. Kingston tells me that he's taking you to see the wild beasts today, right?" She looked expectantly at them, a twinkle in her clear blue eyes. Tommy could barely see a small bit of her hair peeking out of her head covering and what he could see was a pure snowy white. She reminded him of Mrs. Claus from the Christmas specials that he still watched every year. He half expected her to pull out a tray of milk and cookies from behind her back, but he didn't know if cookies had been invented yet.

"Y-yes," he managed to stammer out, "Mr. Kingston is taking us to see the animals."

Mrs. Kingston gave a small shudder, drawing her arms around her plump body. "Not for me, my dears, not for me! I can hear that bloody lion roaring in his cage at all hours of the night sometimes. Sends a chill through my very bones it does. But I suppose that two strapping lads such as yourselves won't mind a bit of excitement after being locked up in here!"

Tommy found himself smiling at her. "Yes, Mrs. Kingston, and thank you for all of the wonderful meals that you've sent us."

Nick chimed in, "Yes, they were wonderful! I really liked that stew that you sent last night."

Mrs. Kingston beamed all the way up from her toes. "It is *so* good to be cooking for young ones again! My children are all grown and gone. I'm sure that Mr. Kingston has told you that I do a lot of the cooking for the higher-born prisoners, but they are nearly always adults and they have all of their people with them. I've never been out to actually speak to any of them, so this is quite a treat for me."

"What do you mean all of their people?" Nick wanted to know.

Mr. Kingston explained, "When a noble person is imprisoned in the Tower, they are given several attendants to wait upon them during their stay."

"What do they do?"

"They assist the prisoner in washing, dressing, and keeping busy. Many of the ladies work their embroidery or sewing for the poor and the gentlemen write many letters. Of course, their letters must be read and approved before they are sent out to prevent any escape attempts or plots against the king."

"Who reads the letters?"

"First, myself, then if I believe that it's necessary, the king's advisors. Sometimes, they even make it to the King himself. I also keep very close watch on any visitors that come in here. Not everyone can have visitors and I have to make sure that nothing gets smuggled out. You'd be surprised how clever some of them are!"

Tommy and Nick exchanged a glance. What would Mr. Kingston do if he knew that they carried a magic amulet? No matter how nice he was to them now, he'd probably turn them in to the King in an instant. That would be bad; very, very bad. Any kindness that they had been shown so far would disappear in an instant.

Nick blurted out, "Did you ever see Anne Boleyn here?"

Mr. and Mrs. Kingston's eyes widened at that and Mrs. Kingston looked around in alarm, crossing herself. She stepped toward them quickly and suddenly, the grandmotherly softness had disappeared and she bent down toward them, pulling their heads close together. Tommy could see that several of her teeth were missing as she began whispering to them.

"Never, never mention that name here my dears; never ever! The King despises any talk of her at all. We are never to mention her, not even in idle talk. It could mean a load of trouble for you if it was known that you had asked about her!"

Mrs. Kingston looked so very grim that Tommy knew she was trying to help them avoid a terrible mistake. Mr. Kingston stepped in closely to add his own warning.

"Listen, I attended Mistress Boleyn while she was here. It was only a short time, but she came to a very tragic end. Whatever you feel about her or her sentence, you mustn't speak any of it! There are spies all over this palace and they are very willing to report back to the king. You must be on your guard *at all times*, even when you think you're alone. Remember, the walls have ears, and mouths, too. Great men have fallen for simply their opinions. These are very dangerous times that we live in, lads. If it gets back to the king that you were inquiring about Mistress Boleyn, he would no longer look kindly upon you. Promise me that you'll be careful at all times!"

Tommy and Nick nodded, scared suddenly by the Kingstons' seriousness.

"Now then, lads, let's put this talk away from us and get ready for our adventure today!" He stepped back and clapped his hands, saying a little too loudly, "Eat your breakfast before it gets cold and thank you for permitting me to introduce Mrs. Kingston to you. I shall return in half an hour to show you the menagerie. Will that be sufficient?"

They nodded and Mrs. Kingston stepped forward, returned to her former demeanor, all dreadful seriousness gone. "I shall come to visit you again later in the day when my duties are done. Mayhap I'll bring my knitting and we'll have a proper conversation." She scuttled out the door on her tiny feet, casting a final smile over her shoulder at them.

"Mayhap" must mean "maybe" Tommy thought. He'd have to catch on to the way of speaking, maybe, *mayhap*, he should even concentrate on his accent. It couldn't hurt to sound more English. It would make them sound less strange.

True to his word, Mr. Kingston was back very soon, apparently excited to show them the menagerie, as well as the rest of the Tower. It was easy to tell that although it had a terrible history, he was very proud of the Tower itself and proceeded to fill them in on all of the history as they made their way to the small section that housed all of the animals.

While the history was interesting at first, beginning with William the Conqueror building the Tower in 1066, as Mr. Kingston droned on about all of the Henrys, Richards, and Edwards that had lived and died there, Nick felt his attention slipping away. He glanced over at Tommy and saw that he was intently focused on Mr. Kingston as he talked. Tommy obviously liked the impromptu history lesson and even Nick had to admit that being in a building as old as the Tower was a pretty cool thing. He just didn't care about the details as much as Tommy seemed to.

At last, they finally reached the section of the Tower that housed the royal menagerie. They could smell it before they actually got there. It was a smell that was partly familiar, like the inside of one of the animal buildings at the zoo when it was a hot, steamy day. They closer they got, the stronger the smell became. Tommy wanted

208

desperately to cover his nose and mouth as Mr. Kingston selected a key from the massive ring around his waist and began to slowly open the heavy wooden door.

Just before he pulled on the handle, he turned to look at the boys and gave them a stern warning. "These animals are wild, so don't go and try putting your hand in any of the cages. You may not come out again as a whole person!" He laughed at his little joke and Tommy rolled his eyes at Nick. As if either one of them needed to be told to not stick their hand in a lion's cage! He was excited, though, to see what was inside, regardless of the smell.

They weren't disappointed. The zoos back home were fun, but never had they seen a lion from that close up before. The big male was sleeping right up against the iron bars, close enough for them to reach out and stroke a part of his mane that was sticking through. Tommy almost did, and then remembered Mr. Kingston's dire warning before they went in and retracted his hand, just in case.

In addition to the lion, there were also several mischievous monkeys leaping around their own cage. As soon as the monkeys spotted Mr. Kingston and the boys, they began screeching at the top of their lungs, jumping all around their cage, and landing on top of each other. They were so funny to watch that Tommy and Nick found themselves laughing out loud at their antics.

Mr. Kingston smiled down at them. "Now there's a sound I haven't heard from the pair of you, yet. We must try to get you to laugh more often. Let's move away from these creatures, though. There are times when they throw their own, um, waste, through the bars. Rather unpleasant."

They agreed that getting hit with monkey poo would be *quite* disagreeable and went to look at the other animals in the menagerie. They stayed for quite a while, looking at the exotic birds, reptiles, and other small mammal-type things that neither one of them could identify. After a while, Mr. Kingston said that it was time to go back.

"I need to get on with the rest of my duties. I'm going to show you the way to one of the outside gardens where you can get some fresh air for a while. As entertaining as this place is, it wants for some clean-smelling air, wouldn't you agree?"

They nodded vigorously and let Mr. Kingston lead them out back through the maze of hallways that made up the Tower. They followed him to the opposite end of the Tower and let them out into a garden the likes that Tommy had only seen in old books. It was small, but there were blooming summer flowers everywhere; he recognized roses, and the air smelled sweet, a nice contrast to the menagerie. There was a stone lined path that wove its way through the tiny garden. The only thing to show that it was still a part of a prison was that it was surrounded by high walls all around with no way to climb up. Mr. Kingston must have noticed their stares. He let them know that there were guards watching from the parapets, or higher towers, around them so that if anyone ever tried to scale the garden walls and get out, they would be stopped by an arrow. Although Mr. Kingston said it in a friendly way, Tommy felt the undercurrent of warning in his voice.

Tommy shivered at that thought as Mr. Kingston told them that he would return for them in an hour or so and to enjoy the garden. With a click, he locked the garden door behind them and they were on their own again.

Silently, he and Nick walked to one of the wooden benches that lined that stone path and they both sank down heavily. For several minutes, they said nothing at all. The day was a beautiful one. Overhead, the sky was the bright flawless blue without a single cloud. The early afternoon sun shone down almost directly overhead and since it was August, it was beginning to warm up. Not as warm as it had been at home in Michigan, where even in May the temperature and awful humidity seemed to begin as soon as the snow melted, but pleasantly warm.

At least the weather was better here. Tommy wondered what it would be like in the fall. Abruptly he shook his head. They wouldn't be here in the fall! Hopefully, they wouldn't be here very much longer at all. The thrill of traveling through time was starting to wear off.

Nick was the first one to break the silence.

"So, what do we do now? What's the grand plan, Tommy?" There was an edge of irritation in his voice and he kicked a small rock across the gravel walkway as he waited for Tommy's answer.

Tommy felt awful. He was starting to seriously doubt that the king would do anything to help them and he knew that Nick desperately wanted to go home. He really did, too. He especially wanted an adult's help about now, someone who knew what to do. He raised his head and prepared to tell Nick that it was over, that they could pull out the amulet and go home, that it didn't matter any more.

He looked over at Nick's angry face, sighed, and said, "Well, how about going…" when he suddenly noticed some movement in the bushes a little way down the path from them. At first he thought it was an animal, a bird maybe, rustling around, but as the movement continued, he saw a hand come out from behind the bush, slowly, and beckon to them!

Not wanting to alarm Nick or to call unwanted attention to them, he nudged Nick's arm and nodded toward the beckoning hand. At first, Nick shrugged his shoulders angrily, as if to say *What?* But when Tommy more aggressively nodded his head toward the bushes, Nick finally saw what Tommy was trying to show him. Instead of looking afraid, Nick looked excited.

"C'mon," he whispered to Tommy and began to get up, going toward the beckoning hand.

"Wait!" Tommy hissed and tried to grab Nick's shirt to pull him back down. "It could be a trap! Remember what Mr. Kingston said about the walls having eyes and ears?"

Nick gave him a cold look. "It couldn't be any worse than what we're doing now." He jerked himself free and walked casually along the path toward the clump of bushes. The hand had disappeared now; whoever the hand belonged to had obviously seen Nick walking over. Tommy held his breath as Nick got closer and closer, stopping along the way to pretend interest in the other plants that lined the walk. When he got to the bush he stopped, looking closely through the branches for the owner of the hand. Tommy waited anxiously as Nick peered closer and closer inside.

All of a sudden, Nick disappeared inside the bush! There was a small rustle of leaves and he was gone. It was almost as if the bush had swallowed him whole! Tommy's heart raced like it did the first time he saw those soldiers coming for them. What was he supposed to do now? Should he shout for help? Should he go over to see where Nick was? He could be hurt, or, Tommy gulped, dead.

He knew what he had to do first. Shaking, but getting to his feet slowly, as to not alarm the guards in the small towers, he ambled nervously down the same gravel walkway as Nick had just a few moments earlier. Like Nick, he looked at the delicate flowers that grew along the path. As he got nearer and nearer to the bush, his heart was pounding so hard that he could hear the blood pumping through his ears. Arriving at the bush, he slowly leaned in to look for his friend, scanning the dense branches for any sign of him or the thing that took him.

"Nick!" he whispered. "Nick!" His heart was in his throat as he struggled to hear something, *anything*, which would let him know Nick was okay. They had been so close to going home!

A hand clamped over his mouth and he was jerked off of his feet in an instant by an arm around his waist. There was no time to scream or yell; he was simply pulled into the bush seamlessly, with hardly a rustle of leaves. Squeezing his eyes shut, he landed hard on the ground and wondered if he was about to die. Was this what had happened to Nick? Was it going to hurt? With his eyes still tightly closed, he realized that no hands were grabbing him any more, except for the one covering his mouth. He took a deep breath and slowly opened his eyes to look his captor in the face, perhaps to meet his doom. What he saw shocked him more than anything else that had happened to him so far since landing in that field of grass many days ago. The person that had been holding a hand over his mouth and was now looking at him with a mixture of relief and anger was none other than Mr. Barnhart!

Chapter Ten

Tommy's eyes widened in shock. *Mr. Barnhart?* How could

he have gotten here? What was he doing here? Tommy looked

around frantically and saw Nick sitting on the ground nearby, under the cover of the bush. He was grinning from ear to ear. *He's probably glad that a responsible adult is here* Tommy thought. Before he could say anything, however, Mr. Barnhart grabbed him by the shoulders and looked him square in the face. Tommy had never seen him look so angry.

"What the hell were you thinking to come here like this? I'm amazed that you're still alive. Do you have any idea what your poor mother is going through?" He shook him a little with every question he asked. Almost as suddenly, anger flooded him and he whispered ferociously back at Mr. Barnhart, still mindful of the guards in the towers.

"I'm here to find my father. I found out that he's from this time and that he came back here! I found the letters! I found the amulet and nobody would tell me anything about him, just to wait until I was old enough. Well, I was tired of it! If he could do it, so could I! I'm not a little kid anymore and no one would tell me the truth! And what are *you* doing here anyway?" His face felt hot and tears were springing up in his eyes. He wasn't sure if they were tears of anger or tears of relief at seeing Mr. Barnhart. He was so confused.

Mr. Barnhart sighed and sat back on his heels. "This was the reason for all of the interest in Henry VIII, then?"

Tommy nodded.

"Have you seen him?"

He nodded again. "Twice. He wants to get us tutors and look for my dad."

Mr. Barnhart groaned and held a hand to his forehead, as though he was getting a headache. "Tommy, you have no idea what kind of man he is. If he even *suspects* you to be something else, he won't hesitate to make you disappear! You're a kid with no connections and no one is looking for you here."

The feeling of fear welled up in Tommy's stomach and he understood that this was going to be a lot harder, still, than he had thought. With Mr. Barnhart here, actually here, it made the situation seem much more impossible. The tears that he was trying to hold back sprang into his eyes and he could barely control them as they threatened to roll down his cheeks.

"I just want to go home now!"

Mr. Barnhart gave another sigh and put his arms around Tommy. "Shhhh…okay, okay, it's going to be okay. We'll figure this out, don't worry. Do you still have the amulet?"

"Here!" Nick whispered and pulled it out from around his neck by the chain.

"Good! Tuck it back in and keep it safe. Show it to no one. I'm going to have to leave you for now so the guards don't get suspicious, but I'll be back. If you see me around the Tower at all, you must pretend to not know me. My name here is Sir Edward Barnhart and the king knows my family. Whatever happens, just play along. Remember, I need to be a stranger to you here for a while, until I figure out a way to get you out. Don't even tell Kingston about me. He's a kind man, I know, but not even his kindness will let him forget about his duty to the king to keep you under guard at all times. Go now and don't talk about this at all! I'll think of something."

As quickly as he had materialized, he disappeared through the bushes, leaving Tommy and Nick sitting there in astonished silence over what had just happened. Mr. Barnhart was with them in 1540! The man was actually, physically here and he had obviously been here many times before. Sir Edward? They didn't know what to make of this or even how to start. Tommy was still absorbing it all when Nick gave his shoulder a little shake.

"We'd better get out of these bushes before we get into trouble," he whispered. Tommy nodded and they crawled out as quietly as they could, one at a time. They stood up, brushed off the dirt and leaves from their clothing, and began walking around the little gravel path that wound its way through the prison garden. With the knowledge that Mr. Barnhart was there and going to help them, the sky looked bluer, the flowers brighter and the feeling of not knowing what to do next wasn't as strong as it had been. Just knowing that someone was on their side made the boys feel a million times better.

"What do you think is going to happen to us today?" Nick asked Tommy. They were out of the bushes now and he used his normal voice. Whispering might look bad right now and bring more unwanted attention to them.

Tommy shrugged. "I don't know. Maybe Henry will want us back again."

Nick's eyes widened. "I hope not! I never know what to say when we're there. He scares me!"

Tommy wholeheartedly agreed with that, but his mind was still on Mr. Barnhart. "How did Mr. Barnhart get here? I mean, there must be another amulet or something and it sounds like he's been here a lot. He said that the king knew his family. Who is his family exactly?"

"Shhh…" Nick looked around nervously. "He said that we're not supposed to talk about this, remember? Anyone could be listening in! We could get our heads chopped off!"

"Okay, okay, I'm just curious, that's all. I want to now how this all works."

"Me too, but let's just wait, okay?"

"Okay." Tommy agreed.

They began to shuffle around the path a bit more when Nick came up with the idea to race. "We've been cooped up for a few days. Let's run!"

Caching the excitement, Tommy agreed. There really wasn't much else they could do out here. They didn't have a baseball or mitts to play catch with or anything else. Racing would have to do.

They ran several times back and forth around the path, getting all sweaty in the process but feeling better than they had the whole time. Running was normal at least and it felt good to move. After racing back and forth several times they heard a chuckle from the gate. They turned to find Mr. Kingston there, grinning at them.

"Good lads! It's good for the body to run! I'll have to take you out here more often, mayhap even a fencing lesson. It would do those twiggy arms a bit of good, I dare say."

Twiggy! The boys laughed. Yes, there was no denying it. Their arms were pretty scrawny. They walked over to the gate, arguing about who had the scrawnier arms, knowing that their time outside was over.

"Come now, and catch your breath. Mrs. Kingston has prepared a hearty meal for your dinnertime and I believe that the king wants to see you again this afternoon.

Nick's heart sank as Tommy glanced his way. The king? Again? Hadn't he had enough of them already? How was he supposed to enjoy his meal now, knowing that the king was waiting to pounce on them yet again? But maybe Mr. Barnhart had already come through. Mr. Kingston noticed how quiet they had gotten and turned to them after he had locked the gate behind them.

"Now then, lads, don't let the king frighten you. I'll wager that he's taken quite a fancy to you. There are hundreds of orphans wandering around London and he's chosen to show kindness to you. That's something to be grateful for."

The boys knew it. This king could have their heads on a pole over London Bridge if he wanted to; knowing that made them even more nervous that they might somehow screw up their good luck.

After a hearty meal back in their cell, they stretched out on the bed while waiting to see what was going to happen next. It was so tempting to talk about Mr. Barnhart; they knew that they couldn't, not just yet, anyway. Tommy was anxious to see what plan he would come up with to help them.

Thankfully, they didn't have long to wait. They heard the familiar shuffle of Mr. Kingston coming down the corridor, a little faster than normal, but still they knew it was him from the jangle of his keys. When he arrived and let himself in to the cell, his face was beaming with a large smile.

"Lads!" he cried, "I have heard the most wonderful news! The king has been pleased with the reports of your conduct and is convinced that you are no threat to him. It appears that he happened to see the pair of you running races in the Tower garden during a visit to the Tower today and thought, rightly so in my opinion, that you are merely children, not Catholic spies from the Pope. He is releasing you from the Tower to go and live with a family who will be in charge of caring for you and for your education. He will receive weekly reports on your progress and will take a special interest in your future. I am to take you now to his Privy Chamber here at the Tower to meet Sir Edward and go with him immediately."

The King had seen them in the garden! That had been a very close call. He couldn't have seen them disappear into the bush or reappear from it or something bad would have happened.

"The King was here, Sir?" Tommy asked, trying not to sound too anxious.

"Yes, lad. He sometimes comes to do business, or when a matter needs his immediate attention. He just happened to see you boys running your races from the window. It made him glad to watch. He even thought of sending his son here to play with you, but that was before he found a place for you."

"Sir Edward, right? Who is that?" Nick asked innocently.

"Why, Sir Edward Barnhart. The Barnhart family has been well-favored by the king in the past. They have lands that go back several hundred years. I believe that a Lord Barnhart even went with King Richard on his Crusade to the Holy Land long ago. The king has made a very wise choice. His father, Thomas Barnhart, did a wonderful job raising his son into manhood and I expect the king knows that Sir Edward will do the same for you."

Tommy and Nick looked at each other in astonishment. Mr. Barnhart *had* stepped in! It had only been a short while since they had seen him in the garden and now they were going to leave the Tower with him. Tommy felt lighter than air as he and Nick jumped up off of the bed and followed Mr. Kingston out of the cell and through the Tower again. *Hopefully this will be the last time that we ever see this place,* Tommy thought to himself. He knew that Nick was thinking the same thing. Nick was happy, too, but he would prefer to leave the Tower without seeing the king again. Henry VIII gave Nick the willies.

They were ushered into the king's chamber in the Tower by the same guards that had been there the time before, except now the guards didn't attempt to rough them up at all. They stiffly and courteously led them into the chamber and presented them to the king and the queen.

They know that the king likes us now and don't want to get into trouble for harassing us, Tommy thought. He wished that he could trip the guards or something else to get even with them, but there was no time for that. A moment later, his mind was completely off the guards as he also saw who else was in the room: Mr. Barnhart! He was dressed in complete Renaissance finery and looked every bit like a gentleman should. Tommy and Nick, who knew next to nothing about how the clothing was supposed to look, knew immediately that in the whole scheme of things in this crazy time period, Mr. Barnhart seemed to be a fairly important person. He was so impressed with looking at him that he forgot to bow to the king until Mr. Kingston nudged him forward.

"Bow to His Majesty," he whispered into Tommy's ear, breaking the spell. Tommy knelt down on the floor, touching his forehead to the carpet until he heard the king say, "Rise."

He and Nick, who hadn't forgotten his manners, stood up and faced the king, anxious to hear what he had to say.

"Well then lads," his squeaky voice boomed from the throne, "Has Mr. Kingston informed you as to why I have called you before me today?"

They nodded respectfully, glancing over at Mr. Barnhart. *Pretend that you don't know him yet,* he tried to telegraph to Nick's mind.

"This is Sir Edward Barnhart, loyal subject to England and to the king. His family has been among my most trusted acquaintances since my father's time and they have done me many a good turn. Sir Edward had graciously offered to take the both of you in after hearing of your situation and will be informing me weekly as to your progress. Not only will he provide a tutor for you, but he himself will instruct you in the art of fencing and other sports. In the meantime, he has also generously offered to assist my scouts in finding any word they can about your father, Geoffrey Andrews. If your father cannot be found, he will find an occupation for you in time, as he has no sons of his own. What say you to this?"

Tommy knew that he had to be as gracious as possible. Kneeling to the floor and bowing he said, "Your Majesty, you are very kind. We don't deserve all of this."

That sounded so hokey to him that he felt sure the king would see right through it but to his surprise, the king seemed to be very pleased with his response.

"Nay, my lad, you may prove yourself to me by being a good student and ward to Sir Edward. You are to leave with him this day. Sir Edward, shall you stay to sup with us this evening?"

Mr. Barnhart shook his head. "Nay, Sire, I wish to arrive home at my estate before nightfall and it is a few hours ride. If it pleases Your Majesty, we shall make our departure now."

King Henry waved his hand in agreement. "So it shall be, but the next time you must stay longer with us. Methinks it has been too long since we've had the pleasure of your company at court. Mayhap we'll find you a wife next time! It's not good for a man to be alone when he can have a lovely rose at his side." He turned and beamed at the queen, who lowered her eyes and gave a small smile. "Although, not as lovely as my dear Katherine!" Apparently, he was still very happy with her.

"Yes, Sire. Until next time then." Mr. Barnhart, *Sir Edward*, rather, bowed stiffly from his waist and motioned to the boys to come with him. Mr. Kingston followed closely behind, not wishing them to leave without saying a proper goodbye. When they were out of the Tower and preparing to mount up on the horses that Sir Edward had secured for them, Tommy heard a small voice calling to them from a window in the Tower. Looking up, he saw Mrs. Kingston waving a cloth from one of the windows and calling to them, "Goodbye! Goodbye! Be good lads now!"

Tommy nudged Nick to turn and look at her and they both waved, feeling a little sad about leaving her and her fine cooking. They called out, "Thank you!" to the kind lady and turned to where Mr. Kingston was holding his hand out to help them on to their horses.

"Ah, Mrs. Kingston will miss you boys greatly, I'm sure. It's been a long time since she's been able to look after any young ones, especially since ours are all grown and gone."

"Tell, her goodbye for us, Sir, and thank her for all of the wonderful food that she made us."

Tommy was touched as Mr. Kingston looked a little teary-eyed himself. "That I will, lad; that I will. When you're grown and a proper gentleman, you come back to visit then, both of you. I'll be curious to see how it is that you turn out under Sir Edward's care." He boosted Tommy onto the back of a swayback old nag that looked to be at least one hundred years old. At least it wouldn't be bucking him off any time soon. He glanced over at Nick to see how he was doing. Nick's horse looked to be even older than Tommy's and Tommy knew that Mr. Barnhart, er, Sir Edward, knew that they didn't really know how to ride horses.

"Never fear, Mr. Kingston. I plan on turning these two into men that the king will be proud of."

"Maybe they'll be put onto better horses later?" Mr. Kingston inquired with an eyebrow raised. The old nags did look rather silly in the setting of such a grand palace. They were better suited for a petting farm than to be used in the service of a royal family.

"Well, Mr. Kingston, I didn't know how much riding experience they had and thought it best not to introduce them to any of my wilder steeds. These will do nicely for the ride home so that I may get to know them better at a slower pace."

230

Mr. Kingston nodded his head in agreement. "Quite right, Sir Edward, quite right. Forgive me my meddling."

Sir Edward gave Mr. Kingston a kind smile. "Not at all, Sir. I know that you have looked after them well."

Mr. Kingston looked gratified as he dipped his head in a bow and waved a hand goodbye as they turned and began to ride away. Tommy and Nick waved and called out their thanks to him as he grew smaller and smaller in the gateway of the Tower.

They made their way through the crowded streets of London. After being locked in the relatively quiet Tower for almost a week, the noises and the smells of the city assaulted their senses. The throngs of people, however, were amazing to see. Everyone had their business to attend to, it seemed, and there was something to buy on every corner. Sir Edward looked behind him at the boys and saw that they were both fascinated and repulsed by what they saw. As angry as Sir Edward was with them, it still made him chuckle a little.

"London will always stay with you, boys," he called over his shoulder. It wasn't a moment too soon that they got through the most populous part of the city and the buildings began thinning out. The amount of people on the streets grew smaller and smaller and they were soon out of the City all together, riding out into the open fields of grass.

They followed the dirt road that had been worn into the middle of the fields for centuries. Nick was thinking to himself that the Romans may have traveled in and out of London using this very same road! All the time they were riding, Sir Edward didn't say a word and neither did the boys. They knew they were in trouble. When they were about half an hour out of the city, he finally stopped his horse and turned it around to face the two of them.

"Don't think for one minute that I'm happy to have to go and find the pair of you. Tommy, your mother knew almost right away what you had done. She called me immediately and told me that you had been getting more and more curious about your father lately. When she realized that the two of you were gone, she found the box and saw that you had taken the amulet. Nick, your parents have no clue where you are! Do you realize what lies we had to tell to your parents to explain where you disappeared to? When we get to my house, we're going to sit down and talk everything out. Then you two are going back to where you belong, as soon as possible.

Hopefully, it's not too late, but you will know everything before the night is over."

"Can we go back to the same day that we left?" Nick wanted to know, feeling very guilty now. He couldn't imagine his father being too terribly upset at his having gone, but he knew that his mother really did love him.

Sir Edward fixed his eyes on Nick as he answered, "No, it doesn't work that way. Yes, we can travel through time, we can go to any time that we want, but when we are returning, it's just as if we've gone on a long trip. For example, if you left on April 23rd, which you did, and you were gone for two days, you would come back on April 25th. You can go to any time outside of your own, but when you want to go home, that's how it works. Thank God I have another amulet so that I could come after you!"

"So that's how you got here!" Tommy exclaimed. Sir Edward glared at him.

"We'll talk about this later. Try to get those nags to keep up with me. I wasn't kidding when I said that I wanted to make it home before dark. There have been too many robberies on these roads lately and I don't want to have to dig you two out of another mess!"

He whirled his horse around and the sleek chestnut stallion reared up on his hind legs before cantering off down the road, making Tommy's and Nick's horses seem even more pathetic.

They edged their horses forward as fast as they would go and tried their best to keep up with Mr., er, *Sir Edward* as they made their way through the seemingly endless sea of grass. From time to time, they passed small houses and two very grand ones, but they didn't stop at any of them.

The sun sank lower and lower in the sky and finally the boys saw a very large stone and timber house off of the grassy path. They followed Sir Edward's horse off to the left onto a smaller path and as they got closer, the landscape became a bit tamer. Tommy could see that there were fields, full of wheat growing. There were smaller gardens up closer to the house, many of them with summer flowers planted in them, some that Tommy knew from what his mother liked to grow: marigolds, chrysanthemums, and poppies. The closer they got to the house, the more impressive it was. They could also see now that there were several smaller outbuildings, one that they recognized as being a barn that was about fifty yards from the house. They followed Sir Edward around the now gravel path that led

234

directly to the barn. By the time their old nags had made it there, a groom had already taken Sir Edwards horse to the stables to be watered and brushed. Another groom was waiting with him, presumably for the other two horses. They were surprised, though, when they stopped their horses at the barn to hear what Sir Edward had to say next.

"George," he said, speaking to the groom, "You can go on. These two need to learn how to put a horse away."

George gave a smile and walked back in to the barn, shaking his head. Sir Edward looked up at Tommy and Nick, still seated in their saddles.

"Alright, you two, come on down. Swing one leg over while standing in the stirrup and then hop down to the ground. If you're going to be here, you need to know how to do what everyone else does. You're not princes and I'm not going to treat you like royalty. You'll have to work to earn your way."

The boys were too tired to answer him. Neither one had spent any length of time on a horse, except for pony rides at the county fair, and hadn't realized how tiring it could be to spend hours on horseback. They swung off without too much trouble but landed on the ground with legs that were suddenly wobbly.

Sir Edward showed them how to take the horses by their halters and lead them into the barn. There, the horses needed to be fed and watered and while they were eating, the boys learned how to brush them down with curry combs. As they brushed, the horses' muscles twitched under their dusty coats and they stamped the flies away prompting Tommy and Nick to watch their own feet so as not to end up with broken toes.

"No, no, no," Sir Edward told them, "You're being too gentle. Watch how John brushes Charlemagne. Put some muscle behind your brushing; it feels good to them after having you their backs for hours."

They redoubled their efforts and at last Sir Edward was satisfied. After the horses were shut into their stalls for the night, he told the boys to follow him. Silently, because they knew that they were still in trouble, they followed him up the almost dark path and to the big stone and timber house that sat on a small hill.

As they walked along the gravel path, Nick nudged Tommy and pointed upwards. There, Tommy saw more stars than he had ever seen in his entire life! The sky was full of them; twinkling, sparkling, and winking at him from the velvet blackness of the night sky. Just on the horizon, a few pale bands of pink and orange from the setting sun still hung in the west, but were quickly receding as the night sky took over. He thought he'd never seen anything so beautiful, or so enormous, in his entire life. He felt very small.

They were almost stumbling with tiredness by the time they reached the door. Sir Edward pulled it open with the iron handle and they followed him inside. Immediately, the rich aroma of some kind of meat cooking met Tommy's nose and he immediately felt hungry. They had had nothing to eat since Mrs. Kingston's stew earlier that afternoon and now it was nighttime.

"Wash up over there," Sir Edward pointed at a wooden basin in the corner. Apparently, someone had seen them coming because it was full with steaming hot water. A lump of the familiar brown soap sat in a dish next to the basin and a clean towel hung from the side. As they began scrubbing their hands with the slimy soap, they heard someone enter the room. They turned to see a woman, who looked a bit like Mrs. Kingston, bustling in the same busy way, looking very pleased to see them.

"Oh, Sir Edward, here you are, home at last! I was beginning to worry that His Majesty would keep you another day in London. I see that you have brought some guests with you?"

"Yes, Mildred, I have. May I present to you Master Thomas Andrews and Master Nicholas Jones? They will be staying with us for a short time. I am on a quest to find Master Thomas's father, Geoffrey Andrews."

Tommy's eyes lit up. He didn't know that Sir Edward was going to help him! He thought that they would be sent home right away but it sounded like Sir Edward wanted to find his dad for him. Mildred, however, had given an involuntary gasp.

"Geoffrey Andrews, sir?" she asked, a bit frightfully. "The same Geoffrey Andrews that grew up with you here?"

"The very same, Mildred. I'm afraid that my boyhood companion's son has come looking for him and King Henry has charged me with finding him for this lad."

Mildred fixed them with a piercing stare.

"Sir Edward, are these boys from..." she trailed off and gave Sir Edward a questioning look.

"Yes, Mildred, they are," he told her in a very low voice. "Geoffrey married Thomas's mother some thirteen years ago, before he came back. The lad found out about him and decided to take matters into his own hands to find him instead of asking for help, as he should have." Sir Edward glared at Tommy.

"Wait, so she knows about all of this stuff, too? And you were friends with my dad? Why didn't anybody ever tell me any of this? Why was this all kept a secret from me all this time? Where is my father?" All of the tiredness had drained from Tommy, replaced with a righteous anger. He felt like such an idiot, like he had been lied to.

Nick was standing there watching the exchange with his mouth wide open, not quite believing what was happening. So much for keeping this a secret; it appeared that more and more people knew about this whole time-traveling thing every day.

Sir Edward sighed heavily. "Yes, Tommy, Mildred knows about it all. She has been with my family for many years. I would trust her with my life, and I have. She keeps the secret and the house for my father and me."

"Does your father know about this, too?" Nick wanted to know.

Sir Edward sighed again, sounding very tired. "My father used to know about it, before his mind began wandering more and more in the last few years. In your time, I believe that you would call it "Alzheimer's disease" or dementia, something close to that. He barely remembers who I am, most days. Thankfully, his memories seem to be focused on the days of his youth, before I was born and certainly before he knew about those cursed amulets. Therefore, he cannot give our secret away to listening ears. If there is a blessing in all of this, than that is it. He'll enjoy seeing the pair of you, though. Children always give him cheer."

"Does your father live here with you?" Nick asked, trying to be polite.

"Yes, he resides upstairs in a grand bedroom. He can't manage the stairs anymore and he prefers to be in his own room. Mildred makes sure that he is well taken care of." Mildred blushed a little at his praise and began urging them to come to the table to eat the supper that she had prepared.

"Come now, come now, I've been cooking all day, so excited I was to have you back! You can all do all of your talking there. Things are better understood when folks have a belly full, that's what I say."

Tommy, however, would not budge from his spot. "You still haven't told me how you know my father, how you grew up together."

Rubbing his beard with his hand Sir Edward told him, "Mildred's right. Let's discuss this over our meal. I have a feeling that we will be awake long into the night with this talk."

Reluctantly, Tommy followed behind Nick and Sir Edward to the table where Mildred had brought out steaming bowls of some kind of soup at each of the three set places. It smelled delicious and the warm brown broth was just salty enough to be really satisfying.

"Don't fill yourselves on that, now! I've got some roast boar that it so tender that the meat is falling off the bones."

"Wherever did you get roast boar, Mildred? Don't tell me you've taken up hunting in my absence!" Sir Edward teased.

Mildred blushed and a girlish giggle escaped her mouth. "Sir Edward, you are still a naughty child! 'Twas a gift from one of the tenants, Mr. Stewart. He nabbed a large one he did, and so decided to gift a bit of it to our household. It was a good thing that you arrived home when you did so that it didn't go to waste. Your father wouldn't have been able to eat it all."

"My most humble thanks for this wonderful meal, Mildred," Sir Edward told her. "I cannot wait to taste the boar." He glanced over at Tommy who was taking long sips of the soup from his spoon, but was still glaring at him. Tommy was right; the time had come to tell him about everything, right from the beginning.

"All right then, Tommy. You want to know the truth?"

Tommy nodded.

"Then let's have at it." Sir Edward took a deep breath and began to tell his story.

Chapter Eleven

"Well," Sir Edward began, "I was born in this house in 1501."

"So you're forty," Nick interrupted.

Sir Edward smiled. "Not until next year. Anyway, this is the house where I was born, the same year as Anne Boleyn, some say, and only eight years before the king's first marriage to Katherine of Aragon. I still remember the festivities in London on their wedding day. My mother died when I was very small and my father, while a very loving man, was away on business for the king much of the time so I was left in the care of Mildred."

"My family has been in England for several hundreds of years, farther back than we've been able to really trace. They were always on the lowest rung of nobility in rank, but high enough so that they never suffered poverty or hunger. We've always managed to be of good use to whichever king was in power at the time without ever having to choose sides and lose everything, as some families have had the misfortune of happening. My several greats-grandfather was one of the entourage that King Richard the Lionheart took on his pilgrimage to the Holy Land in the 1200s."

243

"King Richard?" Tommy asked. "He was the one from the story of Robin Hood, right?" He nudged Nick.

Sir Edward nodded. "Yes, the very same. King Richard led a crusade to go to the Holy Land and was killed on the way home. His brother, Prince John, was then crowned King of England."

"Turned out to be the worst king we ever had," Mildred piped up.

"Yes, well, we'll save that story for another time, Mildred. Anyway, my grandfather made it home safely from the Crusades, even if the king did not. When he came back, he brought with him the four objects that have been the cause of all of us being where we are now."

"The amulets," Tommy breathed. "There are four of them?"

"Yes, the amulets. He brought them home but he never disclosed how he came into their possession. It's doubtful that he ever tried to use them. They were passed own from father to son for several generations with dire warnings until they were finally passed to my father. I know that my father used one exactly once, well, twice; once to get to the past and once to come back, fast. It frightened him so badly that he never wanted to use them again and put them away for safe keeping."

"Now, about your father, Tommy." Tommy perked up.

"Before he comes into the picture, you have to know a little about my family. As I've said before, my mother died when I was very small. I don't even remember her very well. Anyway, my father never remarried and it was just my father, Mildred, and me living in this house. My father always talked about getting married and having more children, but it never happened."

"When I was eight years old, there came a plague of what is known as the sweat, or the sweating sickness. You didn't see it today riding in, but there is a little village just a mile down the road from where we are. When the sweating sickness hit, more than half of the village was wiped out from it. Whole families were destroyed and most of those who were left moved away to start over again somewhere fresh."

"My father rode down to the village after the danger had passed to see if there was anything that he could do to help. He wouldn't let me go with him, but he told me about it later. The place looked like what you would call a "ghost town." There was almost no one left alive and the families that had fled took everything quickly, leaving everything a mess. Some houses were burned down from fires that got out of control, doors were left wide open, and farm animals were running around and starving. There were even dead bodies in the street and in the houses where there was no one left to even bury them. It was a horrible scene and it stayed with my father for many years, especially the children lying there." Sir Edward gave a small shudder as if he had seen it himself.

"It so happened that as he was riding through the deserted streets, he heard a child crying from inside one of the small houses. He got off his horse and went to investigate. The door of the house had almost been torn off its hinges and the inside was a mess. It stank of garbage and of human waste. In the midst of it all was a child, a boy, who was around six or seven years old. He was sitting in the only chair that was left in the house. Flies were buzzing around him, landing on the spoiled food that was sitting out on the table. My father looked at the boy for a long moment before the boy noticed him. He immediately stopped crying, wiped his face with his hands, and stood up."

""Hello, sir," he spoke, in a small voice. "Have you come to help me? They're gone, they're all gone."

"Who's gone, my son, and where have they gone?" my father asked him gently.

"My family, sir. The sweat took them all. They're all dead, save me. The priest came to bless them and they died, one by one. I buried 'em out back the best I could sir."

"My father went to look out the back of the house and indeed, there were three mounds near the family garden. A small boy like that couldn't dig a very deep hole, but he had managed to mostly cover them up. My father's heart went out to the lad, left all alone in the world with no one to care for him. When it was determined that he knew of no other relatives that could take him in, indeed, there was almost no one in the village, my father decided that the best place for him would be at our home, with us. This boy was only slightly younger than I was and Father thought that we'd get on well together, as brothers."

"He put the lad on his horse in front of him, tried not to shudder at the lice crawling through his hair, and brought him home. Mildred took one look and drew a bath for him, straightaway. She washed the filth away, combed all of the lice from his hair and found some old clothes of mine that he could wear until she could make him some new ones. When he was all combed and polished with a good meal inside of him, my father called me in from the field where I had been helping with the spring planting. Sitting in one of the chairs at this very table sat your father, Tommy; young Geoffrey Andrews."

"He was small for his age, not having had a lot of good food to eat when he was growing up, and very sad looking. I would expect the same from any child who had endured the hardships that he had. My father introduced him to me and explained that Geoffrey had lost his entire family and was now to be my new brother. My father was going to adopt him as his ward and would live with us from now on."

"Were you mad?" Nick wanted to know.

"Why would he be mad?" asked Mildred. "Sir Edward has always had his mind about him!"

Sir Edward chuckled. "He doesn't mean "mad" like Father is, Mildred," he explained, "Nicholas means "mad" as in "angry"

Mildred smiled and shook her head. "Sorry to be a bother. I don't understand all of these new words."

"You're not a bother, Mildred!" Nick exclaimed. "You're perfectly wonderful!"

Mildred lightly boxed his ears, teasing him. "Oh, go on with you, Master Nicholas," she said as she went, grinning, into the kitchen to bring out the roast boar.

"And, no, Nick, to answer your question, I was not mad. On the contrary, I was delighted. I had always wanted a brother and was very happy to have one who was already at a proper age to play with. I had seen the new brothers and sisters of my playmates and they were always crying or had dirty clouts. Dirty diapers, you would call them in America."

"Anyway, Geoffrey seemed to me to be the perfect brother and he was. We spent every waking moment together and even slept in the same room, although the house is large enough that we could have each had our own room. We learned to ride horses together, we learned our lessons together and when we were old enough, we courted young ladies together. He was a year or so younger than I, but we got along with hardly a quarrel between us, until I was twenty and he was around eighteen or nineteen."

"What do you mean, around eighteen? Didn't you know when his birthday was?" Tommy wanted to know.

"Birthdays now are not like birthdays where you come from. Many of the common people don't know the exact day that they were born, although they do keep track of the time of year. If someone is born on a holiday, or a saint's day, that makes it easier, but many just don't know and they are content with that."

"Do you know your birthday?" Nick asked.

"Yes, I do. It's November the twelfth. My father kept excellent track of dates and times so I was always aware of it, but Geoffrey never knew when he was born. I'll wager that his parents didn't even know the exact date. We just figured that he was a year or so younger than me and left it at that."

"What happened when you were twenty?"

Sir Edward sighed. "I had told Geoffrey about the amulets. My father had told me about them many times, but thought it was safer to keep it just between the two of us. It was one of my favorite bedtime stories when I was smaller. He would tell me about the

Crusade, not all of it, of course. Much of it was too disturbing for a small boy, but he would recount all of the exciting parts for me, about the deserts and the people that lived there with dark skin and how they were so different from us.

He told me of the caves that they explored and about all of the treasure that was there, just waiting to be found. My favorite story, though, was when he would tell of the one time, just the once, that he used one of the amulets to take him back to see himself as a small child. As you know, it is an intense experience to travel through time. After only catching a glimpse of his young self, he came back to his time immediately, swearing that the amulets were unnatural, evil, and locked them away in his chambers."

"I had been telling Geoffrey the stories, too, for many years in our room at night. I didn't think, after hearing what my father went through, that he would ever want to try it, but when he was about fifteen, he began pestering me to find the amulets and to use them when my father was gone. I refused to show him where they were; terrified that something would go horribly wrong. I wasn't even sure if I could find them. He backed down for a while. He had a good heart and always tried very hard to please us, as if he were afraid that we would put him back in that miserable shack that my father found him in. That would never have happened, of course. My father loved him as a son."

"In the meantime, Geoffrey and I grew closer. I don't think that two natural brothers could have ever been better friends. When we disagreed about something, sometimes we'd punch it out in the back of the barn, but those scuffles never lasted long and we'd always end up laughing, forgetting what it was that we were fighting over."

"He mentioned the amulets from time to time, always very cautiously so as not to upset me, but I knew that if my father ever found out, he would be absolutely furious, and that would be if we managed to make it back in one piece. I must admit, the idea was appealing to me and became more attractive over time, but I still wasn't ready to risk my father's wrath and disappointment."

"Finally, one year, when I was twenty and Geoffrey was about eighteen or nineteen, I gave in. I was at a point in my life when I wanted to show how manly I was and how I wasn't a child anymore. My father had gone on business for the king and Mildred was to be in the village all day, which by then had been built back up. If we were going to do it, the timing was perfect. Geoffrey and I went into my father's chamber and to the loose floorboard where I knew that he kept the amulets. We read the paper that had come with it and, just like the pair of you, I imagine, determined that we would both hold on to only one of them."

"We decided to go to the future, a place that we had only dreamed of. For the place of our landing, we decided on going to the New World, a place which right now is little more than an enormous forest with the Native Americans living their lives with almost no European interference. We had heard of it from the tales of Christopher Columbus and other explorers, though England wasn't very involved in it yet. Regardless, it sounded fascinating. We vowed to not bring anything back or to alter anything while we were there. We also agreed that we would only stay for a matter of hours and then come back before anyone was the wiser."

"The New World is a pretty big place," Tommy interjected. 'Where did you end up going?"

"We weren't specific; we just told it that we wanted to go to the New World in the year 1630. We figured that going about one hundred years into the future was a good start."

"1630? Weren't the Pilgrims there already?" Nick asked.

Sir Edward smiled. "Very good, Nicholas. You've been paying attention in class. Yes, the Pilgrims and several other groups of people were living there. Fortunately for us, we were dropped near a village in the middle of the night when no one was about. Can you imagine what the Pilgrims would have done to us if they had seen us drop from the sky? They'd have surely hung us for witchcraft."

Tommy asked, "What did you do then?"

"We scouted around the village for a while and we probably would have stayed longer if we hadn't run into some Indian scouts in the woods. We took one look at them and pulled the amulet out. I was frozen to the spot at the sight of those wild men, but Geoffrey could think on his feet. He grabbed my arm and told the amulet exactly where we wanted to go: year, time and place and as quick as a wink, we were right back in my father's room. We barely made it to the chamber pot to get sick."

Nick and Tommy exchanged glances. They knew exactly what Sir Edward was talking about and it wasn't a pleasant memory.

"Anyway, after that first attempt, we got bolder and bolder. I probably shouldn't be telling you this, but those amulets are very specific. We traveled to many different times and to many different lands before landing in the twentieth century. The more times that we did it, the less sick we became with each journey. We saw the ancient Greeks and Romans, watched part of the Great Wall of China being built, and even saw George Washington riding through New York."

"No wonder you're such a good history teacher!" Tommy exclaimed.

"Yes, well, that's where I got my interest and most of the artifacts that I use in class. When I decided to become a teacher in your time, I couldn't understand why students didn't like history, why they didn't enjoy it like I did. I understood much better when I saw the history books that you work out of. I decided to become a history teacher and make it exciting for kids rather than dull and boring, names and dates, all of that." It was true. As a teacher, Mr. Barnhart was definitely a favorite among students, and not just for his good looks or his accent.

"But how did you travel to all of those times without being seen?" Nick asked.

Sir Edward thought for a moment before he answered

"I don't know. We were always dropped somewhere out of sight or outside of cities and villages where we could be seen. I think that's just part of the magic of the amulets." He continued on, "We went on several more adventures, none lasting terribly long. Geoffrey carried one amulet, I carried another, and the other two we left here for safe-keeping. After a couple of years, however, I found out that Geoffrey had been going off with one of the amulets on his own, without me. To this day, I'm not sure when it began, but I caught him being dropped in one day, behind the barn. He apologized profusely, of course, and promised never to do it again, but he had a confession to make, he told me. I asked him what was so important that he could betray my trust, that he could just take an amulet and travel alone. I was furious! He bowed his head and said that he had met the woman of his dreams; that he was in love with a lady from the future, from 1998! We had never been that far in the future together, mostly because we didn't think the earth would last that long."

Tommy couldn't hold it in any more. "Was that woman my mother?"

Sir Edward gave a small smile and nodded kindly. "Yes, she was your mother, Thomas. Your father was charmed by her. He was enchanted by the time that she lived in: cell phones, fast jets, the Internet, he loved it all. He had been there several times, he said, and was on the verge of telling her who he really was. He wanted to bring her back with him, to live here with us. He said that in her time, it didn't matter who your parents were or how high you were on the social ladder. If you fell in love and got married, people were usually happy for you. I guess that meant a lot to him, seeing as how he had lost his entire family and had to depend on my father's status in life. He wanted to feel accepted, and she accepted him."

"He begged me to come with him, to meet her. He had made a date with her the following evening and wanted me to give him my blessing. I wanted to be angry with him, wanted to yell at him some more for breaking his promise, but there was something so joyous in his face that I couldn't. I caught his excitement and was happy for him. I agreed to go with him the next night to meet this lady, Elizabeth, or Liz, as you know she prefers to be called."

"We dropped into the back of her small apartment building in Dearborn, closer to Detroit than we all live now. It wasn't really an apartment building, but a large, old, house divided into four small apartments. We went up the stairs to her apartment and knocked on the door. It opened right away, as if she were expecting us, and there stood your mother, a vision. She had been expecting Geoffrey, of course, but not me and was surprised to see me there. Geoffrey introduced me as his adopted brother and that he really wanted her to meet me. She was a little cautious, but invited us in. I was shocked to see that she lived alone! There was no father, no mother, or even older brothers for her protection. When I commented on that, she laughed and said that she was perfectly capable of taking care of herself. She was working and taking classes at the university, something that numbed my mind. A woman at a university? Impossible! She laughingly assured me that it was true and even showed me her schoolbooks. Although I could understand them, they weren't written in the same English that I was used to."

"I was growing more and more enamored of this strange woman who lived alone, worked, and attended a university. I could tell that Geoffrey was, too. He hung on her every word. Over the

258

dinner that she had made us, she told us that she was studying to be a teacher and that she was almost done with her degree. I was most impressed, as was Geoffrey."

"We drank our way through a couple of bottles of wine and that's probably why we were feeling bold enough to tell her more about ourselves. She asked about where we lived and before I could stop him, Geoffrey began to tell her the truth. She thought it was a joke, but Geoffrey tried to convince her. She began to get angry, saying that it wasn't funny what we were doing and maybe we should leave. It was then that Geoffrey pulled out his amulet and showed it to her. He told her to hold on to it and asked her where in time she wanted to go."

""You're joking!" she said sternly. There's no such thing as time travel! How can you play around like this? I thought you loved me!""

"Geoffrey looked heartbroken and took her hands. "Please, trust me", he pleaded, "You'll get very sick to your stomach but at least you'll believe me then. I can't bear the thought of you thinking that I'm a liar." She tentatively took hold of the amulet and I scrambled to my feet. Wherever they were going, I was too. I wasn't about to let Geoffrey leave me here in this noisy, blinking world. We all three put the chain around us and found a piece to hold onto. Liz said, fine, that she wanted to see where we lived, our house in England. She still didn't believe us, but she wanted us to prove it to her. Father was out of town at the time so we agreed and told the amulet, very specifically, where we wanted to go. We landed right behind the barn, as usual, and Liz crawled off to get sick, just like we told her she would."

"Wait a minute," Tommy said, "Do you mean to say that my mom, my mother, *time traveled*?"

Sir Edward nodded. "Yes, I know it's hard to think of your mom taking that kind of risk, but that was before you were born and people do crazy things when they're young. Your mother was very brave but I don't think she felt that way at first. Geoffrey and I had landed safely, of course, and waited for her to feel better. After a moment, she stood up and we began to walk her to the house, only to come face to face with Mildred!"

"Mildred!" they exclaimed.

She came bustling into the dining room. "I thought I heard my name being called."

"Mildred, you saw my mother when she dropped in?"

"Ah, yes, the poor thing. Sick as a dog and wearing a skirt that would have gotten her burnt as a witch, the lamb. I took her straightaway to the house and found her some decent clothing to wear; clothing that had belonged to Mistress Barnhart. They weren't fashionable but they'd do for the moment. Then I gave those boys a piece of my mind, I did!"

"Did you know what they were doing, Mildred?"

"Not exactly yet, but I knew that they had been up to something naughty. I made your mother go and lay down for a while and then sat those two down to make them tell me what had been going on. I didn't believe it at first, but they told me of such wonderful, and terrible, things that were going to happen in the future. Then, I looked at your mother's clothing. I had never seen a "zipper" before, is that the right word? The fabric was such as that I had never seen in the marketplace. I couldn't believe it when young Master Geoffrey told me that it was man-made; it hadn't come from a plant or a sheep or even a silk worm! It was then that I began to believe what they were telling me, that a long-ago Master Barnhart had brought back those wicked things from the Holy Land and that

261

they had been using them. At first, I planned on going to their father with every last bit of it, but after a while I just couldn't. I became the keeper of their secret instead, naughty boys. Now how are you enjoying that boar?"

Truthfully, Tommy thought that it wasn't as good as the provolone pork chops that his mother made but it wasn't bad. He quickly took another bite so as not to hurt Mildred's feelings, but he really wanted Sir Edward to get on with his unbelievable story. He still couldn't believe that his mother had used one of the amulets!

"Why didn't you tell Sir Edward's father about them?" Nick asked.

Mildred stopped her bustling for a moment. "Because, young Nicholas, I could see that Master Geoffrey was in love with Mistress Elizabeth and that she felt the same way. I couldn't be the person to ruin that. I may be an old widow, but I know what it's like to be in love." Mildred reddened to the tips of her elf-like ears and scuttled back into the kitchen. Sir Edward smiled at what she had said and took a gulp of his wine before continuing on.

"Your mother stayed for only a few hours. Geoffrey and I thought that she might be frightened off, that he would never see her again after we took her back home, but that was not the case. If anything, she fell more in love with him."

"He took her home that night, back to her time. I stayed behind, here, feeling like a bit of a third wheel. He returned home about an hour later. When he got back he said that she wasn't as sick as she had been the first time, just like us, but he wanted to make sure that she was alright before leaving her five hundred years away. I knew it was just a matter of time before he'd want to stay with her all the time and I was right. He spent more and more time with Liz, which wasn't difficult because my father was beginning to lose control of his mind by that point. He did less and less business for the king. Geoffrey could disappear for days and Father would think that he'd only been gone a few hours. We took full advantage of that, I'm ashamed to say."

"One day, Geoffrey came home from seeing Liz and told me that they were going to get married, in her time. He would still come back to visit, but planned on living in Liz's time. As fascinated as she had been, she had no desire to live in a place where she couldn't be an independent woman, even if she was married. Liz wanted to teach and to raise a family with all of the comforts of modern medicine and I couldn't blame her. As I told you before, my own mother died while giving birth to a baby sister; the baby died, too. I know that Geoffrey was still haunted by the memories of his family as well and didn't want the woman he loved to be without those comforts in her life. The twentieth century was new to him, to, but there he wasn't an orphan; someone without connections. He could begin a new life as a brand new person."

"But why did he come back here? Why did he leave us?" Tommy blurted out before he could stop himself. Now, more than never, he wanted to know this man who had moved heaven and earth to be with his mother.

Sir Edward looked grave. "Let me get to that in a minute. You need to know the beginning."

"I went to their wedding. It was a small affair and your mother looked like an angel. She had made her own dress and had designed it to look a little bit like the dresses do now in honor of your father. She wore a crown of flowers in her hair and carried only a single red rose. Your father was dashing in his modern tuxedo. He didn't want to wear the long stockings and breeches that we were used to, already trying to fit into his new life. Several weeks after the wedding, he arrived back at home to tell me that they were expecting you in about eight months. He was so happy that he couldn't stop grinning the whole time! He was going to bring Liz back to visit Father and Mildred but after he found out that she was pregnant, we didn't know how traveling would affect the baby, so Liz stayed home. She had graduated by then and was working as a substitute teacher until after you were born. We didn't see a lot of Geoffrey after that."

"From then until the time you were born, he popped in and out and I sometimes went to visit them at their new house in the town, where you and your mom live now. Geoffrey had gotten a job with a museum, his boss being very impressed with his knowledge of the past. They were very happy together, up until the time Abraham showed up."

The boys perked up. "Who is Abraham?" they asked.

Mr. Barnhart took another gulp of wine and poured himself some more before answering. He appeared to be thinking very hard about what to say next.

"One day, when Liz was teaching and Geoffrey was home alone, someone knocked at the door. When he opened it, he was pushed aside and the man forced his way into the house, almost as if by magic, Geoffrey said. He wasn't very tall or muscular, but he had dark hair and almost colorless eyes that would scare the devil himself.

The man told him, quite casually and quietly, that he knew that he had one of the precious amulets from the East which were stolen from his family centuries ago. He informed Geoffrey that his family wanted them back, that many people had died because those amulets have been missing for so long. Geoffrey thought that it would be best to play dumb and told them and that he didn't know what he was talking about. The man laughed in Geoffrey's face and said that he didn't believe him. It was all quite menacing."

"He said that his name was Abraham and that he had been secretly following us for a long time to make sure that we were the right family, the ones who had taken the travel stones. He'd observed us being dropped into various places, had followed us and waited for us back at home unseen. Long ago, his family had been the keepers of great treasures, magical treasures that had slowly disappeared over the centuries. These treasures had been taken by soldiers of different lands or stolen by rival kingdoms in order to

266

gain power, killing off much of his family. The family now had greater numbers and could now hunt for all of their lost treasures, wanting to restore their power and prestige."

"He knew about me, my father, and he knew about Liz. He went as far to threaten you, Tommy, saying that he would even come after you, and that he would return soon. He told Geoffrey that he would give him two days to think about it, so that the matter may be resolved peacefully. If Geoffrey didn't give him the amulets at the end of two days, our entire family would suffer for it. He then whirled out of the house and disappeared into thin air, apparently using another item to do so, perhaps another amulet or something that we didn't know about. We still don't to this day"

Geoffrey was stunned. All this time, the amulets had been something fun, a wonderful, mystical toy. It never occurred to him, or to any of us, that the original owners of those amulets would come back to claim them. He knew, though, that it was a serious situation and came to me right away."

Tommy asked in disbelief, "He was another time traveler?"

Sir Edward nodded. "We figured that and decided that it was better to not panic, to let things settle down and to see what happened next. For Liz's sake, we decided not to tell her at first, worried what might happen to both of you. We would save that for after you were born, thinking that we could hold him and his family off until then."

"I agreed to stay at the house with them until you were born, for safety. Liz thought that something might be up, but didn't pursue it. We told her that it was because of her, how there would always be someone there for when she went into labor, just to be safe. She was used to having me around and had other things on her mind, anyway. After two days had passed, there was no sign of Abraham and eventually, we foolishly forgot all about him and his family. We had something to look forward to, after all!"

"The day you were born, safely and in a modern hospital, I might add, Geoffrey was so happy! He must have personally introduced you to every nurse and doctor on the floor, holding you aloft in the air. You'd think a child had never been born before!" He chuckled at the memory. Tommy felt a warmth move up through his heart. He didn't remember his father but the more he found out about him, the better he felt. Sir Edward went on.

"I stayed with the three of you for a while, with no sign of Abraham. After a few weeks, I went back home to give you all some privacy. I thought that you would be safe and that the man was just a crazy lunatic who maybe had a magic amulet like we did. I truly didn't think that he would ever show up again and I don't think your father did either. We did tell Liz to not open the door to anyone, or to let any stranger in. We told her a partial truth, that we didn't know how many of these amulets were out there or who had access to them and we just wanted to be doubly sure. She agreed but then laughed."

"'I should be cautious about letting strange time travelers into my house? Well then, how do I explain the two of you?' She thought it was a bit funny and tried to make a joke about it, but reassured us that she understood the precautions that we were taking. Even after all that time, the whole idea of her husband leaping back and forth in time must still have been strange to her, so she trusted us to know what we were doing. It's still strange to me and I've been doing it for more than twenty years!"

"Nothing much happened in the next few months. I went back to take care of my father and life for the three of you seemed to proceed normally, although Geoffrey confessed that many times he felt as if he was being watched by unseen eyes. He wasn't sure if someone was really watching or if he was just becoming paranoid about the whole thing."

"Liz had your baby pictures taken and he brought them back to show me. He was as proud a papa as any man I had ever seen. He tried to tell Father about her and you without betraying too many details. Father would understand and be interested for a while, but then the madness would set in again and he would ask for his mother and father, wondering where they had gone, leaving him in this strange place. He still does that, even to this day. 'Tis a sad state of affairs."

Nick, not wanting Sir Edward to get too sad, or distracted, by thinking of his father, asked, "Did Abraham ever come back?"

"Yes, and he's the reason that the two of you are in so much danger being here!" Sir Edward banged his fist on the table, remembering the reason for this talk in the first place. "Well, it appeared that the feeling of being watched wasn't all in Geoffrey's head. When you were ten months old, Liz got a teaching job in the neighborhood school where she's still teaching to this day. She put you in the care of an older lady named Mrs. Edwards who lived just a few minutes away in the neighborhood. She would take you there every morning and pick you up every afternoon."

"One day that October, just before your first birthday, she brought you home to an awful scene. The door to your little house had been kicked in and the whole place was trashed. Papers had been shredded, the television screen was shattered, even the fish tank had been smashed and the whole floor in the living room was soaking wet. Nothing was taken, but someone had definitely been looking for something."

"She called Geoffrey right away at the museum. When he got home, he was horrified! Of course, his first thought was of Abraham and knew that he had been looking for the amulet, which Geoffrey wore around his neck at all times to protect it. He would never have left it in the house, but apparently, whoever had been there though he might. While Liz took you back over to Mrs. Edwards's house so that they could begin to clean up, Geoffrey came back to get me. He was more scared than I had ever seen him; terrified that the next time they came, it would be when Liz and you were home and he didn't know what the man was capable of yet."

271

"I came back and helped them clean up the entire mess. The police were called and a report was made to satisfy the neighbors' curiosity, but since nothing had been taken, Liz and Geoffrey told them that they would handle it. We put your room back together first and brought you home to sleep."

"As soon as you were in bed, Liz sternly sat us down and made us tell her the whole thing. We did and then promised that we would never hide anything from her again. She was so angry with us! We spent the rest of the night cleaning up the entire mess. By morning, we had it almost back to normal, except we had to throw out the carpeting. A forty gallon fish tank holds a *lot* of water and there were a lot of dead fish scattered about as well. What they thought they were going to find in a fish tank, I don't know."

"Geoffrey took some time from his job while Liz returned to work as usual. Geoffrey's plan was for the two of us to stay in the house and wait for whoever had done all of the damage to return, without his wife and baby there. He felt as if it was his sacred duty to protect his family."

"We waited for three days. Nothing happened. I learned that daytime television was very silly and boring, especially soap operas.

I learned to play Uno and began working on a one thousand piece jigsaw puzzle. I was planning on going home after the fourth day, but it turned out that we didn't have to wait any longer for Abraham to show his face."

"The morning of the fourth day, after Liz went to work, Geoffrey and I were settling in for another morning of *The Today Show* when we heard a large *BANG* against the side of the house. We jumped to our feet and quietly ran to look out the window. There, in the flower bed on the side of the house were three men. Geoffrey nudged me and pointed at the shortest one, communicating that he was the one who had been there before; Abraham. He was with two larger men, goons, presumably for their strength."

"They made their way around to the back door of the house, the same place that they had entered from the last time. Geoffrey and I had gone to the hardware store to buy a new door after the last attack, one that was steel enforced. It's still hanging there today. The man smirked to see it, probably thinking that he would have no problem getting past this door."

"Geoffrey, meanwhile, had quietly gone to get his sword from the bedroom. During the past few months, he wisely thought that having his sword with him would be a good idea. I, however, didn't have the foresight to bring anything with me so after glancing around the kitchen, my eyes settled on the large butcher knife in the wooden block next to the stove. I grabbed it out and stood by Geoffrey, prepared to battle to the death if need be. We had both been trained in swordplay as children and young adults, as every young man is in case of war, so we knew what we were doing."

Tommy was listening in amazement. His *teacher* knew how to use a sword?

"Just as one of the goons began running at the door with his shoulder poised to ram into it, Geoffrey flung the door open and let him run by. The goon, who had his eyes closed to brace for the impact, was surprised as he ran through the now open door and slammed face first into the refrigerator. Not giving him a chance to recover, I slammed him in the groin with my knee and while he curled up on himself, struck him hard over the head with the flat end of the knife. He fell to the ground, unconscious, but I knocked his head into the wall once more, for good measure and to make sure that he wouldn't be creeping up behind us any time soon. I could always kill him later if I had to."

At the mention of Sir Edward killing someone, the boys' eyes widened. He noticed and explained, "If it is a choice between your life or an attacker's, you must preserve your own in any way that you can." He yawned. It was getting very late and the boys could tell that he was growing tired, but they desperately wanted to hear the end of his story.

"What happened with the other two bad guys?"

"Things kind of paused for a minute while I took care of the first one. With him gone, the odds were a little more even now than they had been before. Geoffrey brandished his sword before Abraham and his remaining goon. "What do you want with my family?" he shouted at them."

"Abraham smiled, showing pointy little teeth and gave a slight, mocking, bow before replying. 'It's a pleasure to see you again, as well, Mr. Andrews, and wonderful to meet you, Sir Edward. It does get confusing; all of this time-jumping and deception doesn't it? I have been chasing your family and the travel stones that you have for many years now. When your English soldiers came to my country, they took with them part of my family's legacy which includes those very travel stones.'"

"'We had them in our possession for three thousand years and we've spent much of the last four hundred trying to find them. We know that your family has them and that you don't belong here, in this time, so we will offer you a deal, as you say. We will allow you to choose between your time and this one, for a permanent stay. Oh, and we shall not kill you. I'm afraid that I can't do much more for you than that.' He stopped and looked at us, those clear eyes boring into us. I could feel him trying to make us bend to his will. I looked over at Geoffrey and he was as mad as a hornet! His eyes were bright and his face was red with anger."

"'How dare you!' he shouted at Abraham. "How dare you frighten my wife and child, destroy our house! Do you think that I'm going to just hand anything over to you after the destruction that you have caused? No, sir, you will leave this place, never to return. If you do come back, I will see to it that you never get back to your own time, whenever that is! Now, leave us at once!' He did make a bit of a frightening figure, your father was rather tall, standing there with his sword drawn and ready to defend his home to the death, but I didn't know if he actually had it in him to kill someone. How would we explain that to the police? Things like that are much more

276

difficult to hide in your time than they are here. I decided to step in and see if I could help the situation. I pushed in between Geoffrey and Abraham."

"'Gentlemen, let us not forget that we are all grown men. We can settle this without any bloodshed,' I told them. From the look on Geoffrey's face, I didn't think that he agreed with me, but he reluctantly lowered his sword a bit and I went on. 'How did you get here, Abraham, if we have your amulets?'"

"He sneered at me. 'Fool! Do you think that there are only those two jewels that possess the powers I seek? I come from a family of very powerful sorcerers. For thousands of years we have collected mystical objects from around the world and since the discovery of these stones, we've also been visiting different times to ensure that we find everything that we can. I have been entrusted with the last remaining stone and instructed to take back what is ours.' I could see Geoffrey starting to say that there were actually five stones and that we had four of them, but I gave him a sharp look and, luckily, he understood to keep quiet about it."

"I stared at Abraham, steely-eyed. 'What is it that you and your family want? We've never heard of you in all of history.'"

"He grinned again. 'Ah, Sir Edward, that is part of our grand scheme of things. We are not from one area; we are from many lands: China, Russia, Lebanon, Egypt, even your precious little continent of Europe. We have people in high positions that you would never suspect are a part of our family. Some of them don't even know about our magical background, but we have put them in those high places to make the world work the way that we want to. You've heard of Ramses II, the Emperor Nero, yes? They are a part of us, among others.'"

"'Unfortunately, there seems to be only those three amulets that make time travel possible and our scientists have not yet figured out how to make more, although that is a project in progress. That is why it is so crucial for us to take your amulets back. We need all of them to accomplish our goals and make no mistake, we *will* get them back.'"

"'I'm a patient man, but not overly so. I will leave now and come back in twenty-four hours. You will give the amulets to me or I will take them by force. I hope, Master Andrews, that you do not make the wrong decision. It would be a shame for your young son to grow up without his father. Or a father to grow old without his son', he added. With that, he beckoned to the other goon that was still standing. The goon grasped the unconscious one under his arms and dragged him over to Abraham. The three of them disappeared at the same time, leaving Geoffrey and I standing in his kitchen, still stunned by what had just happened."

"'I have to leave,' Geoffrey said after a minute. "I can't let Liz go through this, dragging her and Tommy through time while these people are chasing me. I have to leave.'"

"'Wait, Geoffrey, are you sure?' I asked him. I knew that it would break Liz's heart if he left. What would become of you, Tommy, if your father were to leave?"

"He paced around the room, thinking out loud. 'If I run, if I take the amulet and go, he'll never be able to find me. I can blend in anywhere, any time. Liz and Tommy will be safe. You can bring her letters from me from time to time. I'll send her money from wherever I am, but I must never visit. They'll be sure to track me here and I can't take the chance that Abraham will hurt them to get to me and the amulets.' He ranted on for a few more minutes about his plans and then stopped to put his hands on my shoulders."

"'You will need to take care of them for me, Edward. Guard them with your life, as if they were your own.'"

"'Me!' I cried. 'You don't think that he's going to come after me when you're gone? I use an amulet, too, you know.'"

"'Yes, but you can stay at home and tell him that I left with both of them, that you are very angry about what an ungrateful orphan I turned out to be, leaving you stranded in 1540. He doesn't know that we have four of them!' He gave me a cocky grin. 'Make it look very believable and say terrible things about me so that he will leave you all alone and come after me. You know, lie your head off.'"

I didn't think it was funny. 'But how am I supposed to take care of your family and my father, too, with you popping in and out of different times all over the world? What if he overpowers me and really does take my amulet? I'll be stuck in our time and no one will be able to take care of Liz and Tommy.'"

"'Please, Edward, I'm begging you. Find a way. I swear to you that I will repay all of your efforts. I'll leave an amulet with you so that you can go back and forth to watch things here, just don't do it very often so that Abraham doesn't become suspicious. I think that he will be watching. Come back with me on my amulet, leave one here, and then the three of us will all have one, with one still hidden at home. Stay with your father, but once in a while, go and see how my wife and child fare. I will meet with you at certain times to exchange information. I will owe you my very life if you do this. Please, brother.'"

"What could I do? I made the promise to him and for the rest of the afternoon, until Liz came home, we planned out what we were to do for the rest of our lives."

"How did my mom take it?" Tommy asked. He was amazed that all of this; goons, bad guys popping in and out, had happened right in their little kitchen, where his mother made pancakes and lasagna, and he had never known.

"She was upset, of course. She begged Geoffrey to stay and told him that they could handle it, that they should call the police, even offering to come with him, jumping through time, anything to get him to stay there but Geoffrey was determined that the both of you should be protected and convinced that the only way to do that was for him to leave. In the end, she sadly agreed. I asked her to come back here to live with me, but there was no way that she wanted to raise you in our time with all of the diseases and the hard life."

"She cried all night but knew it was for the best. You see, she had only read about things like this, magic and all. People here don't believe in this kind of thing, what with science, computers and all. She was still trying to come to grips with time travel and a husband that continuously visited the sixteenth century. The idea of Abraham coming back to harass her made her very nervous and she wanted you to be safe. The quiet life of a single teacher and her son seemed to be the best solution."

"It all went as planned. Geoffrey and I went back to our time the very next morning with one amulet, warning Liz to be very careful when she came home the next day, but when I checked with her later, she said that nothing had happened. She told people there that Geoffrey had been called away on urgent family business in England and she had no idea when he'd return. Eventually, people stopped asking about him out of politeness, figuring that he had decided to stay there, leaving the two of you behind. She hid the other amulet safely away, or so I thought until yesterday", he glared at them, "but at least Abraham hasn't discovered it yet."

Tommy felt sheepish about using an amulet but was still puzzled about a few things. "Yes, I get that, but when did you come back to stay?"

Sir Edward smiled. "That was tricky. Abraham had, of course, visited me in England with Father and tried to make me give up what I knew, but I stuck to the story and managed to throw him off, although he did do a fair amount of damage to the house. Geoffrey was an ungrateful orphan, I told him, and had disappeared, taking both amulets with him, leaving me stranded and not able to go to you. I could tell that he didn't believe me; the house was broken into a few times and there have been figures lurking about, watching me to see if Geoffrey came back or if I would disappear anywhere, but I had hidden the amulets well and I didn't pop into see you for a long while."

"Eventually, they got tired of watching and, I assume, focused on looking for Geoffrey in some other time. With only one amulet, Abraham can't afford to stay in one place for too long. That's our advantage; that and he doesn't know that there are actually five of amulets."

"After a year or so, I began sneaking back to check on the both of you, but I didn't get too close in case you were also being watched. I left notes for your mom, letting her know that I was okay. After a while, I started spending more and more time there. I even started visiting your mom, but only for very short periods. I forged some documents and took a few classes at college to get a teaching certificate, then made sure that I got a job close to you. I went home every weekend and vacation, telling everyone in your time that I had business to attend to."

"But how did you see my dad to get the letters to pass on to my mom? Did you meet with him?" Tommy still wanted to know.

Sir Edward shook his head sadly. "I haven't seen your dad since that day. The letters were always just waiting in my room, addressed to your mother, so I delivered them. He occasionally left a note for me as well, but with very little information. He only said that he was still alive and evading Abraham, but he never popped in to see you. He was too afraid that he was being followed and didn't want to bring any harm your way. That had to be killing him. That's always been his main focus, keeping you and your mom safe."

"I know that you think he abandoned you, Tommy, but in truth, he loves you very much. He always has." Sir Edward covered Tommy's hand with his own as this news sank in, patted it and sat back in his chair with his wine goblet, exhausted. Tommy could see that telling the whole story had worn him out.

The room was very dark now, except for the flickering of the candles that Mildred had lit around the room while they had been talking. Tommy hadn't even noticed. He'd been too enthralled listening to Sir Edward's story. At last he knew his father's background, knew more about him now that he ever did. It was wonderful to know that his father had really cared about him, that he had rearranged his whole life for him, but the reality of Abraham and his family disturbed him. They had to still be out there, somewhere, looking for him. Suddenly, he had a question.

"Sir Edward, when was the last time that you got a note from him?"

"Not for a few years. I've even searched Father's room, thinking that he might have wandered in and taken it, but nothing has turned up. Mildred keeps an eye out as well. I wouldn't even know where to look for him now."

"But he might be in trouble! Maybe Abraham captured him, or he caught some horrible disease! What if he needs our help? We can't just sit here!" Tommy had sat up in his chair at the thought of his father being in trouble, but Sir Edward gently took his arm.

"Tommy, think about it. He has an amulet. We can't just go zipping through random times looking for him when for all we know he might not even be alive! If Abraham has caught him, that would explain why he hasn't been around for a while. Of course, our recent travels may tip him off."

Tommy's face blanched. That would be so unfair, to come through all of this only to discover that his father was dead. He shut his mind to the possibility.

"No! We have to try!"

Sir Edward gripped both of his arms and looked him in the face. "How, Tommy? How? We can travel through time but we can't determine where someone is. I believe that Abraham has something, some kind of magic, that can track people who use the amulets but we don't! Out of all the times in the history of the world and of all the places that there are, how would we find one man, one small person in the middle of it all unless he communicates with us? This isn't the internet; we don't have some sort of time travel GPS, we have nothing! I'm afraid that we're simply going to have to wait until your father decides to show himself again. Don't you think that I miss him, too? He was as dear to me as a brother!"

"Don't say "was!"" Tommy yelled and pulled away. The tears came rolling down his cheeks and, embarrassed, he wiped them away with his sleeve. "He's alive, I know it!"

Mildred came bustling in at all of the shouting and put her arms around him. "There, there now, my lamb, it'll be alright. Your father's a smart one, he is, and perhaps he's just staying out of sight for a while."

Sir Edward groaned and massaged his forehead with his fingertips. "Mildred, don't feed the boy a fantasy. It's been too long! We have to be realistic about this."

"Sorry, sir, but he just as well may be alive! I don't want the boy getting all upset if there's nothing to be upset about. Why don't you all get to bed now? It's late and clearer heads may prevail in the morning. You'll all think better after a good night's rest, aye?"

"Aye, Mildred, I won't argue with you there. I believe that we all do need a rest. Please show the boys to their rooms, Mildred, and pull out some of my old nightshirts for them to wear."

"I already have, sir," Mildred replied, looking pleased that she had anticipated his thoughts. "Come along then, my young gentlemen."

Tommy and Nick followed her up the dark staircase, following the bobbing light from the candle that she held. As they left the table, they saw that Sir Edward didn't get up after them, but reached to pour more wine into his goblet. Tommy, still upset from the conversation, wiped his tears and tried to calm himself while Nick, fascinated as he had been with the whole story, was almost dead on his feet and ready for a long sleep.

Mildred led them into a room that already had a cozy fire burning, casting flickering light on the walls and taking off the chill of the air. There was a large, furry rug on the floor and comfortable-looking quilts on the large feather bed that stood in the center of the dark room. Mildred stirred the fire a bit and left them quickly.

"You'll be needing a good rest after all of that, young ones. I'll leave you to it and will bring your breakfast in the morning", she called over her shoulder and went out the door, closing it behind her. They could hear her shuffle down the stairs. Nick didn't waste any time. He kicked off his shoes and hurriedly changed into one of the long white nightshirts that were lying on the bed. Pulling back the heavy cover on the bed, he slid his way in and before Tommy could even get undressed, he could hear Nick's breathing deepening. Incredible. He was already asleep.

Tommy stood there for a moment, trying to take in everything that he had heard. It was all swimming together in his head: the story of his father surviving a plague, his mother and father meeting, his mother actually time traveling for crying out loud, Abraham and his family, it was so surreal and overwhelming. He wanted to talk to Nick, but at the same time, he didn't want to talk any more.

Exhausted, he let the feeling overtake him. What he needed was sleep to sort everything out. It would all be clearer in the morning. Yes, that was it. He pulled on the nightshirt left by Mildred and crawled under the covers next to Nick. What he needed was a deep sleep and for his mind to rest. In seconds, his body did just that.

Chapter Twelve

The next morning dawned brightly through the window, the sunlight forcing Tommy's brain into "awake" mode, even though the rest of his body fought it. His brain was winning out, however, and not for the first time, he had to remind himself where he was and what exactly had been going on. He moaned as he stretched out under the heavy coverlet on the bed and bumped Nick in the process.

"Ow!" Apparently, Nick's brain was intent on waking him up as well.

"Hey, can't you keep your arms to yourself?" he asked sleepily.

"Sorry, had to be done," Tommy replied. He sat up and rubbed the sleep from his eyes, not wanting to leave the comfortable feather bed. He was glad that he waited for a moment because Mildred bustled in a moment later, carrying a tray of food.

"There, then, Sir Edward thought that you would still be abed! He was only half right. One of you is sitting up at least. Sir Edward wanted me to tell you that after you eat and dress, he wants to see you down in the barn, to teach you a little something about the horses, I would imagine. Don't you have horses where you come from?" she asked quizzically.

"Yes, we have horses there, but not everyone has them. We live in a town and there are horses that aren't far away, but we don't have any. We've never taken care of any," Tommy tried to explain.

"Then how do you go from place to place?" Mildred wanted to know.

"We have cars," Nick piped up.

"Cars?" Mildred's brow wrinkled. "What are cars?"

Nick had to think of how best to describe them. "They're like carriages, or wagons, you see, but they're not pulled by horses or by any other animal. They're powered by gasoline."

Tommy broke in, "Gasoline is a fuel and when you put it into a car, the car can go. Didn't Sir Edward ever tell you anything about the future?"

Mildred shook her head as she went to tend to the fire that now seemed like a dead pile of coals. Almost magically, she was able to have it sparking again in a matter of seconds.

"It always sounded like sorcery to me, like those amulets. Sometimes, I wish to Jesu that old Lord Barnhart had never found them! Not that I mind meeting you two lads," she tried to backtrack, but it was obvious that she was afraid. "If King Henry ever found out about those, you can be sure that he would have some new heads along London Bridge!"

Tommy shuddered with the memory of actually seeing the heads there. He quickly reassured Mildred, "The amulets may be magic, but gasoline isn't, Mildred; it's science. There's no magic in it at all." He thought for a moment. "People will figure that out in about three hundred years."

"Well, I still prefer to know what's pulling me, not that I ride in carriages a lot, mind you, but if I did, I'd want a nice sturdy horse rather than that gasoline you're talking about. The future doesn't sound like a place where I'd like to be." She gave an emphatic nod and finished tending to the fire and making sure that they were eating their bowls of hot porridge and honey with small plates of ham, then turned and bid them to hurry down to the barn as soon as they had finished.

"Leave the plates on the tray, lads. I'll come to collect them later." She left the room and suddenly it was quiet. They finished eating in silence and then washed and dressed themselves in the same clothes they had worn the day before.

Hurrying down to the barn, they were able to see the inside of Sir Edward's house a little more clearly now that it was daytime. The walls were white and rough, bordered by dark beams of wood. It looked as if it had been around for a while. There were trophies of animals, deer and boars, mostly, hung on some of the walls and a large coat of arms in the room across from the dining room where they had been the night before. They made their way out the door that they had entered through and found themselves standing in the brilliant sunshine. Like the previous day, the sky was a brilliant blue with not a cloud in the sky. The air smelled a lot sweeter than it had in London, with just a touch of barn smell to make them feel as if they were really in the country. They breathed deeply and Nick especially was glad that the smells of the city were gone.

When they entered the barn, Sir Edward wasn't in sight so they walked around slowly taking it all in. There were the horse stalls, of course, but there was also a spot for pigs, several of them, lolling about in mud and straw. There were chickens running about everywhere and from outside they could hear the lowing of the cows.

Rounding a corner, they almost bumped into the man they had seen last night in the stable, John, who was carrying two pails of milk.

"Whoa, sorry," Tommy said to him. John glared at them and motioned over his shoulder.

"Sir Edward wants you over by the horses this morning", he snarled. "You've already missed the milking but you can help get them started today." He made his way off through the barn with out a backward glance.

"Man, what's wrong with him?" Nick whispered. Tommy didn't have time to answer because Sir Edward came around the corner at just that moment. He was dressed in working clothes, not the grand outfit that he had worn to see the king the day before. Clearly, he was more relaxed here.

"There you are, lads!" he boomed in his teacher voice. "I was just going to head in to see if you were awake yet. You've missed the milking." He seemed a lot more cheerful this morning.

"Yeah, we know. John told us," Tommy replied, exchanging looks with Nick.

"Well, let's get the horses taken care of. While we're doing that, you can tell me about your first days here. One thing I've never been is locked in the Tower! Fill me in up until I came to get you."

While they brushed and fed the horses and then shoveled out all of the manure, Tommy and Nick told Sir Edward all about their experiences: meeting Henry VIII for the first time, the soldiers' nasty breath, their invented story about losing their memories, and the kindness shown to them by Mr. and Mrs. Kingston.

"Say, "Mistress" Kingston. That's how it's done in this time," Sir Edward explained. "It's a good thing that they took a liking to you and that they believed your tale. Things could have gone very badly for you if they hadn't."

"Seriously!" Nick exclaimed. "Did you see those heads on the bridge? Just like you told us! It was totally nasty."

Sir Edward agreed. "It's a pretty bad way to end up." He looked at them sternly and spoke to them in a low voice.

"I want you two to realize just how much danger you are in here. As much as I've told you and as much as you've learned in the past few days, you're still outsiders and people know it. You don't understand everything yet and, God willing, you won't be here long

295

enough to learn it all. Abraham or any of his family could be watching and waiting for us to slip up. The last thing he needs to know is that there are other amulets and that you two are using one! I wouldn't expect him to go easy on you because you're children."

"I thought we were almost adults here," Tommy replied saucily.

Sir Edward sighed and closed his eyes for moment before looking at them dead on. "You don't get it. This is not the year 2013! This is 1540 and, yes, you're almost considered adults here, but you haven't been taught the same things that you would have if you had been born in this time! You know nothing about class, status, or what manners you're supposed to use, things that kids now have been taught since they were born! As much as you're learning and having fun, you stick out like sore thumbs! If Abraham is looking for us, at us, you'll be a sure giveaway to what we've been doing. He'll know that Geoffrey didn't take the remaining amulets and that we pulled a fast one on him."

"I've been so very careful these last ten years and he seems to have vanished completely, but I know that can't be true. Even if he himself is gone, he said that his family is out looking for the amulets so he would have a replacement, someone who we wouldn't even know! It could be anyone! That is why we have to get you two back to your own time, except now I have the king after me trying to make sure that we find your father and that I educate you. Damn, what a mess this is!" Sir Edward held his face in his hands for a moment and took a deep breath before looking at them again.

"What if we went home now and came back when the king wanted to see us?" Tommy asked. "We already know how to read and write."

"Can you write with a quill and ink? Do you know Latin? Do you know religious teachings? No! These are the things that King Henry wants you to know. If you were constantly popping in and out, you would definitely attract the attention of Abraham and we can't have that. No, we'll have to figure something else out, something that will make the king forget about you entirely. I need time to think. Finish cleaning these stalls, the cows' area, too. John will be glad of a bit of a break. After dinner, I'll introduce you to my father, Lord Barnhart, although he'll probably forget you five minutes later. Then, we'll begin instruction on writing and Latin so you'll have something to show the king in case you're still here when he summons us back to court."

"We can't just write him and tell him that we're coming?" Nick asked.

"No, you must wait to be summoned. That could be a matter of days or a matter of months, depending on what mood he's in. If we're lucky, he won't summon us before he goes on his summer progress. That's only a couple of weeks away. Then, I think we'll be quite safe. He'll have enough to think about. I do want you to keep an eye out for anything suspicious, however. Abraham could be anywhere."

"In the meantime, I need to think. Finish your work now and I'll be back to check on you later." He strode out of the barn quickly, his boots making clomping noises on the dirt floor and raising a cloud of dust behind him.

Tommy and Nick were quiet after that. There was a lot to think about. Not only were they in danger from King Henry, but also from this unseen Abraham who had it in for them. Tommy turned to Nick, who was scooping up a particularly gross load of horse manure to toss into the waiting cart and making an awful face.

"Look, Nick, I'm sorry that I got you into all of this. I just wanted to come and find my dad. I never thought that this would turn into such a crazy thing. I would understand if you wanted to take the amulet and go home right now."

Nick continued shoveling for a moment before he stopped, leaned on his pitchfork, and looked at Tommy.

"We can't, and anyway I don't want to go home. I'm in the middle of this with you now and, as crazy as it sounds, I'm having fun, especially now that we're out of the Tower and that Mr. Barnhart is helping us."

"Sir Edward," Tommy corrected him with a grin. "Remember that here he's Sir Edward."

Nick laughed and rolled his eyes. "Yeah, you watch, I'll finally get used to calling him Sir Edward and then we'll have to go home. Can you imagine the look on peoples' faces when I call him Sir Edward in class? They'd all think I'd lost my mind for sure!" They both cracked up at the thought.

"Boy, would Susan Wright ever freak out if she saw those heads on London Bridge!"

"Yeah, and could you see her cleaning out this barn? She'd never make it!" They went on and on about their classmates as they finally finished scooping and then sweeping out the horses' stalls. When they went around the corner to get a load of new straw to lay down, they nearly ran right into John again, who seemed to be just standing there rather than walking around the corner.

"Watch where you're going!" he snapped at them again.

"You were the one just standing there!" Tommy shot back. "What were you doing, listening to us?"

John sniffed. "Don't you think I have better things to do than to eavesdrop on a pair of lazy lads like yourselves? I was coming to tell you that dinner is nearly ready and to hurry up with your duties. Your very *light* duties," he added.

"Are you always this grumpy?" Nick asked him, getting a little braver. "We didn't do anything to you."

Now John looked angry. "You're a pair of foundlings who are living better than you deserve to! I work hard for my living and your hands are as smooth as my lady the queen's! Now I have to get behind in my work so that you can learn what it's like to do an honest day's labor. You would do well to stay out of my way!" He brushed past them, purposely bumping Tommy's shoulder as he did. Tommy looked over at Nick.

"Jeez, what a grouch! I still think he was listening in. We should probably tell Sir Edward. He said that we shouldn't trust anybody." Nick nodded in agreement and they hurried to finish their chores.

***

Later, after a good dinner of roasted rabbit and parsnips, Sir Edward took the boys to meet old Lord Barnhart. He was sitting on the edge of a large feather bed dressed in a nightshirt, robe, and soft looking shoes. His hair and beard were pure white and had grown down past his shoulders.

"He refuses to let us trim it," Sir Edward whispered to them.

In louder voice he said, "Father, may I present to you Geoffrey's son, Thomas and his friend, Nicholas Jones." He gave them a slight push forward.

"It-It's a pleasure to meet you, sir," Tommy stammered nervously. Leaning on his ornately carved cane, the old man scrutinized him closely with filmy blue eyes.

"Geoffrey? Geoffrey has a boy? Thomas, you say, Edward? Well then, my boy, where is your father?"

Shocked by the question, Tommy nevertheless answered, "I don't know, sir. He has disappeared."

The old man's eyebrows shot up. "Disappeared, you say? But where has he gone?"

Sir Edward stepped in. "We don't know, Father, but I will be taking care of young Thomas until Geoffrey is found."

Lord Barnhart nodded. "Yes, yes, very well. Now, then, my boy, let us prepare to leave for court. You know that the young king has very recently married and has invited us to court for the festivities. I'll need my new coat and my…" he trailed off and the boys were very surprised to see that Lord Barnhart had fallen asleep sitting up. Sir Edward gently laid his father back on the mound of pillows and set his cane next to him on the bed.

"He never uses it," he explained softly, "but he likes to hold onto it when he's awake." He motioned them out of the room and gently closed the door behind them. They followed him down the flight of stairs and into a room where they hadn't been yet. It was small and had a wooden table in the middle with two chairs. On the table were two inkpots, a variety of feather quills for writing, and several sheets of parchment to write on. There were bookshelves lining two of the walls which contained several books, all of which looked dull and boring to the boys.

"What's all this?" Nick wanted to know.

Sir Edward smiled. "Surely you didn't think that I was going to ignore the king's wishes! I promised to educate the two of you while you're living here and while we're figuring out our next move, you may as well begin your education."

"But we already know how to read and write!" Tommy protested.

"Not in Latin, you don't, and you need to know how to use a quill."

It was amazing how quickly Sir Edward could transform from Renaissance nobility into twenty-first century teacher. In no time at all, he had them memorizing roots of Latin words and writing them down on clean sheets of creamy parchment, which quickly became smeared with berry ink as they made their first attempts to write the alphabet with their quills.

It wasn't as boring as they had anticipated and was actually quite fun and messy at the same time. After a few hours, they were actually getting some decent, legible words and had been working on some Latin nouns, which weren't nearly as much fun as learning to write with a quill.

It wasn't until the sun began to go down and they were wrapping things up that Tommy suddenly remembered to broach the subject of John with Sir Edward. He listened as Tommy and Nick described the scene in the barn from that morning and was thoughtfully quiet for a moment before answering.

"I really don't know John all that well. He's only been here for a year and doesn't talk much, but he definitely should not be talking that way to my guests, even if they are learning how to clean out a barn. I'll have a word with him tonight after supper."

"Do you think he could be part of Abraham's family?" Tommy asked.

At the mention of Abraham, Sir Edward's jaw tightened. "I suppose it's possible, but if he's here to spy on me, I haven't given him much to be suspicious of, until recently, that is," he add dryly, looking at the boys with his teacher look. Tommy and Nick knew that one very well from when anyone acted up in class. They looked sheepish as he went on.

"Now that you've said that, it's gotten me thinking about him. We'll have to keep a closer watch on him, all of us. If he's innocent, we don't want to offend him, he's a good worker, but if he is working for Abraham we'll have to watch out. Keep me informed if he does or says anything else. Now get cleaned up in here. Mildred will have supper on the table soon." He walked out of the room and left the boys to clean up.

After a dinner of leftovers from the midday meal, Sir Edward went out to the barn to talk to John. Tommy and Nick waited a minute and then quietly followed him out to the barn. When they heard voices, they ducked behind a stall door so that they wouldn't be seen. A moment later, they heard Sir Edward's voice raised in anger.

"How dare you be insolent toward me! I am your master and I will not be spoken to in a rough manner by one of my servants! You are dismissed, sir, immediately!"

Shocked, Tommy and Nick peered around the corner at the last bit of that speech to see Sir Edward with his face red and his arms gesturing as he spoke. John was sniveling in the corner but he was watching Sir Edward with hatred in his eyes. As Sir Edward stopped shouting and waited for him to leave, John slowly stood to his full height, short as he was, and pointed an accusing finger at Sir Edward.

"I will leave, but you will be sorry; very, very sorry, Sir Edward. I know what you have now, thanks to your foundlings, and I will be back for it when you least expect it," he said in his high voice. He turned to leave, but Sir Edward wasted no time.

In a flash, he had slammed John up against the wall of the barn, pinning him to the wood with his arms behind his back. The skinny John was no match for Sir Edward's strong arms and he began to stutter and moan.

"You may have me here, Sir Edward," he wailed in a crazed voice," but Abraham is coming! He knows! He's biding his time before he comes to take his revenge on you and the boy!" Tommy's stomach felt sick as Sir Edward slammed John against the wall again.

"Where is he, you little weasel?" he thundered. "Where is your coward of a master who hides in the shadows? Why won't he come and face me like a man?" He threw John to the ground with all of his might and planted his boot on his back; the past twelve years of waiting and watching had taken their toll on his patience.

"Tommy! Nick! I know you're there. Show yourselves!" Sir Edward called.

Fearfully, they stepped out from behind the stall door, not able to tear their eyes away from the struggling man on the ground. Sir Edward was breathing heavily with anger as he held him fast. It was clear that John wasn't going anywhere.

"Run in the house and tell Mildred that we're leaving for London, immediately, and that she needs to pack us some provisions to take."

"We're going back to London?" Tommy managed to eke out. Sir Edward glared at John on the floor.

"Yes, we'll be turning in a traitor, for one thing. He'll be dumped in the dungeon where all of his talk will seem like madness to the other prisoners. They'll never believe him and may even tear him to pieces for being mad!" At this, John stopped struggling and looked up with fear in his eyes. Sir Edward gave him a grim smile.

"Oh, yes, my fine man. They don't take kindly to crazy codgers who speak of magic stones and witchcraft. You may be dead before morning." He looked back at Tommy and Nick. "We're not safe here, anymore. Tell Mildred to send the scullery maid to town and alert Lord Hastings to come and bring her and Father to his home. He knows of Father's situation and will be happy to help. Mildred will know what to tell him; just leave it to her. Make haste, now, make haste!" he barked when they didn't move fast enough.

They raced back into the house where Mildred was cleaning up in the kitchen. There was a girl helping her, about their age, whom they hadn't seen before. They blurted out what had happened in the barn and what she was to do. Without wasting anytime, Mildred instructed the girl, who she called Mary, to run and fetch her cloak and be ready to run to town. Then she pulled out a piece of parchment and began to scribble something down with one of the quills that the boys had put in the kitchen earlier.

"You can write?" Nick was surprised. Sir Edward, when he was still Mr. Barnhart, told them that not many women were educated in this time.

Mildred looked up with a little grin. "Aye, Sir Edward and Master Geoffrey taught me when they were learning their letters. Said it would come in useful one day; I'd say they were right." She finished her message, folded it, and stamped it with a wax seal before handing it off to Mary, who had rushed back in with her cloak around her shoulders. Mildred took her face in her hands, gave her a kiss on the forehead, and put the sealed letter into her hands.

"Now, run, lass, run like the wind to Lord Hastings. I'll take care of everything here." The girl flew out the door, not having said one word the whole time. Mildred turned to look at them as she began pulling food out of the pantry.

"Sir Edward said that this day might come, that we would need to be ready to leave quickly. Now, you'll be needing some bread and some cheese, perhaps some dried meat. That should see you through the night to London." She hurriedly began putting the food into a leather bag.

While she was packing, Tommy asked her, "Mildred, who was that girl?"

"What, Mary? She's a girl from the village. Sir Edward took her in after her father died." She handed Tommy the bag. "There now, and God give you a safe journey! Oh, and one more thing," she said as she bent to give each of them a kiss goodbye, "If you do see your father, will you kindly tell him to come and see me sometime? I watched grow into a fine man, I did. It does me good to see you, looking so much like him."

Blinking back tears, she then shooed them out the door into the night where Sir Edward was waiting with John, now sitting on one of the other horses with his hands bound together and his feet tied to the stirrups. He looked very unhappy and glared at them as they made their way over.

Sir Edward saw the leather pouch and his face brightened a bit. "Good! I knew that Mildred wouldn't let us down. I've got your horses saddled in the barn; go get on and let's be on our way. I want to leave before Abraham decides to check on his favorite spy."

"But what about your father?" Nick asked.

"It's all a part of the plan, Nick. Mildred sent a message to Lord Hastings, who lives not far from here. He doesn't know the whole situation, only that there would come a time when he would be needed to come and collect my father as soon as possible. He worked with my father in the court when Katherine of Aragon was queen and has great respect for him. He's very trustworthy and I know that he will come as soon as he gets the message. Don't worry, I'll check on him later. Now let's get a move on!"

They did as they were told and in a matter of minutes, were traveling back down the road to London at a much faster pace than the day before John's horse was bound to Sir Edward's and Tommy and Nick trailed behind on the old horses that they had ridden in on. It was a beautiful, cool, summer night; the stars were huge and bright, so close that Tommy felt he could reach out and touch them, nothing like home where the city lights made the stars look like tiny pinpricks. The air was cool with a chill, but riding on the big, warm horses kept them very comfortable, even without a cloak like Sir Edward was wearing.

As they went along, Sir Edward began to question John about Abraham and his mission. At first, John wasn't willing to talk, but as Sir Edward promised him more and more brutal punishment when they arrived at the dungeon, eventually, he began to give up little bits of information, hoping to save his skin. Listening to the threats that Sir Edward was making, the boys couldn't believe that this was the same teacher that seemed so tolerant in the classroom!

"Where is Abraham now? How do you give him your information?"

John smirked. "That only shows how naïve you truly are, Sir Edward. Abraham appears to me once a week or so; he has ever since I've been working for you. He stays for but a moment to collect information and then disappears."

"Are you the only one he's ever sent?"

"I'm the only one who managed to work on your land. The others before me were only able to disguise themselves as peddlers or travelers. They were never able to stay long enough to get any real information. When your other stable-hand grew too old, Abraham saw an opportunity and sent me to you. I was always good with dumb beasts."

Sir Edward sighed, not rising to the insult. "I grew careless in those twelve years, believing that Abraham had given up on watching me. It appears that Mildred is the only one I can trust. Wait!" He sat straight up in his saddle as a thought occurred to him.

"Mary! Is she one of Abraham's servants as well?"

John gave a snort. "That little mouse? One look from Abraham and she would have fallen in a faint. No, we choose our members carefully to accomplish our goals. You're not the only one we're tracking, you know."

Sir Edward raised an eyebrow. "Oh? What else do you seek?"

John smiled to himself before answering. "You cannot imagine the wealth out in the world, yet undiscovered or needing to be brought into the Family." He spoke of it as one might speak of the Mafia.

"Abraham is the one in charge of the amulets and with going through time in order to recover the treasures that have been lost to us. There are others who are assigned other tasks, all for the same purpose of making the Family strong."

"So, Abraham isn't in charge?" Tommy asked.

"No, there isn't one person who is in charge, it is several. They all make the decisions together. We simply carry out our orders."

"And what do you get in return?"

"Wealth, special privileges, a chance to move up in the Family, although I have set myself back quite a bit after the events of today."

Sir Edward smirked a little at that one; that was definitely the truth. He couldn't imagine that Abraham would be too happy to hear about the capture of a valuable spy.

"When is Abraham supposed to check in with you next?"

John shrugged sullenly. "I don't know. He would pop in and out randomly. He never said when he would be back."

"All the more important that we hurry, then. For all we know, he could be back now!" Sir Edward spurred his horse on a little more, Tommy and Nick urging their old nags to at least attempt to keep up with him.

***

The large luminous stars were just starting to fade when the outline of London came into view. In fact, they were almost upon it; it was as if it had appeared magically out of thin air! Tommy was amazed at first but then he remembered that there were no electric lights in London. The city would be almost completely black at night. He shuddered, thinking of how dangerous it would be to be out in the streets after dark.

They entered the city as the sky in the east began to turn gold, then pink. As they finally reached the jail, the blazing ball of a sun began peeking up over the buildings, casting bright rays through the streets.

The jail smelled horrible, even as far away as they were. Sir Edward quickly found a guard and was able to have John secured inside with almost no trouble at all. He mounted his horse again and began to lead the boys away from that frightful place.

"How long will he be there?" Nick asked.

"He'll stay until his trial, if he lives that long."

"Then what?"

"I'll give my testimony that he worked for me under false pretenses in order to betray me to a villain, every bit of it true."

"What will happen to him?"

Sir Edward merely looked back at them and raised an eyebrow.

Nick was shocked. "They'll kill him?"

Sir Edward's voice was grave as he spoke. "Justice is done a little differently here. It's not what you're used to, but then again, you might want to get used to it. Now that Abraham will be looking for us, it may come down to your lives or someone else's." He turned to face forward again and none of them said another word for the rest of the ride.

They followed Sir Edward through the crowded streets until they finally stopped, not at the Tower, but at a large dwelling near the River Thames. The area was a little quieter than the general hubbub of London and the boys were still too shocked by what was going to happen to John that they didn't ask any questions, although they looked at each other to exchange worried looks.

Immediately after riding to the small barn behind the house, a groom appeared from around the corner. Sir Edward handed him the reins of his horse and gestured to the boys' horses. The groom silently took all three sets of reins and began guiding the horses back around the corner. Tommy watched for a moment and then shook his head.

"Sixteenth-century valet parking," he whispered to Nick, who cracked a smile.

They followed Sir Edward up to the door. He knocked at it smartly and a moment later it was opened by a wizened old man who looked as if he barely had the strength to hold himself up. When he saw Sir Edward, his toothless mouth opened wide in a huge grin, making him look like a week-old jack-o-lantern.

"Sir Edward! How very good of you to come and see me! Come in! Come in! Are these your sons? How long has it been since you've been away?" His wrinkled face screwed up in thought as he paused. "You never had sons before. Has it really been that long?"

Sir Edward chuckled and patted the old man gently on the back, careful not to knock him over.

"No, Sir James, these aren't my sons. May I present to you Nicholas Jones and," he paused for a moment, "Thomas Andrews." There was a silence as the little pumpkin-faced man caught Tommy's name, as if he knew that his name meant something but couldn't quite place it. Then, all of a sudden, it dawned on him.

"Andrews, you say? It can't be!" he gasped. He quickly glanced up and down the street and then hurried them inside.

"Quickly now, quickly." He ushered them past the large doors, which he firmly shut and locked from the inside behind them. Then he ushered them down the hallway and into a small dining room, where a fire was roaring in the grate.

"Sit, sit," he told them and they all pulled up chairs to the old wooden table. There was a decanter of what appeared to be wine in the middle of the table and Sir James poured himself and Sir Edward a glass before continuing on. His face wasn't as happy now.

"It was a dangerous thing to bring him here, Edward, very dangerous indeed. If King Harry were to suspect…"

Sir Edward broke in. "They've already met the king. His men are the ones that found them. He gave them to me to take care of, with progress reports, of course."

Sir James visibly relaxed. "They've already met the king, you say? Well, there's one hurdle passed. How did you get them released to you?"

Sir Edward spent the next ten minutes or so filling Sir John in with a brief version of what had been happening so far; their arrival in England, spending time in the Tower, their meeting in the garden, even the news about Philip. During the entire conversation, Tommy and Nick exchanged looks. Sir James must be in on all of this as well. *How many more people know about these amulets?* Tommy thought.

Sir James looked at them. "I think I'm the last one, young Thomas."

His eyebrows shot up. How did Sir James know what he had been thinking? Sir Edward glanced at them and laughed.

"Sir James is, shall we say, skilled in determining your thoughts, among other things."

Sir James gave a slight bow before continuing on. "I have certain talents that need to be kept quiet around here. The king and the bishops don't take kindly to any kind of magic, but I think you already knew that. I trust that my secret is safe with you?" His large watery blue eyes looked at them both and waited for an answer. They vigorously nodded.

"I thought as much, after being through your ordeal. You're Geoffrey's son then? Yes, he would have done the same thing if he had been in your shoes. Boys will be boys, I suppose. Now, then, we'll have to find a way to get you back to where you belong without Abraham interfering. That's going to be difficult, especially once that he finds out what has happened to his spy." It was clear that although Sir John looked like a dotty old man, his brain was as sharp as a tack.

"I will need to try and get inside of his mind, which may or may not work, bouncing from time to time like he is want to do."

"You can do that?" Nick asked. Sir James reached over and patted his hand.

"Sometimes. This isn't an exact science, you know."

"But how do you do it, go inside other people's minds, I mean?"

"I'm afraid that I don't know. It's something that I've always been able to do and something that I've always had to hide from most other people. I don't use witchcraft, I don't worship any devils or demons, I don't consult any cards, dice, dead animals, spirits, ghosts, talk to trees, or do anything else that would be illegal; I'm simply able to read the thoughts of others, if they're strong enough. I'm afraid that I don't have the mechanics worked out just yet. Do you mean to tell me that no one has figured it out in your time either?"

The boys shook their heads and Sir James sighed. "I had such hope for the future, too. Ah, well, it's been working well for me so far."

"Excuse me, but how do you know about the amulets?" Tommy wanted to know.

"My many-greats grandfather was on the Crusade with Sir Edward's. My grandfather knew that he brought them back, the only soul he told, actually, and the story was passed down through the generations. Where they originated from, I'm afraid I don't know. They left that part out."

"Our families have been friends for over four hundred years," Sir Edward added.

"Edward came to me when he and you father began using them. He knew that I would understand. I was intrigued and, as someone who believes in such things, I was eager to hear all about their travels. I'm very sorry that Geoffrey has vanished, though. If it helps, I believe that he's still alive, though," he said, patting Tommy's arm. "I can *feel* that he is alive, but I can't get into his mind. Don't worry, though. Now that I know you're looking for him, I'll try harder. Maybe I can get a little bit of information."

Tommy's heart leaped in his chest at the thought of his father still being alive. "What about Abraham?"

"I'll try him first, since he's the danger right now. I'll need some quiet, though."

Sir James closed his eyes and scrunched up his brow. Tommy wasn't sure what to expect. It just looked like the old man was thinking hard rather than trying to read someone's mind. His expression didn't do much for his pumpkin-like appearance.

He stayed like that for almost ten minutes before letting out a big breath and looking around the table at them. He blinked, once, twice, three times and then said, "He's strong, very strong. I feel rage, but he won't let me in to actually read. I don't want to poke about too much; he may be able to tell what we're doing here and where we are. I don't know how much magic he has himself."

"I'll put you up for the night, but I suggest that you find somewhere else to go in the morning, not that I don't enjoy your company! I don't believe that you'll stay hidden for long, though, even in a city such as this. Again, not that I don't enjoy having visitors." He smiled that toothless smile at them again and stood up.

"My cook shall make us something to break our fast. After I rest a bit, I'll try your father, Thomas. Reading is difficult work and I'm not as young as I once was."

322

Breakfast was delicious. Fried ham, gravy, and bread were served by Sir James's cook, a woman that was more ancient-looking than him. Afterward, Sir James announced that he was going to rest and Sir Edward requested that they be shown to their beds as well, saying that they could all use a rest after riding all night. The three of them were to stay together in one room for safety reasons. If Abraham was faster than they thought, it wouldn't do to have them separated throughout the house, Sir James explained.

Tommy didn't think that he would be able to sleep after all the excitement, but the beds were soft and before he knew it, he was snoring away with Nick and Sir Edward.

After a short, but refreshing, sleep, they awoke to the sound of thunder outside the window. It was the first time that it had rained since they arrived and Sir Edward told them that this was normal for England. "Those sunny skies have been unnatural for us. We are more used to the rain."

For the rest of the afternoon, they listened to the sound of the rain and worked on their Latin lessons while Sir James slept and the air turned cold. The ancient woman that worked for Sir James, Joan, came in and built up the fire a number of times, announcing that she would serve a full dinner when the master awoke, placing before them some cheese and bread to chase off their hunger pangs.

When the sky began to darken, they finally heard Sir James's footsteps coming down the stone staircase.

"Ah, my friends, there you are!" he exclaimed. "I apologize for keeping you waiting for so long. Readings take a lot from me these days. I'll call Joan for dinner and then after, we'll try to find your father, eh, young Thomas? In the meantime, let me show you the rest of the house. I'm very proud if it. We've had to rebuild in some spots, but parts of it date back to the time of Henry II and Queen Eleanor."

"How long ago was that?" Nick wanted to know.

"It was about the time that those blasted stones were brought back, in the late 1100's."

"London has been around that long?"

"London has been around since the Romans built it, more than one thousand years ago. It has endured countless hardships, but is still standing and still changing. I expect that it looks very different in your time." He clapped his hands for Joan and she appeared at the door, nodding to show that she understood it was time for dinner.

"It does look different, but many of the old buildings are still there," Sir Edward told him. "The Tower, for instance, is still there, and Westminster Abbey."

The old man's eyes gleamed. "And does it still hold prisoners?"

"No, not for many years, I'm afraid. People from all over the world flock to see it now, especially to hear nonsense, like ghost stories of King Henry's wives. Many items survive from this time and are housed in the palaces themselves or in museums. Stories from this time have become quite romantic."

"I should like to hear some one day when we're in different circumstances." Joan stood in the doorway.

"If you please, sirs, dinner is ready." The quickness of her preparing dinner made Tommy think that this was not the first time Sir James had slept the afternoon away. They filed into the dining room where there was a wonderful meal waiting for them. They all ate and sat without much conversation. The events of the past few days had them all very tired and it was enough for the moment to just eat. Sir James asked them a few questions about themselves, but for the most part, they ate in silence.

At one point during the meal, Tommy thought to himself *I wonder if this guy is really for real. Can he really read minds? Can he really help find my father?*

He was startled when Sir James raised his head from his trencher, looked at him squarely in the eye and said aloud, "I very much hope that I can," before nonchalantly going back to his meal. Tommy shocked, didn't know what to say and Sir Edward laughed at his expression while Nick just looked confused.

"It's a bit unsettling at first, but you get used to it."

Sir James looked up again with a twinkle in his eye. "Just don't think any thoughts that will make me blush." Tommy was the one who blushed at that and hurriedly went back to his dinner, trying to not think of anything at all.

When they were done and Joan had cleared away the small dishes of custard that they had for dessert, Sir James stretched up his arms and gave a great yawn.

"I know that you are all anxious to move on to the next part of the evening, so let's get to it, shall we?" He led them into the small parlor where they had spent the afternoon. The fire was roaring now, attempting to fight off the dampness from the rain.   Sir James sat down and motioned that they should sit as well. Then he closed his eyes and scrunched up his brow again. Tommy and Nick had to fight the urge to giggle at his appearance. He looked like an old monkey.

After a few moments, accompanied by some crazy eyebrow movements, Sir James opened his eyes and looked at them. After a moment, he began to speak.

"Your father is alive, but very difficult to get in touch with. The fact that I was able to reach him at all means only that he is in this time, at least. Although you have the power of time travel, my ability does not and can only enter the mind of someone who is living at this present time. He may have even been able to build up defenses in his mind, like Abraham has, to keep people like me from getting inside."

"So you know where he is?" Tommy asked eagerly.

Sir James shook his head. "Alas, I cannot know where they are unless they are thinking it. What I did get from him is worry, lots of worry." He shook his head full of white hair. "I'm sorry that I

327

couldn't find out more for you. I can try again tomorrow if you'd like."

Sir Edward nodded. "Maybe once more before we leave."

"Where are you going next?" Sir James asked him.

"I'm not sure yet. There are a couple of possibilities, but I haven't made a final decision. I need to choose a place where Abraham won't think to look for us. That's going to be difficult, seeing as how I don't know who's working for him. How long has your groom been with you?" he joked.

Sir James laughed. "I think you can trust Gregory. His father worked for me before he did and I read his mind quite frequently. I know that he's honest and a bit of a simpleton, but he has a way with horses and he's fiercely loyal to me. No need to fear there. Now, I suggest that we all retire for the night. You must still be feeling the effects of your long ride last night and you'll want to be awakened early, I'm sure. Joan will provide a handsome breakfast for us."

They said goodnight and went to their room. Tommy was sleepy but happy, too. His father was alive! He was in this time! Of course, the world was still a big place, even in 1540, but still, he was here somewhere. As he found a comfortable position under the heavy quilt, he listened to the rain, still pounding on the roof, and drifted off to a place of no dreams.

***

Crash! The loud noise pulled Tommy back from a dreamless sleep and into the blackness of the room. It was still night and there were no lights shining anywhere except for the last few remaining coals in the fireplace. He looked around frantically, willing his eyes to become accustomed to the darkness and jabbed Nick, who was lightly snoring beside him, with his elbow to wake him up. As Nick mumbled and sat up, Tommy's ears strained to hear any more movement and he grabbed Nick's shoulder, whispering *"Shhh...".*

As his eyes adjusted to the dark room, he looked over to the bed where Sir Edward was sleeping. He was there, a big lump covered with another heavy quilt. In the darkness, he could not detect anything wrong and after not hearing anything else, decided that it had been his imagination. Nick hadn't woken up all the way and was now lying back down, mumbling something about horses. Tommy sighed. They had all had a long week and he was a bit jumpy. It was to be expected.

He listened for a few more moments, waiting to hear any more noises, but it was silent. He lay back down on the feather pillow and closed his eyes, hoping for sleep to come back to him as quickly as it did before.

Just as he was trying to go through the alphabet backward, he heard another sound; a long, low, moan coming from the hallway. That was definitely *not* his imagination. At first, he thought of all of the ghost stories about castles and old buildings. This as definitely an old building but Sir James hadn't said anything about a ghost and he would be the type to mention such a thing. Tommy hadn't really believed in ghosts before, but he hadn't believed in magical amulets or the power to read minds, either.

He heard the moan again and his heart began to race. There was definitely something wrong. He pushed the heavy quilt aside and carefully walked over to Sir Edward's bed. He began shaking his shoulder.

"Sir Edward!" he whispered. "Wake up! There's something wrong outside!"

Unlike Nick, Sir Edward was up like a shot. All those years of looking over his shoulder made him a light sleeper.

"What is it?" he whispered.

"I heard a moan in the hallway, twice, and before that a crash woke me up. I thought I was dreaming at first."

"Okay, okay." Sir Edward was up and out of his bed as silent as a cat. He quickly pulled on his trousers and grabbed the large sword that was lying right beside the bed. Tommy was glad that he hadn't gone to that side to wake him up. Stepping on a sword would not have been a good thing.

Sir Edward moved to the door and as quietly as possible, lifted the iron latch. There was a small *click* and then he slowly swung the door open, just a bit. Tommy's heart was beating so fast that he was sure he could hear it. After a moment, Sir Edward beckoned to Tommy, who could now see everything.

Sir Edward whispered close to Tommy's ear, "Sir James is lying on the floor. He was the one who was moaning. I want you to go to him and see if he's sick or if it's something else. I'm going to watch your back, just in case. This could be a trick."

Tommy nodded and slowly crept forward through the door, Sir Edward shadowing him closely. He walked over to where Sir

James lay on the ground and knelt beside him. He touched the old man's shoulder.

"Sir James," he whispered. "Sir James," he said, just a little bit louder and giving him a gentle shake.

Sir James moaned again and turned his head toward Tommy. Even in the grey darkness, Tommy could see that his head was bleeding from a gash on his forehead.

"Sir James, what happened? How did you get here?"

"Thomas," he gasped, "Thomas, you must flee! Abraham…"

Just then a shout rang out from the staircase followed by more behind it. Sir Edward sprang in front of Thomas and Sir James, brandishing his sword and adding his own shout into the mix.

In the darkness of the hallway it was difficult for Tommy to see but he thought that he could make out three hulking shapes; more of Abraham's goons, no doubt. His heart thumped wildly as he looked for somewhere to run. He sprang to his feet as the clang of Sir Edward's sword met with one of the goons sounded into his ear. Disoriented, he almost fell over when Sir Edward's hand yanked him closer.

"Out the window", he hissed into Tommy's ear. "You and Nick. NOW!"

Tommy scrambled into the room where they had all been sleeping peacefully just moments before. He slammed the door behind him and latched it, hoping that the goons wouldn't try to follow him in. Nick, who was definitely awake now, jumped out of bed.

"What is it, Tommy?" he asked anxiously.

"C'mon! Abraham is back, well, at least his goons are. They attacked Sir James and Sir Edward is holding them off. He told us to go out the window."

"Do you have the amulet?"

"Around my neck. Let's go!"

"But what about Sir Edward?" Nick jumped as the sounds of shouting and clanging came through the heavy oak door.

"He said to go! He can take care of himself! He knows that we have to protect the amulet. We'll think of something on the way out."

They ran over to the window, still eyeing the bedroom door, expecting it to crash open at any moment.

The ground was a long way down, but there was a strategically placed pile of straw underneath, as if someone knew it would be needed.

"Do you think Sir James knew that we'd be doing this?" Nick wanted to know.

Tommy shrugged. "I don't know, but I wouldn't doubt it. Now *jump*!" Tommy swung his legs over the windowsill and willed himself to just do it. He felt himself free-fall, for too long, he thought, and he started kicking his legs in the air, the ground rushing up to meet him. For a moment, he thought that he was going to miss the straw but then, *WHUMP*, he landed in the musty-smelling pile. It wasn't pleasant, but at least he didn't hurt himself. He scrambled out and called to Nick, "C'mon! Jump!"

He saw Nick's legs go over the edge of the window and then heard him scream as he threw himself out. Nick almost did miss the straw; it was clear he hadn't been aiming, and Tommy saw why. As Nick did manage to safely hit the pile, a face appeared in the window and it wasn't Sir Edward.

"Come back here!" the goon yelled after them .Tommy just ran to the first place he could think of: the barn. He could hear Nick panting behind him as they scuttled in to where the sleepy horses barely gave them a second glance. They ducked through the granary door and into the tack room where they ran into Gregory, Sir James's groom, who was still up and polishing their saddles beside a small fire. He looked up in shock as the boys ran in, wild-eyed and panting.

"What is it, lads?"

"Sir James... Sir Edward... under attack!" was all that Tommy could stammer out. Gregory leapt up and pulled a sword out from under a pile of straw.

"Where?" he demanded.

"In the house. They attacked us while we were asleep. Nick and I went out the window."

Gregory took off at a run through the dark stable and shouted over his shoulder, "Come on!"

Tommy looked at Nick and they knew what they had to do. Sir Edward was fighting for them up in that house. He had saved their lives and taken care of them the entire time they had been here. Now it was their turn to help him. How to do it, they didn't know, but they couldn't let him suffer up there alone.

They ran after Gregory into the London night. The city, amazingly, was quiet at this time. Even the beggars seemed to have retired for the night, unaware of the commotion going on at Sir John's house. Their footsteps echoed on the cobblestones as they came up upon the house. Tommy put on a burst of speed, trying to catch up to Gregory. As he went around the corner, he ran smack into a man on the other side. The impact knocked Tommy to the ground and he jumped back up, apologizing profusely to the stranger he had almost run over in his excitement.

"I'm so sorry, Sir. I'm in a hurry and…" Tommy stopped as the stranger suddenly gripped his shoulders tightly and looked into his face. With a leap of fear, Tommy thought for sure that he had been captured by one of Abraham's goons who had come looking for them.

This is it, he thought, *it's all over now. I'll never see my mother again.* He called out, "Nick! RUN!" as he struggled to break free and raised his eyes to look at the stranger who was surely going to kill him. Strangely enough, the stranger held him fast and just looked at him with an odd expression. After a long moment he whispered, "Tommy?"

Confused, Tommy stopped trying to get away and looked at the man more carefully. He wore a hood that almost covered his face, but Tommy could see that his cheeks had dimples, just like his. The man released the grip he had on Tommy's shoulders and slowly pushed the hood back from his face.

In the light from the almost-full moon, the man's eyes, as blue as Tommy's, looked back at his own. His brown hair, pulled back in a leather thong, looked the same as the picture in Tommy's house. The man's eyes filled up with tears and the realization of who this was began to wash over Tommy. For the first time in his life, he spoke the word that had been aching to come out for so long.

"Dad?" he whispered unbelievingly and his father pulled him to his chest for the hug he had always been waiting for.

Chapter Thirteen

Tommy's mind swirled with so many feelings that he felt dizzy. Was this really his father? Could this really be happening? He clung to the man for a moment, but then remembered the reason that he was out in the darkness to begin with. He pushed his father away.

"Sir Edward is in the house with Abraham and his creeps! We have to help him!"

Geoffrey Andrews smiled and drew out a sword from inside of his cloak. "That's my boy! Let's go!"

338

Tommy led the way, catching up with and passing Nick, who only had a few seconds head start.

"Who is that?" Nick asked breathlessly as they pounded through the first floor, Geoffrey right behind them.

"My dad", Tommy managed to tell him over his shoulder before they began running back up the stairs, not knowing what might still be up there. Nick stopped in his tracks.

"Your dad?" he asked, puzzled.

Tommy called out, "Yes, I'll explain later. Come on!" He ran as fast as he could to get into the house and stopped at the foot of the stairs, listening. Was Sir Edward dead? Was Abraham there? How in the world were they going to fight off those goons? He was glad that his dad had a sword but had no idea how to help.

There were sounds of commotion still coming from the bedroom. Just as he was about to charge inside, he felt a hand on his chest. Geoffrey was suddenly beside him.

"Wait here, son, let me see what I can do first." Tommy watched his father size up the situation through the door. By now, the pale dawn light had taken the edge off the darkness and they were able to see a little more clearly than they had before. Tommy saw Sir Edward and Gregory inside, exchanging blows with the two remaining goons. There was a dark shape lying on the floor; apparently Gregory had been able to surprise one of them. If Tommy and Nick had ever had any doubts about Gregory's loyalty, they had long disappeared. The stable hand was defending himself with everything that he had, trading blows and swipes with his attacker as well as Sir Edward was. Although Gregory and Sir Edward were excellent swordsmen, the goons were larger and their sheer size was beginning to win out.

Without hesitation, Geoffrey threw himself into the mix, surprising the creep who was fighting Sir Edward, who looked back at him in surprise.

"It's about damn time!" he shouted and grinned at Geoffrey, who grinned back through the clanging steel.

"Better late than never!" Geoffrey shot back as, together, they began to overpower the goon. As Tommy watched, Geoffrey's sword managed to sneak in and strike the goon in the chest while Sir Edward warded off a blow. The goon staggered, realizing what had happened, and then fell to the floor, clutching his chest and making funny choking sounds.

Sir Edward and Geoffrey then turned their attention to helping Gregory. He had been doing well but the goon was beginning to back him against a wall. Now, with all three of them brandishing their swords, the only remaining henchman realized that he wouldn't last long. He paused, looked at the three of them, dropped his sword and then turned to run down the stairs.

"Stop him!" Sir Edward called out, "He's going to Abraham!"

Nick very quickly stuck out his foot, just as the goon was running through the door. It caught him in the shin and with a very surprised, "Oof!" he fell to the floor with a crash, narrowly missing Sir John, who was still lying there. Without thinking, Tommy and Nick jumped on top of his back while Geoffrey and Sir Edward secured him. They yanked him to his feet and began to hustle him downstairs while Gregory began to attend to Sir James.

"Master! Master!" Gregory softly called to the old seer as he moaned and moved his head. He was alive, at least. Nick and Tommy scrambled to his side to see if they could help. They could hear the protests of the goon as Sir Edward and Geoffrey maneuvered him down the staircase.

Sir James opened his eyes with another small moan and looked at the faces around them.

"Gregory? Where am I?"

"In your hallway, my lord. You were knocked unconscious."

"Where is my attacker?"

"There are two dead in the bedroom, my lord, and Sir Edward has taken the other downstairs. We had another savior come in from the street…"

"It was my dad!" Tommy blurted out before he could stop himself. Sir James slowly turned his head and fixed his watery eyes on Tommy's face. He smiled at the boy.

"So he came, did he? I knew that his life force was strong, that he couldn't stay away. I believe that he could sense you were here, young Thomas. You've met him at last? And where is he now?"

"Downstairs, helping Sir Edward. One of the attackers is still alive."

"Then why are you up here with a sick old man? I have Gregory and Nick to help me; go and see your father, boy!" Gregory nodded at him, a small smile touching the corners of his grimy

342

mouth. Tommy noticed that he had sustained a few wounds from the fight himself. How lucky Sir James was to have someone so loyal! Tommy, his heart jumping for joy for the first time since they came, leapt up and raced down the stairs.

He found Sir Edward and his father in Sir James's kitchen, the goon tied to one of the heaviest chairs that they could find. He came in quietly, but his father looked up and noticed him immediately. He crossed the room in three long strides and had enfolded Tommy in his arms. Tommy hugged his father tightly and breathed in his scent; a mixture of leather, horses, wool, and some kind of soap. His father let go after a long moment and took Tommy's chin into his hand, studying his face.

"You look a lot like your mother, you know", he said to him.

"She says that I look like you", Tommy said.

"Well, you have my eyes, that's for sure, and my chin. Your hair is dark like hers, though." Geoffrey shook his head. "I've done badly by you and your mother, Thomas. You must believe that all I've ever wanted to do is to protect you and that I wanted to be a normal father for you. I never expected for all of this to happen." He swept his hand around the room, gesturing at the goon, who was watching all of this with interest.

"You'll never stop Abraham!" He shouted out from his chair, struggling against his bindings. "He'll have those stones yet! You can't hide from him, Andrews; he's been after you for a long time. That boy will be your undoing." His head slumped to his chest as Sir Edward, standing behind him, delivered a smart blow to his scalp with the handle of his sword.

"That should shut him up for a while. I don't know how long you two will have to catch up, but you should have a little time to yourselves before we have to move again. I'll go check on Sir James." He tousled Tommy's hair as he went past, giving him a little smile that was hard to read. All of a sudden, after all the years apart, Tommy and his father were alone together for the first time, if you didn't count the unconscious goon in the chair across the room. It was a bit of an awkward moment. Tommy had spent all of his energy in the past few weeks trying to get to this moment. He hadn't thought of what he would actually do if it happened.

Geoffrey, feeling the awkwardness, suggested that they sit down at the table.

"Where does Sir James keep his ale? I do believe that I could use some right now. Ah, here it is." Geoffrey poured himself a tankard and sat down. He took a long drink and set his mug down on the table with a thud. He looked at Tommy straight in the eyes and, with an accent that sounded very much like Sir Edward's, said, "You must hate me for being absent most of your life."

Tommy shook his head. "I don't hate you. I never have. I've only wanted to know why you weren't there with us."

Geoffrey sighed, a sad sigh. "It's a very long story. You see…" But Tommy interrupted him, laying a hand on his arm.

"Sir Edward already told me. He told Nick and me everything a few days ago, from the very beginning. I understand what happened. I heard all about Abraham. Really, I get it."

Geoffrey wrinkled his brow. "So, Edward told you everything, did he? Have you known him long?"

Tommy nodded. "He's my social studies teacher. I mean, he *was* my social studies teacher. I don't know what he is now. He rescued us from King Henry and we've been trying to find you ever since."

Geoffrey's eyes widened in surprise. "He rescued you from King Henry? Is Henry after you?"

"No, no, nothing like that. He talked the king into letting him raise us for a while. The king thinks that we've lost our memories and he felt sorry for us. I feel kind of bad about lying, but it kept us alive"

"Well, I suppose that's not the worst thing you could have done. If Henry found out what you had really done, you may be hanging from the gallows right now. These are very dangerous times to have anything to do with magic."

"I know. Sir Edward told us."

"So, you know where I came from, and how I met your mother. You've heard all of that?"

"Yes. He told us while we were staying at his house."

"You stayed at Edward's house? How is his father? Does your mother know that you're here?"

"Not very well and she does now, although we left without telling her", he admitted sheepishly.

Geoffrey tried to look stern, but Tommy could see a little admiration in his eyes. "By the stars, I never would have guessed that you'd get this far. Not that you don't have what it takes, but Henry could have had you killed on the spot! Abraham must be slowing down, too. He used to do all of his work himself instead of sending underlings." His eyes suddenly filled with tears as he looked at Tommy. He reached across the table and grabbed his hands with his own.

"I swear to you, I will never disappear from your life again except through death. I can't lose you again. All these years, I've been tortured with the thought of what might be happening to you and your mother. Thank God that Edward was able to give me details now and then. I've been wracked with guilt for leaving the both of you and for dragging him into it. I have so much to make up for! There's so much lost time! Never again, I swear it." He kissed Tommy's hand and pressed it to his chest, tears falling from his eyes as he smiled at him. Tommy felt a little uncomfortable but at the same time he was just so glad to see his father!

"My son. The thought of you has kept me alive. How does your mother? Is she well?"

Slightly scared from all of the emotions that he was feeling, Tommy shook his head yes. "She's fine. She's still a teacher. We still live where we did before. Sir Edward said that he had been keeping an eye on us all the time."

"And Abraham has never bothered you?"

"No. I don't think that he knew my mother had the other amulet."

Geoffrey smiled. "That's good. Our plan worked, then. Of course, now, we will have to come up with another one, I'm sure." A flicker of concern shadowed his face. "Your mother... has she ever... remarried?"

"No. She's never even been out on a date, but...", Tommy stopped himself. He did not want to tell his father that he thought Sir Edward liked his mother in that way. That would be too cruel. His father heard the slip.

"Hmm", he said, knowingly. "Was it Edward? Are they close?"

Tommy didn't say anything for a moment. He could feel his father's sadness. He burst out, "It wasn't like that! They never went out or anything! He came over for dinner because I invited him. He never tried to be her boyfriend and she never tried to be his girlfriend. She never cheated on you and neither did he."

Geoffrey gave a long sigh. "I suppose it's only natural for them to develop feelings for each other, they went through some very difficult times. I wasn't much of a husband, was I? Well, let's just see how things go, shall we?"

Although Tommy was relieved that his father wasn't angry, he knew that the news was upsetting to him. Why did he have to slip up that way? He hoped that he hadn't messed things up between his dad and Sir Edward.

He could hear footsteps coming down the stairs and knew that they were making a lot of noise on purpose. Sir Edward, Nick, and Gregory assembled in the kitchen and another awkward moment happened until Geoffrey went over to Edward and gave him a huge hug, nearly lifting him off the ground. Sir Edward returned the hug, slapping Geoffrey's back, the two suddenly smiling at each other and laughing.

"Welcome home, brother!" he said. "I suppose you've had the chance to begin to know your son?"

"Aye", Geoffrey said, "we've had a bit of catch-up. I still have a lot to make up for, though."

"Before we start atoning for past sins or planning family reunions, let's see what we can find out about Abraham. When his men don't come back, he may come looking for them. We need to be ready for him and whatever else he may bring with him or we need to be gone. Personally, I would like to be gone rather than to stay and fight. There's been enough bloodshed here tonight." They all nodded at this and with a sinking feeling,   Tommy suddenly remembered those two bodies upstairs. He had seen his father kill the second man. The reality of what had happened hit him and he felt sick to his stomach. He had seen someone die. He knew that his father and Sir Edward had to do what they did, that the other men were trying to kill them first, but it didn't make him feel much better. Would Abraham send more men after them now? Who else would die?

As if he had heard them talking about him, the goon in the chair groaned. Relieved, Tommy could see that although he had a lump on his head from the butt of Sir Edward's sword, he looked like he was going to be okay. When they heard the groan, Geoffrey and Sir Edward walked back over to the chair. Sir Edward patted his face a bit roughly, but enough to try and bring him round.

"Hey, there! Time to wake up now, sleeping beauty!" Sir Edward said loudly. Tommy grinned a little. This guy was definitely not a beauty. His gorilla face was heavy with fat and had several scars. The goon groaned some more and opened his eyes, squinting at the first rays of sunlight that were beginning to filter in through the window.

"Ah, there you are! We need some information from you, my friend." The goon shook his head.

"I won't say a word." He looked like a very large, defiant, child, pouting after a tantrum.

"Oh, but I think you will." Sir Edward got right down in front of his face. "Your friends are dead. There's no one here to help you. Abraham hasn't shown his face here at all. You have nothing going for you and the sooner you spill your secrets, the easier it will be." Sir Edward sounded menacing in the same way that he had been when talking to John. He hoped that the goon wouldn't be hurt any more that he already was. All of the men looked as if they'd been through a battle, with scrapes, cuts, and angry bruises beginning to show up on them.

The goon, however, didn't seem to be intimidated by Sir Edward and shook his head fiercely.

"I won't say a word, I swear to you! If Abraham finds out that I've told you anything, I'll die a horrible death and he'll go after my family. I've seen it happen with my own eyes to others who have betrayed him. I won't have my family suffer that! You may as well run me through with your sword now." He closed his eyes as if he thought they would kill him right then and there but neither Sir Edward nor Geoffrey pulled their swords.

"We're not going to kill you, you great oaf! What good would you be to us dead? We need your information and we're prepared to wait until Judgment Day to get it! This has gone on long enough!"

"Indeed, it has", said a voice from the still-dark staircase. Sir James was slowly walking toward them, supported by Gregory, who was almost carrying him. Sir James looked dreadful. As he came into the light, Tommy could see a large lump on his head and his face was drained of color. Still, he wobbled into the room, Gregory shaking his head disapprovingly.

"I told him to stay in bed, my lords, but there was no reasoning with him! Said he had to talk to you and it was urgent."

"Thank you, Gregory. Sir James, he's right, you shouldn't be up! That's quite a goose egg on your head, sir." Geoffrey hurried over to help Gregory lower Sir James into a comfortable chair and to wrap a shawl around his frail shoulders.

"Oh, bosh, I can do as I please. Quit treating me like an old lady! I came down to be of some service. This man's mind is calling out to me. I don't believe that he wants this chase to go on any more, either. His mind is racing!" At Sir James's announcement, the goon went pale and began to shake.

"No! No, my lord! You are mistaken! I've heard about you! I don't want you to know anything!" All of his former bravado was gone now.

Sir James looked at him fully in the face. "I know that you don't want me to, but I must. You aren't giving me the information as much as I am taking it from you. Abraham can't fault you for that now, can he? You may as well relax. This won't hurt a bit. Gregory, please go and wake Joan. I may need some tea after this, perhaps something stronger with it. It's been a very long night."

"Yes, my lord." Geoffrey bowed slightly and went to wake the ancient housekeeper who had remarkably slept through the night's events.

Sir James closed his eyes and got the same dreamy, monkey-like, look on his face that he had had the day before. The room was absolutely silent as he probed the goon's mind. The goon, it seemed, was having trouble relaxing. He was still shaking and Tommy began to feel the tiniest bit sorry for him. The thought of failing Abraham really had him scared.

The reading didn't last as long this time. It ended just minutes later when Joan came shuffling in, clearly perplexed at seeing her kitchen full of men at this early hour. At her footsteps, Sir James opened his eyes.

"Ah, there you are, my dear. Could you put the kettle on right away?"

"Yes, sir." While Joan went bustling about, the rest of them looked expectantly at Sir John.

"Well?" Sir Edward finally said.

"Well", said Sir James, "well, indeed. This young man has a very easy mind to penetrate. You've only been with Abraham for a year, I see, young Walter."

The goon, Walter now, moaned with fright. He had clearly been hoping that Sir James was not the mystic he claimed to be, but this was not the case. It seemed that Sir James could see right through him. Sir John looked at the others.

"Abraham has retreated a bit. He wasn't expecting full success on this attempt. It was more of a training session for the three of them, to prove themselves. Obviously, they're not cut out to be his best men, and at least two of them never will be." He glanced over his shoulder up at the still-dark stairway where two of Abraham's men lie dead in the bedroom. He closed his eyes again.

"I don't think we'll have to worry about our friend, here", he said a moment later, opening his eyes. With his withered old arm, he lifted Walter's chin.

"Listen to me. We're not going to give you back to Abraham or put your family in harm's way. We're going to give you some money and set you free." He nodded silently at Joan and she ambled off, seemingly understanding exactly what he wanted her to do. Sir

James looked back at Walter, who was staring at him, open-mouthed in shock. "Abraham will surely kill you if he finds you here because you failed him miserably. You need to go, as far as you can from this place. Find some work on a farm or in a town, preferably not in England. Somewhere Italy or even Russia would be good. He won't hunt you down. You're not that important to him. You're young enough to labor for someone and maybe even have a normal life one day."

As Sir James talked, Walter's face brightened up a bit. He asked Sir James, "Do you really think I could get away from him?" Sir James nodded.

"Only if you leave immediately. He's sure to be here at some point, once he's decided what to do and it would definitely be best if you were gone."

"But what about my family? Won't he go after them?"

Sir James shook his head again. "Not if you don't go back to them. What's the point in hurting your family if you're not there to see it? Go far away, into the Continent and disappear for a long while. Who knows? Perhaps in a few years this whole nasty business will be over and you can live with them peaceably again. Now, untie him, if you would please, gentlemen."

Reluctantly, Geoffrey and Sir Edward cut the ropes loose that had been binding Walter's hands and feet to the chair. Walter rubbed his wrists and ankles silently, apparently not knowing what to say at this turn of events. The room was filled with an awkward silence. No one seemed to know what to do next when Walter suddenly spoke.

"The other stone. I know where he keeps it", he said in a low voice. Tommy's eyes widened in surprise. Sir James leaned in closer to Walter.

"Yes?" he asked.

Walter sighed. "I'm telling you because you spared my life, because you're helping me to escape. One good turn deserves another, right?" He looked at Sir James squarely in the eyes. "I'm not all bad. My father would be so ashamed if he knew that I had been dabbling in dark magic. Maybe after a while I can go back and see him someday. He raised me to be honest in all that I did, not to use magical stones to hurt people."

"So you don't have an amulet yourself?" Tommy blurted out.

Walter shook his head. "Abraham uses his to send us where we need to go. He doesn't trust us to hold onto one ourselves. There's only the one more." Clearly, this was a shock to everyone in the room. They had been by led to believe, by Abraham, of course, that he had many amulets and ways of traveling. Walter was giving up quite a lot of information, indeed. They stayed quiet, however, so as not to alarm Walter and to keep him talking. It was difficult.

"How does he send you?" Sir James asked.

"We all touch the amulet, Abraham tells it where we need to go, and as we begin to vanish, he snatches it back and steps away. That's how he sometimes gets rid of people who he thinks are useless. He puts them in different places in time where they don't have much chance of surviving. That's probably what he'll do to me if he catches me here", he added glumly.

"But he won't catch you here!" exclaimed Tommy, warming to him. "You're going to get away!"

"Yes, but first", Sir James stepped in, "would you be so kind as to tell us where Abraham keeps his amulet?"

"Oh, of course", said Walter. "It's in a small leather pouch attached to his belt with a chain. He always keeps it there. He even sleeps with it attached, just in case. It's the one thing that he never lets out of his possession. It will be most difficult to take it from him."

"Well then, my friend", Sir Edward stepped in. "You had better be on your way. You've done us a great service and we don't want you to suffer any more for it." He extended his hand to help Walter up. The now ex-goon looked at it for a moment, the grasped Sir Edward's strong hand with a small smile. They all paused for a moment, wondering if he really was going to do as he said, but they didn't wonder for long. He simply stood up, dusted off his clothes and began to walk to the door.

"Wait!" said Sir James. At that moment, Joan came bustling through the entryway, a small bulging purse in her hands. As she gave the purse to Walter, Sir James clapped a hand on his back and said, "Daylight is just upon us. You have the entire day to travel. You can probably catch a ship up the Thames right now and out to the sea. Go, and I wish you well."

Walter's eyes filled up with tears of gratitude and he couldn't speak. He nodded briskly at them all and squeezed his huge frame out the door and into the early London morning. They were all silent for a moment.

"Man, oh man", Nick mumbled from his place in the corner. "This has been one crazy night."

"Yes, indeed", Sir James answered him. "Joan, shall we have a bit of something to break our fast?" Joan seemed to have been thinking way ahead of the rest of them, the dead men in the room above hadn't deterred her from preparing a large breakfast for them all. She smiled her kindly smile and called them in to eat. Geoffrey put his arm around Tommy and together they walked into the dining room.

As they sat around the oaken table eating bread, cheese, and fried ham, they were mostly silent. After he had finished eating, Geoffrey sighed, folded his hands on his stomach, and leaned his head back on the chair. "What a day this has been for us all", he said, looking at Tommy. Tommy smiled at him. The enormity of actually, no, *literally*, running into his father in London while in the middle of the sixteenth century still hadn't sunk in. There hadn't been much time to think about it, with all the goons attacking them. Sir Edward had a suggestion.

"There's time for us to all catch up with you later, Geoffrey. Sir James thinks that Abraham isn't coming straight here just yet. Why don't you and Thomas go for a walk about London and get to know each other a bit? Nick can stay here with us and help Gregory with the barn. There's also the small matter of the bodies upstairs. We'll have to fetch the lord mayor for that, don't you think, Sir James?"

Sir James nodded his head. "He's an old friend of mine. The Lord Mayor is aware of my peculiar talents and has called on me from time to time. This will not be a problem."

"What are you going to tell him?" Nick asked.

"Simply the truth", Sir James replied, looking surprised. "We were awakened in the middle of the night by those two ruffians. Thank Heaven that Sir Edward and Gregory were there to save us all. Geoffrey, I'm well aware of your contribution, but let's keep you a secret for now, shall we?"

Geoffrey grinned. "As always, Sir James, I bow to your wishes. Now, I shall take my son and get to know him a bit better while you clear that up. We'll be back for dinner and then we'll need to make a plan of where we are to go next." He put his arm around Tommy's shoulders. "Come along, son." Tommy grinned, but that grin faded a little when he saw Nick's face, smiling sadly at him. Nick was probably thinking about his own father, who was constantly on his cell phone, not paying a bit of attention to him. Tommy felt bad. He made up his mind to try and include Nick more often, especially if Geoffrey ended up being able to come home with him. For now, though, he would just concentrate on getting to know his dad.

■■■

Chapter Fourteen

London was just coming to life as Tommy and Geoffrey stepped out into the pale dawn. The walls of Sir James's house were so thick that they shut out most of the noise but now, Tommy could hear the sounds of the city quite clearly: the roosters crowing, dogs barking, and the lowing of cows waiting to be milked. Peddlers were wheeling out their carts, calling out to them to sample all that they had to offer. Warm milk, roasted nuts, eggs, all of these were available to anyone with a coin or two.

They seemed to walk aimlessly, without speaking, through the crowds of people that were getting bigger as the sun rose slowly into the sky, warming the chilly air just a bit. As they wound their way through the endless streets and alleyways, Tommy took it all in. The crowds reminded him of the time that he had gone to Comerica Park with his class to watch a Detroit Tigers game. There were people everywhere in downtown Detroit, all having somewhere important to be, just like now.

Tommy followed his father's lead through the confusing city streets and occasionally snuck a glance at him, studying his face. His dad was handsome, just like in the picture at home. His long brown hair now had wide streaks of grey and his face had some lines and creases beginning to form. He really didn't know what to say to him. He hoped that his dad would ask him a question, talk about the weather, anything to make conversation as they walked swiftly on, but Geoffrey didn't say a word.

At last, they came to a quiet doorway and Geoffrey led the way inside to a small tavern. At this early hour, there was only one other person inside besides the owner behind the counter and they had no trouble finding a table in the corner for privacy.

The owner came over to take their order.

"A pint of ale, Michael, and a weak pint for my son." Obviously, his dad had been here before.

The owner's eyes widened. "Your son, Geoffrey? Where've you been hiding him? Coming right up." With a wink and a wide grin, he disappeared behind the counter and brought their drinks a moment later. Tommy was nervous. He took a sip of the bitter weak ale and waited for his father to speak. At last, the silence was broken.

"Well then, Tommy, here we are." Geoffrey smiled at him from across the table and sipped his own ale. "What shall we talk about?" Tommy shrugged, not knowing what to say. Geoffrey gave him a small smile, sighed, and shook his head.

"I'm sorry, son. All of this is my fault. I shouldn't be asking you to talk. I do want to know, however, how it was that you managed to get yourself here. Did your mother finally tell you?"

Tommy shook his head and began to tell the story of how he and Nick had broken into the box, how they had gotten Mr. Barnhart, *Sir Edward*, to tell them about the time period, and how they had finally done it. The time flew by as Tommy, keeping his voice low, spilled everything that had been pent up inside of him for the past several days: meeting Henry VIII, seeing Queen Katherine and knowing that she was going to be beheaded, Mr. Kingston, the Tower of London, the treachery of Sir Edward's groom, John, and their journey to London. It felt good to finally tell him all that had happened. Of all the people in the world, his father would understand.

Geoffrey sat and listened for a long while, fascinated as his son told him the entire tale. His eyes filled with tears as he realized just how much Tommy had missed having him around all of those years and wondering how he could ever make up for it all. When Tommy was finished, exhausted, he reached across the table and covered Tommy's hand with his large, calloused one.

"Tommy, I am so deeply sorry. I must tell you that I never would have left you if I felt that it would be safe to stay. Abraham was after *me*, and as long as he thought that I had the only amulet, you and your mother would be safe. I've missed you horribly over the years and I wanted to come back so many times, but I thought that if I did and Abraham found out, he'd attack you again. I did write your mother a few letters. I left them in Edward's room when I'd pop in every couple of years. That doesn't make anything right, though. I'm so, so sorry. A boy should have his father around." Geoffrey bowed his head.

"It's okay, Dad", he said in a quivery voice, "I know all about what Abraham did. Sir Edward explained the whole thing the first night that we stayed with him. I know that he's crazy and I found the letters that you wrote to Mom. She kept them in the box. That's how we figured out all of the time traveling stuff. We thought it was crazy at first, but Nick thought that it might be right so we tried it. I know that you wanted to keep us safe and I'm not mad at you. I promise!" he added earnestly.

Geoffrey lifted his head and gave Tommy a weak smile. "It does me good to hear you say that. Has Edward looked after you all these years?"

"I guess so", Tommy replied. "I never knew it, but he's taught at that school for a long time and he kept an eye on Mom, too."

A strange look passed over Geoffrey's face. "And how is your mother?" he asked. Tommy felt a little weird. He knew that his mother had been thinking of dating Sir Edward, or Mr. Barnhart, but now that his father was back in the picture, how would that work out, exactly? He decided to not say anything about that.

"She's fine. She teaches third grade and takes really good care of me."

"Did she ever speak about me?"

Tommy nodded. "She didn't give anything away, either. She just said that you were from England, that you didn't have any family left, and that the town that you were born in didn't exist anymore. Oh! She also said that you were a terrible cook."

Geoffrey threw his head back and laughed loudly, breaking the tension. "She would say that! I was a terrible cook. I still am. It was torture trying to learn how to work one of those stoves from your time. I almost set the house on fire, more than once." His face turned sober again. "Have the two of you had enough money over the years? I left her as many coins as I could, you know."

Tommy nodded. "She kept them in the box, too. There were a lot there, so I don't think she ever used them. I promised Nick that he could have one when we got back, for helping me with all of this"

Geoffrey smiled. "That would be just like her. I'll wager that she was saving them for you to use. Now then, tell me about yourself. What do you like to do? How do you spend your time? How long have you and Nick been friends? He seems like a good sort of fellow."

Tommy, relieved to not have to tell his father more about his mother, launched into details about his daily life. He told him about Nick, about school, about how much he couldn't stand Susan Wright and her snobby attitude, about how he couldn't cook, either, and about how much he liked Social Studies and his teacher, Mr. Barnhart, who, of course, turned out to be Sir Edward.

Geoffrey stayed silent while Tommy talked on and on, fixing his eyes upon him intently as though he wanted to drink him in. His hand was still covering Tommy's and every now and then, he gave it a squeeze, as though to reassure himself that Tommy was really here. When Tommy was finished at last, the silence was awkward for a moment.

Geoffrey looked at him quizzically. "What is it, son?" he asked.

Tommy looked down at the table. "Well, I was just wondering what happens now? How are we going to live? How are we going to see each other?"

Geoffrey squeezed his hand again. "I've thought about that in my mind a thousand times since I left. The truth is, until Abraham is defeated, I don't know how this is going to work. As long as he's alive and still has an amulet of his own, he may follow us forever, especially now that he knows you have one yourself. Before we can figure out how to be together, we first have to defeat him. That's something that we'll need Edward for."

Tommy agreed. He knew that Sir Edward had spent the better part of the last twelve years trying to protect him and his mother from Abraham. How hard that must have been for him, always watching, living in fear that they would be taken away to

369

another time, traveling back and forth to see his father when he thought it was safe. It was strange how little he had known about the Social Studies teacher who was now so important to him. There was one more thing that was troubling Tommy.

"Um, Dad?" It still felt funny to use that word.

"Yes?"

"How did you come to be outside of Sir James's house last night?"

Geoffrey smiled. "Once in a while, I can feel Sir James trying to get into my mind. I met him when I was growing up with Edward and was made aware of his talents. I could feel him yesterday; Edward and I saw him quite often while we were growing up and he liked to practice on us. It had been a while since he had tried so I thought that I would go and see him to find out what the matter was. I was actually already in this time, but I was a bit of a distance away, in a small village outside of London. You ran into me right about the time I got to the house. I was going to wait until daylight before I went to see him, but running into you changed matters a bit."

Geoffrey gave Tommy's hand one final squeeze and stood up. "We'd better be getting back now. There are plans to be made and things to do." He stopped and looked down at Tommy, shaking his head. "Your mother has to be worried sick. If it wasn't so risky, I'd take you back there right now. She's going to kill the both of us for this, you know."

Tommy felt that stab of guilt again about his mother. "Yeah, I know", he admitted sheepishly.

"As soon as this whole nasty business is done, we'll head back to your time straightaway, hopefully today. I don't want the poor woman worried any more than she is."

With a nod to the tavern owner, he left some coins on the table and they entered into the maze of busy London streets where they wound their way back to Sir James's stately house. There they found Sir Edward, Nick, and Sir James sitting at the dining room table, deep in conversation. They both looked up as Tommy and Geoffrey entered the room.

Sir James smiled at them. "I trust, young Thomas, that you and your father have been getting to know each other?" he inquired.

371

Tommy nodded and Geoffrey answered for them both. "Yes, Sir James. I'm beginning to learn that my son has inherited much of my damnable curiosity, which has led him here. I can't say that I'm too disappointed, however." He reached over and tousled Tommy's hair with a grin and Tommy's heart warmed.

Sir Edward spoke softly from the corner with a smile. "Let us hope that he also has inherited some of his mother's good sense, as well."

Rather than being offended, Geoffrey laughed. "Aye, that would help the lad out. Elizabeth has always had a good head on her shoulders."

"Thomas told me of all the good you have done for him and his mother when I left. I knew that you had delivered my letters to her but not that you watched so closely. I owe you a great deal, brother. It was my fight. You didn't have to stay but you did, and I thank you for that."

Sir Edward sighed and looked Geoffrey straight in the eye. "Well, I got you into the whole mess, didn't I? It took me a little while to actually stay there, though. I was very angry when you left. I didn't want to be stuck in that time, with all of the noise and lights, so I came back here to stay with Father and went to check on Liz and Tommy from time to time. But whenever I left, I wanted to stay with them. I decided that I needed to watch over them more closely so I went to school and became a teacher, a history teacher, of all things." He grinned. "It was the easiest profession that I could think of; after all, I'd lived through much of it! Liz knew that I was there but we didn't make a big show of knowing each other and I didn't let on to Tommy who I was. We didn't want to attract attention in case Abraham was watching."

"Tommy became my student in middle school and always did well in my class. You wouldn't believe how little twenty-first century students know about history! Appalling, really." Tommy agreed. Once, for a Civil War assignment, there had been a student in the class who had written a report about John Wilkes Booth driving off in a get-away car after shooting Abraham Lincoln!"

Sir Edward continued, "Anyway, this year, Tommy began asking rather odd, in-depth questions about this particular time period and I wasn't quite sure if he was merely interested or if he had found something out. I knew that Liz was going to tell him everything about you, but I knew that she didn't intend to when he was twelve! I got myself invited to dinner in order to better answer his questions. I thought then that I could also get a sense of what was behind all of Tommy's questions. It was just as I thought; Liz didn't seem to think there was anything sinister about his fascination with King Henry, except that it was a sudden, new interest. Tommy and Nick told her that they were going to do a report on him."

Geoffrey interrupted, "Did you tell her of your suspicions?"

"I didn't have a chance. We weren't left alone for a moment. You have a very vigilant son there, Geoffrey." Tommy could feel his ears turning red.

"Anyway, the next thing I knew Liz was calling me frantically on the phone, saying that Tommy and Nick were gone and that her box where she had kept the amulet was lying open in the living room. I knew exactly where they had gone, so I called the school and told them that I had a family emergency and that I would be gone for at least a month. I dug out my amulet and came straight here, to Henry's court. I knew that they would stick out like sore thumbs and probably get arrested, first thing. I was right, so I used my influence, or rather my father's influence, to get them out."

"Have you talked to Elizabeth since you left?" Geoffrey asked.

"No, I didn't want to attract attention to her. I left her to deal with Nick's parents. You can bet that Abraham is hopping mad right now. I told her to get out of town for her own protection, but she didn't want to. She's waiting at home until one of us comes back."

"We're going to have to get back there. There's no telling what could happen to her if she stays."

Tommy's heart began to beat fast again. He hadn't thought of that. Abraham might try and get to his mother! The thought of her being hurt or scared filled him with dread.

"And what about this one?" Geoffrey pointed at Nick, who had also gone pale at all of this.

"His parents should be fine", Sir Edward said. "Abraham knows nothing about him or his family. He won't be able to get to us through them. We were also getting acquainted while you were gone. I was able to learn Nick's story quite well. Hopefully, Elizabeth gave his parents a good enough story so that we won't come back to police and sirens." Nick smiled a little at this, but was still scared-looking. Sir Edward tousled his hair.

"Never mind, son. We'll get you back to them alive. Now, how exactly are we going to do this?"

Geoffrey said, "Let's just go back to Elizabeth's time. It will draw Abraham out and we can get this thing over with once and for all!"

Sir Edward nodded. "I think that may be best. There's one thing that I have to do before we go, though, in case we're gone for a long time. I need to tell the king that we're going on journey of sorts."

Geoffrey began to protest, but Sir Edward held up his hand. "I know your feelings about him, but I need to keep up appearances. If I just disappear with these boys, he'll have my head, literally, or he could take my family's lands. My father needs to be comfortable and taken care of." Sir Edward grimaced at the thought of old Lord Barnhart suddenly becoming homeless. "I need to seek an audience with him, today, and tell him that we're leaving for an extended period, shall we say six months or so, so that he doesn't get suspicious about us being gone."

The king again! Tommy's stomach gave a little quake of fear. It was true that the king had been kind to them, but there was something about knowing that he was going to shortly have his wife beheaded that still gave Tommy the chills. He met Nick's eyes from across the room and knew that Nick was thinking the same thing.

"Where is the king today?" Sir Edward asked.

"At Whitehall, I believe", Sir John answered. "They were making ready yesterday."

"It's right in the city", Sir Edward explained to Tommy and Nick. "We won't have to go far."

Geoffrey nodded. "As long as I don't have to go, too", he said.

Sir Edward grinned wickedly. "I told him that you were dead long ago."

Geoffrey's eyes widened. "Truly?"

"Yes", Sir Edward nodded, "He's thought you were killed on pilgrimage years ago, ever since you married Elizabeth. What was I supposed to say? You found a way to travel through time with a magical amulet? Please! I like my head on my shoulders, just where it is, thank you!"

They all laughed at this. It broke the mounting tension over what they were about to do.

Joan had heated water over the great fire and soon they were all washing up and changing their clothes for an audience with the king. Obviously, Sir Edward had thought ahead and had brought changes of clothes for both of the boys.

"These belonged to Geoffrey and me when we were boys. Fashions have changed a little, but not so much for the young. You'll be perfectly presentable in these."

As they struggled to put on the colorful tights, or hose, Nick started to giggle uncontrollably.

Could you see", he gasped, "Susan's face if she ever knew that we were wearing these things?"

Tommy began to giggle, too. The horrible Susan seemed so far away, along with everything else from his own time. They were slowly and surely becoming used to living in the 1500's.

When they were finished dressing, and had choked back most of their giggles, they came downstairs for inspection. They gasped at the sight of Sir Edward. He was dressed in very fine silks, complete with a feathered hat, looking exactly like the pictures in Tommy's history book, the way he'd looked on the day that he had rescued them from Henry. He and Geoffrey fussed over the boys for a moment, straightening their shirts, doublets, they called them, and making sure that their hose had no tears in them. When they had been pronounced as presentable, Sir Edward strapped his sword on and they began to walk out of the house into the busy London streets. Geoffrey was staying behind, to preserve his image of being dead.

They felt very important as the people in the streets made way for Sir Edward's horse. The way he was dressed made it clear that he was someone important and not a commoner. Tommy and Nick followed in his wake on their old but sturdy nags and they soon arrived at the palace.

As they approached the impressive gates, Sir Edward turned to them and said, "This is Whitehall Palace, by the way. It's been here for centuries but most of it does not exist in your time."

"You mean it's gone? They'll tear it down?" Nick asked.

"Keep your voice down", Sir Edward told him, "Yes, most of it will be torn down. Count yourselves lucky that you get to see it while it's still glorious."

Tommy and Nick took it all in. The ancient stones *were* magnificent. Just entering through the gates made them feel very small.

They followed Sir Edward through and to a closed gate where he had words with a guard. The guard left for a few moments and then returned to let them through. He nodded toward some oaken doors, much like the ones at Hampton Court that Tommy remembered from their first meeting with the king. What a difference this was! No smelly soldier was dragging him up any stairs this time. He wondered if he would see the queen again or if she had already been arrested. He tugged on Sir Edward's sleeve as they left the guard behind.

"What about the queen? Is she still here?" he asked.

Sir Edward gave a grim smile. "That's still a little way off, yet. The king and his court will be going on their summer progress soon to look the country over. She won't be found out, or arrested, until this fall; November 1, to be exact."

"Do you think she has any idea what's coming?" Nick asked, remembering to keep his voice low.

Sir Edward shook his head. "She's a foolish child, thinking she can get away with what she's doing. The king does not like to be humiliated." He turned and stood very straight, letting the boys know that this conversation was over.

They followed him up the stairs and waited to be admitted into the king's chamber. Once the guard opened the huge door, they entered and Tommy remembered that they needed to bow. He followed Sir Edward's lead, removing their hats and bowing once when they entered, once when they were about halfway to the king, and once when they approached him. They stayed with their heads down until the king finally spoke. Tommy glanced to the right of the king and sure enough, Queen Katherine was sitting next to him, looking the same as she had the last time they had seen her.

"Sir Edward, a pleasure to see you again."

"Thank you, your majesty. The pleasure is mine."

"And you've brought your wards with you today?"

"Yes, Your Grace. I crave your permission to take them on a progress through England and part of the continent."

The king smiled. "Ah. Furthering their education, I see. Excellent, excellent. Do you have a complete plan of where you will be traveling?"

"I thought we'd leave from London and explore the south of England before crossing the passage into France into Calais. I do so wish to take them to Italy to see the masters of art before bringing them home to view the northern lands, near the Scottish border. Then we shall return home to my estate."

"And how long do you intend on being gone?" the king asked in his reedy voice that did not suit him.

"For at least six months, Your Grace", Sir Edward bowed again, "if it pleases the king."

King Henry thought for a moment, and then nodded his head. "Your petition is granted. I dare say that you have done well by these wards. They look better already! Mayhap it is time you had some sons of your own, Sir Edward", he added with a sly smile.

"Indeed, Sire. I have not found a woman that I wish to marry as of yet."

The king guffawed loudly. "Time will run out for you as it is for me. I have but one son to carry on my kingdom, but I plan to have many more. Find a decent wench before it is too late." He reached over and stroked the queen's cheek with a fat finger. She smiled pleasantly enough at him, but Tommy could see that her eyes were cold. He quickly looked down so that the king wouldn't ask him any questions. There was a long moment before the king gave his final answer.

"Sir Edward I grant you permission to take them on the extended progress, on one condition."

Sir Edward bowed his head again. "Anything, Sire."

"I want you to look for a wife while you are away."

Sir Edward looked up, a bit surprised. "Indeed, Sire, I shall."

"Then I have your word on it?"

"You do indeed."

"Good!" the king roared. "Every man should be as happy as I, with my rose that bears no thorns." He took the queen's hand and squeezed it. She smiled graciously at him, but it looked like it was more difficult for her to do this time. Sir Edward, however, managed to look both interested and grateful for the advice. He bowed again at the king's knee.

"We should all aspire to your Highness's happiness", Sir Edward said.

"Go then. Enjoy your journey, boys, and be thankful to the man that has saved you from a life of utter desolation." The king looked at them with satisfaction and suddenly, Tommy remembered that they were supposed to bow. He hoped that Nick would follow his lead, and he did. They bowed, said, "Thank you, Sire", and stood again to walk out. Tommy held his breath until the big oak doors swung shut behind him, then let out a long breath.

"Whew!" said Nick while putting his hat back on. "That was scary!"

Sir Edward smiled. "You boys handled yourselves pretty well, much better than last time."

"Well, it was a bit different this time, wasn't it?" said Tommy.

"Yes, well, we must still be very careful. C'mon, your father is waiting."

They followed Sir Edward down the steps of the palace and back into the crowded London streets.

Chapter Fifteen
385

It was early afternoon when they arrived back at Sir James's house. The filmy sunlight played lazily through the windows and spilled out onto the floor, giving the place a comfortable, homey, feel in spite of what had happened there that morning. Tommy was exhausted, having been awake since before dawn. He was also ravenous and was delighted to find that Joan had made dinner. A rich, meaty smell hung in the air and the table was set.

"Right then, so have we've decided that we're going back to Tommy's time?" Geoffrey wanted to know as they sat down and began to eat. It fell silent for a while as they all dug in, but soon Sir Edward began to speak.

"For now, I think that's the best plan. If we don't, Abraham's likely to show up here looking for us and I don't want to put Sir James in danger again." As Sir James began to protest, Sir Edward held up his hand and said, "Now, Sir James, I think one lump on the head is enough for one of our visits, wouldn't you agree? Save it for another time."

Gregory stepped forward. "Sir Edward, I would like to go along with you, if Sir James will permit it."

Geoffrey clapped him on the shoulder. "It's a good man you are, Gregory, but won't Sir James need your protection? Abraham may decide to send some of his men back here as a warning. Sir James and Joan will need someone to defend them."

Gregory looked disappointed, but he smiled bravely at Sir Edward and said, "Just remember that my sword is always ready to help you."

Sir Edward nodded and said, "We thank you, Gregory. You were an invaluable help to us this morning and we won't soon forget it. Well, gentlemen, shall we go?"

Tommy nodded, but Nick asked the same thing that Tommy was thinking. "Are we going to throw up again?"

The men laughed. "Bit of a rough landing last time, son?" Geoffrey asked. "We'll try to help you through it. There's a technique to landing properly that won't knock you unconscious that Edward and I eventually learned, but perhaps that comes with experience. It may be that whoever created these wanted to deter anyone from using them again. Come on, everyone together now.

Geoffrey and Tommy held onto Geoffrey's amulet while Nick held onto Sir Edward's. Again, Tommy felt the buzzing in the stone, as though it were powered with electricity, and felt the vibrations go through him.

"Think of the kitchen in Tommy's house, 2013, April 28th!" Sir Edward said.

"I thought it would send me back to that day anyway", Tommy said.

"You and Nick, yes, but your father and I aren't from your time. We have to be a bit more specific", Sir Edward told him.

Tommy concentrated hard on his kitchen, with the refrigerator, stove, and small square table where he had eaten breakfast almost every day of his life. With the picture firmly in his head, he nodded at his father and in an instant, the familiar, whirling, feeling took over and they disappeared from Sir James's kitchen.

Sir James, Joan, and Gregory stood watching the spectacle. One moment, the four of them were there, two pairs holding onto purple amulets. The next moment, they had vanished into thin air, leaving no trace behind.

There was silence in the nearly empty kitchen until Sir James said, "Well, I suppose that anything else we do today cannot possibly compare to what we've already done. Still, we must be on our guard. Gregory, take care to report anything out of the ordinary."

"Aye, m'lord." Gregory, still looking a bit disappointed, went back to the stable to feed and clean. Life at Sir John's house slowly adjusted back to normal.

Meanwhile, Tommy felt that horrid dizziness again as he held onto his father with both hands, gripping his doublet as tightly as he could. He could feel them spiraling down, down, down, and began to brace himself for the eventual impact. His father's arm was tight around his waist as they fell, holding Tommy close. This journey was so different from the one before! That alone made Tommy feel a little better. He wondered how Nick and Sir Edward, (or would he be Mr. Barnhart again?), were doing.

All at once, the kitchen floor was under their feet with a *thud* and Geoffrey held Tommy upright so that he would not land on his head again. He was very dizzy, but nowhere nearly as bad as the time before. Geoffrey laughed at his expression. "Perhaps, son, landing on your head the first time contributed to the throwing up."

A half-second later, Sir Edward and Nick appeared next to them. Sir Edward was holding Nick upright the same way Geoffrey had done for Tommy. Nick looking pale, but conscious.

"All right there, Nick?" he asked his friend. Nick nodded.

"Better than last time." Tommy grinned but his grin faded when saw his mother at the kitchen door, her worried face pale, her dark eyes looking right at him and then sliding around to all of the people in her previously empty kitchen. They opened wide when they came to rest on Geoffrey, looking for all the world like a painting from a book had stepped into their modern kitchen.

"Tommy", she whispered. "Geoffrey, Edward, you're alive! I can't believe it!"

"Mom?" Tommy said. His eyes stared filling up with tears, He couldn't help it. All of the guilt he had felt over the past days was all flooding back into his chest and he couldn't stand to see her worry for one more moment. He sprinted across the kitchen floor and threw himself into her arms.

"Oh, Mama, I'm so sorry!" He hadn't called her "Mama" since he had been a little boy, but somehow that's what came out as he sobbed in her arms and she hugged him tighter than he could ever remember her doing. She kissed him all over his face and stroked his hair, tears running down her cheeks. Then suddenly, she held him by the shoulders and pushed him back, looking at him very intently, mascara streaks running down her face.

"Thomas Geoffrey Andrews, if you *ever* do *anything* like this ever again, you will be grounded for life. Do you have any idea how frantic I've been? Thank God that Edward figured out what you had done! And Nick!" Nick looked down at the floor, shamefaced and red. "Nick, your mother believed that you had a school trip that she had forgotten about, thank goodness, or the police would have been involved, I'm sure."

"How did she believe I had a school trip?" Nick asked, bewildered.

"I told her." Mrs. Andrews said sternly. "I called after Edward left to find you both. I explained that Nick's father had paid for the trip and signed the permission slip ages ago and that you and Tommy would be back in a week. She ranted and raved about your father and then apologized to me, telling us to have a good trip. Then

I called your father and told him the same thing, but that your mother had paid for it. He reacted pretty much the same way. They both think that you're on a school trip. I suggest that you go home and tell her that your trip ended early. It may get very ugly here."

Nick shook his head. "No way. After everything that I went through? I'm staying here and waiting for Abraham with the rest of you."

"That's very noble of you, Nick, but…" Geoffrey was cut off by Elizabeth.

"Abraham? Is he coming here again? Why?"

Geoffrey stepped forward and took her hands in his. He looked down into her eyes and said, "We have to draw him out, Elizabeth. It has to end. This running from time to time is exhausting and now that Tommy knows the truth, Abraham will come after him, too. We have to stop him today or it will never end."

Tommy's mother sighed, a long sigh. Then she gave a sad little smile up at Geoffrey. "I guess I knew that marrying you would be quite an experience. It just turned out so differently from how I thought it would." She looked at him intently. "You look well,

Geoffrey. A little greyer perhaps", she smiled as she gently lifted a piece of his hair that had come loose from its binding, "but well, nonetheless." Tommy noticed that Sir Edward looked away while this was going on.

"And you, my darling, look as beautiful as the day I married you."

Elizabeth looked at him softly. "That was a long time ago", she said gently.

Geoffrey gave a little sigh, "Indeed, it was. Was it too long ago?" he asked.

"I don't know", she said slowly. "Let's get through this first and we can talk about it later." She squeezed his hands, released them, and walked over to the kitchen counter. In the still-awkward silence, she began pulling out the coffee filters and coffee can from the cupboard.

"How many are going to want coffee?" she asked, giving her something else to do.

"Perhaps something stronger?" Sir Edward joked. She gave him a look over her shoulder. Tommy knew that look well. It said,

"In your dreams, Buster!" and she gave it to him when he wanted to something that he knew would never be allowed, like the time he and Nick wanted to ride their bikes all the way to Lake Michigan. Yes, he knew that look.

"Get used to this time again, Edward. You need to keep your head about you. If we get through this intact, I'll personally bring the whiskey."

"All right, then, coffee it is", he conceded.

Geoffrey cleared his throat. "Well, everyone, we need a plan for when Abraham shows up. We know that he can tell where we are, we just don't know when he'll decide to come."

"His lackey, Walter, said that he carries his amulet in a pouch attached to his belt, that he never takes it off. I've never seen his belt; it must be under that coat of his. It's going to be a chore finding it." Sir Edward grimaced.

"Walter said that it was attached by a chain. I'm going to suppose that it is an incredibly strong metal, something that won't break easily. A sword most likely won't be able to sever it or the belt", Geoffrey added. "How will we get it off of him?"

There was silence for a moment and then Elizabeth said slowly, "Bolt cutters."

The men looked at her. "What?" Geoffrey asked,

Elizabeth smiled. "Bolt cutters. They cut through metal. The custodian at school uses them to cut through student locks when they forget their combinations or lose their keys. We actually have some out in the garden shed, Geoffrey, you just never used them."

Sir Edward clapped a hand to his head. "I didn't think of that! I never really had a use for them here, but if we can get Abraham down, it just might work. Just out of curiosity, Liz, why do you have bolt cutters?" Tommy was wondering the same thing.

"They were there when we bought the house. I just kept them in there, figuring they'd come in handy someday."

Tommy shook his head with a smile. His mother was amazing sometimes. The adults began planning out a strategy and Tommy thought it might be a good time to use the bathroom, a *real* bathroom, not a hole in the ground or a patch of grass. It was amazing what normal everyday things he had missed while he was away.

■ ■

After he had washed his hands and opened the door, he stopped and looked at the toothpaste on the sink. *Toothpaste!* It had been so long since he properly brushed his teeth! It was too hard to resist. Since his toothbrush had disappeared on the way to London, he pulled out one of the extra toothbrushes that his mother kept under the sink and piled on extra toothpaste. While he was brushing, Nick came to the door.

"Oh, *toothpaste*! Do you have any extra toothbrushes?" he asked eagerly. Tommy nodded and pulled another one out for Nick. They were both scrubbing when they heard a lot of commotion going on in the kitchen. Tommy spit out his toothpaste and began to start out the door when Nick held him back.

"No! What if it's Abraham?" he whispered. "We don't have the cutters yet! We have to get out to the shed without him seeing us!"

Nick looked scared, but determined, and Tommy saw his reasoning. They couldn't let Abraham know that they were there. He quietly turned off the water and strained to hear what was going on in the kitchen to make sure of what was going on. After a moment, he heard a gravelly voice that he assumed must be Abraham's.

"Did you think I'd give you time to plan things out? Do you think I don't know that Walter betrayed me?" he laughed softly.

"Walter didn't betray you, Abraham. We probed his mind." It sounded like Geoffrey speaking.

"Ah, yes, your mind-reading friend. I'll make sure that he's dealt with later, in a more permanent way, once I'm done with you. Quite the little resistance you've been gathering against me, but now look at you! This ends. Now. You will give me your amulets. All these years I thought there was only one other, but now I see that there are more. Your ancestor robbed the treasury well, Sir Edward. Ah, well, more for us. Now you must decide what is more important to you: your amulets or the woman. No more games."

Tommy's eyes widened. The woman? They had his mother! Neither Geoffrey nor Sir Edward would risk anything happening to his mother; that he was sure of. He knew what he had to do. He motioned to Nick to come further into the bathroom and then quietly shut the door behind them both, turning the lock. He slid open the bathroom window and pulled up the screen. The window was small, but at least the bathroom was on the first floor. Nick gave him a small boost and Tommy wriggled through the small opening. He could barely hear Sir Edward say loudly to Abraham, "Nobody was robbed! Those stones were given to my family!" He hoped that Sir Edward could keep Abraham talking and hold him off.

When he landed on the ground, he reached back in to give Nick his hands and helped pull him out, as quietly as they could. He thought to himself how he had been getting an awful lot of practice going in and out of windows lately.

They silently ran toward the small garden shed behind the house, thankful that it was out of view of the kitchen window. The rusted door, however, gave a loud, protesting screech when they opened it. They froze, looking for any sign from the house that they had been heard, hearts pounding hard in their chests. When none came, they slipped into the shed and began looking around for the bolt cutters.

"What do they look like?" Nick wanted to know.

"Kind of like those pruning things your mom uses on the bushes, but thicker. I've seen the janitor use them." They looked through the dark shed for a few minutes before Tommy heard Nick

say. "These?"

He turned and saw Nick holding the bolt cutters up. "Yep,

that's them. Let's go!"

They ran out of the shed but Nick grabbed Tommy's arm.

"Wait", he said. "We can't just barge in there with these. We

need a plan or they'll take us prisoner, too, or worse!" Tommy

stopped. Again, Nick was right. Those goons were holding his

mother hostage and they needed to come up with something in a

hurry or all might be lost. A plan of some kind started forming in his

mind.

"Listen", he told Nick, "I'll go in and surprise them. While

they're focused on me, you be ready. As soon as they get the chance,

I'm sure that Sir Edward and my dad will tackle him and you can run

in with those. You don't need to find the amulet, just cut off the

whole belt. We'll worry about finding the amulet later. We just need

to get that belt off."

Nick nodded, his face pale again, but he had lost the terrified

look that Tommy had seen at the beginning of their adventure. Nick

had gotten a lot braver in the past week. *I think we both have,*

Tommy thought to himself. Now was the test of how far they had come. Now was the time to put all of what they had learned to use.

Tommy boosted Nick back through the bathroom window after carefully checking that none of the goons had forced open the door to check for them. As he handed Nick the bolt cutters through the window, Tommy whispered to him, "Listen for the commotion. It has to be quick. Be ready." Nick nodded.

Tommy crept around the rest of the house, right under the kitchen window that his mother had opened earlier that day, probably to let in the sunshine. He listened to what was going on inside. He didn't dare to peek in the window. It was a clear view and Abraham might see the top of his head.

He could hear Abraham's voice rising in anger.

"This is the final time that I will ask politely. GIVE ME THE AMULETS!"

Tommy heard his mother tearfully say, "Don't give them to him! He'll be too powerful! Take Tommy and go!" and then she screamed.

"*Liz!*" he heard Sir Edward shout at the same time he heard his father bellow, "*Elizabeth!*" He knew that he couldn't wait any more or his mother might die and he raced through the screen door into the kitchen without another thought. The sight he saw made his knees weak with fear.

His dad and Sir Edward were standing against the wall on one side of the kitchen, their swords dropped to the floor and Tommy soon saw why. His mother was sitting in one of their kitchen chairs, a goon on either side of her. One of them was pulling her hair back with one hand and held a long, sharp knife to her neck with the other hand. The other goon held on to one of her wrists but he was also holding a knife. Tommy could see that the reason she had screamed was because the goon with the knife on her neck was pressing the point of it tightly to her and he could see a small trickle of blood begin flowing down. His heart thumped with fear and he felt light-headed as he stood in the center of the kitchen, taking it all in. Abraham turned slowly to him.

"So, Geoffrey, your son has decided to join the party. I was wondering where you were."

"Tommy, *run*! Ow!" his mother called to him, grimacing as the goon with the long knife pressed the point of it a little harder into her neck.

"No", Tommy said, shaking. "I'm not going to let them hurt you."

"Well then, my boy", Abraham grinned, "perhaps you would be so kind as to give me the amulets, or to tell me where they are. That is the only way you will be able to spare your mother's life. You can be a hero, Thomas. You can save your mother, just by saying the word or you can be the reason that she dies."

Tommy hesitated. Would it really be that easy? His mom wasn't badly hurt, yet, but Tommy had a feeling that even if he did give them the information that they wanted, she would still be killed, along with the rest of them.

He remembered what Sir Edward had told him about Abraham, about how he was part of a "family" that wanted to take over the world using magical objects. He thought of how Abraham had chased his father through time for twelve years, about how his father could never come and see him, how his mother had had to raise him all alone, never knowing if his father was dead or alive. The more he thought about all of the wrongs that Abraham had done, the angrier he got, the trembling left his heart, and strength began flowing back into his legs.

He looked at his mother in that chair, at his father and Sir Edward, disarmed and pressed against the wall so as not to hurt her any more, and he remembered Nick, waiting in the hallway to take Abraham's amulet. A plan started to quickly formulate in his mind.

"Well..." he began slowly.

"Tommy!" his father gasped. "Don't say a word! Run, son, run! Edward and I will handle this! Get away, quick as you can!"

"No, Dad. I think we should give him the amulets. Then he'll let Mom go and we'll never see him again."

"That's right", Abraham purred, a smile appearing on his oily features, "You'll never see us again. You, out of your whole family, finally understand the most sensible thing to do. We'll take the amulets and be gone, forever. Just think, Geoffrey, you can stay in one time with your family. You don't have to lead this chase from year to year. I respect your ingenuity, but it's rather exhausting chasing you from Ancient Greece to Victorian England. Wouldn't you rather stay in one place, with your wife and child? Edward, don't you want to settle down with a family someday?"

As Abraham went on about the benefits of giving over the amulets to him, just past his head, Tommy could see Nick peeking

403

around the corner of the bathroom door into hallway that led into the kitchen. Both of the goons and Abraham had their backs to the hallway and while Abraham droned on, Tommy locked eyes with Nick and gave a tiny nod. Nick's eyebrows rose up, but it was clear that he knew what to do. He gave Tommy a small nod back, raised the bolt cutters and silently ran up behind Abraham, bringing the flat side of them down hard on Abraham's head!

Geoffrey and Sir Edward, who had also seen Nick's approach, were ready. The instant that Abraham went down, they both grabbed their swords up off the ground and rushed the goons that had held Elizabeth in the chair, knocking the knives out of their surprised hands and backing them into the corner. Elizabeth sprang up out of the chair and rushed over to Tommy, hugging him tightly before releasing him and rushing over to Nick to do the same thing. Nick was just standing there, letting Mrs. Andrews hug him but still holding the bolt cutters in shocked silence as he stared at Abraham lying there where he had gone down.

"Are you okay, Nick?" Tommy asked.

It took a moment for Nick to answer, but when he finally looked back up at Tommy and Elizabeth, he had a smile on his face.

"I did it", he whispered. "I stopped Abraham!"

Elizabeth kissed him on the cheek and hugged him tightly to her again. "Yes, you did! Oh, Nick, you were so brave!"

Tommy went over and clapped him on the shoulder. "Yeah, dude, you were awesome!"

"Is that what you wanted me to do?" Nick asked. "I wasn't sure."

"You were spot on", Tommy told him. "It was like you could read my mind! It was perfect! You dropped him like a rock."

"Is, is he dead?" Nick asked.

Elizabeth dropped down and felt for Abraham's pulse in his neck. She looked up at them. "No, he's alive. You didn't kill anyone, Nick, don't worry."

Nick breathed a sigh of relief. "Whew, I'm glad of that."

"More's the pity", Geoffrey said, winding duct tape around one of the goon's wrists. "This stuff was a wonderful invention! It's a shame we don't have it where I come from!"

He finished and walked over to the unconscious Abraham on the floor. Standing over him with his sword still drawn, he said gravely, "He should die for what he's done, not only to our family,

405

but also to the rest of the world. He's stolen treasures, sacred, magical, objects and used them for the gain of his family for centuries! People have been killed, entire families murdered for the sake of power. He doesn't deserve to live!" Geoffrey lifted his sword high and pointed it at Abraham.

"Dad! No!" Tommy yelled and yanked Geoffrey's arm away. "You can't kill him!"

"Why not?" Geoffrey asked. "Tommy, *he's* the reason I wasn't around for all those years. He's the reason for so many bad things! If I don't kill him, he'll be back!"

Tommy shook his head, tears in his eyes. "*Please* don't kill him, Dad! It'll make you a murderer! I don't want a murderer for a father!"

Geoffrey looked puzzled. "What about those two men at Sir John's? You weren't that upset about them!"

"That was in self-defense", Tommy explained. "That's different. Abraham isn't fighting you right now. It's not fair."

Geoffrey sighed, stepped back, and sheathed his sword. "You're right, son", he said. "Forgive me. I almost let my rage get the better of me. I won't kill him."

Sir Edward came over and clapped him on the back. "Well done, brother. But now that we've decided to let the scurvy dog live, what shall we do with him?"

Tommy thought for a moment. "I know! We'll take his amulet, then take him and his goons somewhere in time and leave them there. They won't be able to travel back to their family and we'll have all of the stones! We can keep them safe and you can use them to go and take care of your father", he said to Sir Edward.

Geoffrey and Sir Edward looked at each other for a moment. "The boy makes sense", Sir Edward told Geoffrey. "We could absolutely leave them somewhere."

"Well, let's cut the amulet from his belt first, then we can decide."

Tommy felt excited. They had liked his plan! His father wouldn't kill anyone; Abraham would be taken someplace where he wouldn't hurt anyone and maybe they could be a family again.

Please let us be a family again, he prayed.

He watched as Sir Edward helped Nick clip off Abraham's belt with the bolt cutters. They had insisted that Nick do it, since he was the one who had ultimately stopped Abraham. The belt itself wasn't metal, simply a strong leather, but the chain holding on the pouch with the amulet was most likely platinum, Sir Edward thought.   Nick held up the thick, heavy, belt in triumph and they quickly found the amulet. Walter had truly done a good deed in telling them where to look for it.

"Such a little thing", Tommy said, holding it in his hand and feeling the familiar electric sensation in his fingers. Geoffrey smiled at him and then plucked it out of his hand.

"I'll just hold onto that, if you don't mind, son", he said. I don't want to have to search the Nile River Delta for you during the time of Moses or anything."

"Have you been there?" Tommy asked breathlessly.

Geoffrey paused for a moment, looked down at Tommy with a twinkle in his eye, and said, "Let's just say that Mount Sinai isn't *quite* the same mountain that it used to be." As he walked away, Tommy shook his head in awe. How great it would be to travel to some of these places with his dad! Maybe he could convince him to use the amulets sometimes. He knew better than to ask at the moment, though.

"Well then", Sir Edward began, as he finished wrapping Abraham's wrists with tape in case he woke up, "Where shall we send these fine gentlemen?"

"Russia?" Nick suggested. "We could send him to Ivan the Terrible."

"How about sending them back to dinosaur times?" Tommy said.

Geoffrey shook his head. That won't work. I've tried. I think that it will only send you to places when there are people. Any suggestions, Elizabeth?"

Tommy's mother shook her head. "Not anywhere in particular. Just someplace where they'll have to struggle and won't have anyone there that they know to help them get back."

It was quiet for a moment while they thought. Suddenly, Sir Edward said, "Tommy, go and get your history book."

Tommy ran to his room. His book was still in his book bag, right where he had left it nearly two weeks before. It felt like a lifetime ago. He sprinted back into the kitchen and gave it to Sir Edward, who flipped through the pages until he found what he was looking for.

"There!" he exclaimed as he put his finger on the middle of a page. "That's where we'll take them."

They all leaned in to look and Tommy saw, to his surprise, that it was the Battle of Gettysburg!

"When does this battle take place?" Geoffrey wanted to know.

"Right, I keep forgetting that your knowledge of history spans more than this little piece. The Battle of Gettysburg was the turning point of the American Civil War. It was three days of continuous bloodshed that took place in the farmland of Pennsylvania in July of 1863."

Geoffrey gave him an incredulous look.

"Why the hell would we send them there?"

"Geoffrey! Language!" Elizabeth warned him, giving him a *look*.

"Sorry, sorry, I mean, why on earth would we send them there? Why not a prison ship, or the Sahara Desert, or anywhere else where he can die quickly"

"Because, my un-American friend, it is one of the few places where there will be too many men to listen to Abraham and a mass

410

of confusion, besides. And, as a bonus, there's a very good chance that he won't get out of it alive. Even if he does survive, there's no one living there during that time that's connected to the family that we know of, so it's our best bet."

"Are we all agreed, then?" Elizabeth asked. "That we'll send Abraham to Gettysburg? Personally, I think that we should send the goons someplace else. They shouldn't be able to communicate after this."

"That's good, Mom", Tommy told her. "Let's send them other places."

Elizabeth smiled and held her son's hand. Geoffrey took Tommy's other hand. For the first time in a long time, it seemed, they were going to be a family of sorts, a family that included Sir Edward and Nick.

Chapter Sixteen

So it was decided. Despite much begging and pleading from Tommy and Nick to go along ("Think of the great history lesson it would be!"), Geoffrey and Sir Edward were the ones to deposit a still-unconscious Abraham near a Confederate regiment who was fighting at Gettysburg. They chose to deposit him there after nightfall and they carefully cut off the duct tape from his wrists and ankles before reappearing in the Andrews' kitchen. What would become of him, they hoped they would never find out.

One goon was deposited in Russia, directly in the court of Ivan the Terrible, per Nick's suggestion, and the other was taken to one of Nero's palaces in Rome; Elizabeth's idea.

After all of the traveling was done, Geoffrey and Sir Edward sat in the living room, sprawled out on the sofa, mugs of hot coffee laced with a little whisky in their hands. Even though they were seasoned at time-traveling, especially Geoffrey, four trips in one day proved to be exhausting for them.

Elizabeth broke the silence. "Nick, before you go home, perhaps you and Tommy would tell me all about your trip. I haven't been back to England, in any time, since before you were born. I'm anxious to hear all about it."

So, while Geoffrey and Sir Edward rested and drank several mugs of steaming coffee, Tommy and Nick started from the beginning.

Elizabeth sat spellbound through their entire tale, smiling at how Mrs. Kingston fussed over them and her eyes growing large at how Tommy and Nick had escaped through the window in Sir John's house. As they told their story, Tommy felt like he was reliving it all again. It sounded almost like a movie with all of the sword fighting and narrow escapes, but it had been real, too real at times. He was happy that they were safely home now.

When they were finished, Elizabeth sat back with her own coffee and sighed. Tommy looked at the clock. They had been talking for an hour! He looked, worried now, at his mother. He knew that she was still upset because he had done all of this and that he had scared her badly. He waited for her to speak. Finally, she sat up again and looked at both Tommy and Nick in their eyes.

"Boys", she began, "you have no idea how worried I was. Because of your actions, I had to lie to Nick's parents, which I hated having to do, as well as sending Edward into danger. But could you see me trying to explain where you had gone? I might have been locked up and charged with kidnapping, murder, locked in a mental ward, something! It was lucky for us that your parents don't speak to each other, Nick, or there might have been some serious issues there."

"Tommy, just because everything turned out all right this time, I don't want you to think that going behind my back is the way to get things done. That breaks down trust in a family and we can't have that. Our family situation is a little, well, unusual. It's incredibly important that we tell each other the truth, *always*! I won't have you going about and jumping through time when you get the urge to do something,"

Tommy began to protest that it was just the once, to look for his dad, but Elizabeth raised her hand to stop him.

"I know, I know, your intentions were good. I know that finding your dad has always been important to you and, well, things are going to change now. There's a lot that needs to be discussed: living arrangements, what to do with the amulets…"

Geoffrey interrupted, "They'll be put into a box with a much better lock, one that our clever Nick here can't pick." Nick blushed scarlet all the way up to his hair and began to protest, but Geoffrey continued.

"And your mother's right, Thomas. There are a lot of things that are going to change. Some of them will be easy changes, but some will be difficult. You're not used to having me around and I'm not used to staying in one place."

"Are you going to live here?" Tommy asked.

"We'll discuss that later. There are a lot of decisions to make," Elizabeth said. "Right now, we're going back to the subject of your behavior."

Tommy sighed. He could never get away with sidetracking her for long. He braced himself for the punishment that would follow.

"What you two did was a really stupid thing. You could have been killed or seriously hurt. Abraham was no one to trifle with. But, seeing as how you came through it all right and we've solved the problem of Abraham," she paused and Tommy held his breath, "I think you've been punished enough for this time." Tommy and Nick both jumped off of their chairs and squeezed her tightly, their faces showing their relief.

"Let this be a warning to you, though! Abraham is gone, but there may be others that we don't know about. We can relax a little, but we must stay on our guard. This may have opened a whole new can of worms."

"But in the meantime," Sir Edward stood up, stretching his long-legged frame, "we can celebrate our victory and have a lovely little reunion. Now, Liz, about that 'something stronger' we discussed earlier? I believe we came through this alive and I was promised whiskey, not just in my coffee!"

They all laughed at this and Elizabeth went to get some glasses for the adults and some pop for the boys. They decided that Nick would go home in the morning and they all stayed up late, telling more details from their adventure that they had forgotten earlier and eventually heading for bed.

As Tommy fell asleep that night, after a hot shower, in his own bed that wasn't stuffed with straw, he thought over the evening with happiness. The last thought that crossed his mind before he finally drifted off made him smile. The thing that he had been wanting for so many years had finally come to pass: his dad was home. They were all safe.

■■■

July 4, 1863: Gettysburg, Pennsylvania

The Union doctor walked slowly among the hundreds of

bodies that were lying out in the hot July sun. He had seen so many

men in the past three days. With all of the battlefields he had been to,

he would have thought that one could get used to seeing all of the

injuries and death, but it still turned his stomach to see what was left

after a battle, especially one like this. It was eerily silent in this part

of the battlefield and he listened closely for any signs of life. Not

hearing any, he changed his direction and began walking again,

careful of where he stepped.

A faint moan stopped him in his tracks and he waited for it to

come again. When it did, the moan led him to a small man lying face down in the trampled grass. The doctor rolled him over and peered into his face.

"Son? Can you hear me son?" While he waited for a reply, he scanned the man for injuries. He wasn't wearing a uniform, just some odd-looking clothes. He had on a long coat, even in this July heat. The doctor stripped the coat off of him in order to look at him better. He would worry about what he was wearing later. A bullet hole had pierced his chest, just above his heart and he had a large lump on the back of his head. Perhaps, just perhaps, this one could be saved. He had to try.

"Hold on there, son, I'm going to take you back to the medical tent. This might hurt a bit, but I'll do my best to fix you up. What's your name?" He patted the man's cheeks, trying to bring him around.

Finally, the man opened his eyes, just slightly. The doctor asked again," What's your name, son?" The man blinked in the bright sunshine, looked at the kind doctor's face and said slowly and painfully, "Abraham."

Historical Note

While I have done my best in many areas of this novel to be accurate to the Tudor time period, this is a work of fiction and some of the details had to be invented in order for Tommy's adventure to happen.

While some things having to do with the story were made-up, such as time-travel, the history of King Henry VIII and his six wives is a story that is very real. He actually was married to six different women, beheading his second wife, Anne Boleyn, and fifth wife, Katherine Howard, whom you met in this story. The rhyme that Mr. Barnhart teaches Tommy and Nick is one of a few common ways that British schoolchildren remember the order of his wives. Even after marrying all of those wives, Henry only had four children. Three of them would each rule England for a while. His son, Edward VI, became king for a few years after Henry's death in 1547. Edward died young in 1553 and was followed by his oldest sister, Mary I, who would later become known as "Bloody Mary". Elizabeth, Henry's daughter with Anne Boleyn, would become the Queen of England after Mary's death in 1558 and became one of England's longest-reigning and most successful monarchs. Henry also had another son out of wedlock named after himself, but he would die early without having children. In fact, Henry had no grandchildren at all, so today there are no direct descendants from him.

Mr. Kingston, the Constable of the Tower of London, was also a real person. He was in charge of Queen Anne Boleyn when she was a prisoner and guarded many important prisoners during his time. He and his wife did live in the Tower, but what his personality was like, we don't know. I wanted him to be a friendly face for Tommy, but not too friendly. I set the story in August of 1540 because he died in September of that year.

The Tower of London and Hampton Court Palace both still exist today, as do a great many buildings from Henry's time and before. In fact, I was able to do some of my research while visiting London.

I tried to create as realistic of a picture as I could about daily life in Tudor England. It was definitely a much different place than we are used to! Bathing was rare among common people and London was a filthy place, with garbage in the streets, along with excrement from animals and what was emptied from the waste buckets in the houses. The Thames River, while much cleaner today, was pretty polluted during Tudor times and for many years after. It was a pretty smelly place, according to people from that time who wrote about it. I know how I would feel being around all of that as a modern person and I tried to make Tommy and Nick feel the same way.

The Crusades, led by King Richard the Lionheart, were also real. Soldiers from all over Christian Europe raided countries in the Middle East to try and force the Muslim nations to convert to Christianity and to claim the holy city of Jerusalem. They called the people living in the Middle East and northern Africa "Moors". While it was a time period where many stories of finding the Holy Grail and other sacred objects come from, it was also a time of major wars and bloodshed, understandably leading to hard feelings between Europe and the Middle East for hundreds of years. Soldiers returning from these crusades often brought back objects that they had gotten from the many battles that were fought. That is where Sir Edward's great-grandfather brought the amulets back from that figure into our story.

There are some websites that can give my readers more information on the Tudor time period. Some of them have information and others have games to play. This is only a short list, but these sites also lead to more.

http://www.tudorhistory.org

http://www.hrp.org.uk/toweroflondon/

http://www.hrp.org.uk/HamptonCourtPalace/

http://www.alisonweir.org.uk

Acknowledgements

Thank you, thank you, to my family: Marty Man, you have been my rock and my biggest supporter since I started all of this craziness. Zachary, Anthony, and Andrew, thank you for putting up with Mama writing and letting me put some of your behaviors into Tommy and Nick. Mom, (Toni), thanks for listening to my rants.

Thank you to my beta readers and listeners who gave me feedback on what they liked and what they didn't. Your help was invaluable to me.

Carolyn Buccellato, Melinda Carricker, Corinne Fine, Nicole Fogt-Smith, Tanya Micallef, Anne Musselman, Kathrine Musselman, Sara Schaaf, Maya Audi, Lily Bargamian, Bahijah Bazzi, Batoul Bazzi, Celine Bazzi, Ryan Bearden, Ryan Blanton, Adam Chahine, Liam Diehl, Lana Elzein, Rayan Elzein, Laurel Etter, Layal Farhat, Ahmad Fawaz, André Flemming, Rayanne Hider, Mya Ismail, Fatima Jaward, Alexandria LaJoice, Jonathan Marshall, Hannah Mellatat, Isabella Martin, Ava Nasser, Tarick Nasser, Mackenzie Noah, Tushaunna Pruitt, Ali Saad, Maya Saad, Ramez Saad, Shadi Saad,

Jennah Sabrah, Yasmeena Serhane, Mohammad Shrime, Adam Srour.

Thank you, Brian Townsend, for jumping into this endeavor and designing an amazing cover for Tommy and Nick. I look forward to working with you again soon.

Made in the USA
Lexington, KY
24 August 2018